THE DEMON'S SECRET BABY

PRIDE

TOUCHED BY A DEMON
BOOK THREE

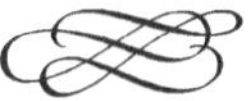

JEANNE OATES ESTRIDGE

The Demon's Secret Baby

Cover art: Deranged Doctor Design www.derangeddoctordesign.com/

Copy Editor: April Reed www.theeditingsoprano.com/

ISBN: 978-1-949451-08-5

First edition

October 2022

Also available as an ebook:

ISBN: 978-1-949451-07-8

✸ Created with Vellum

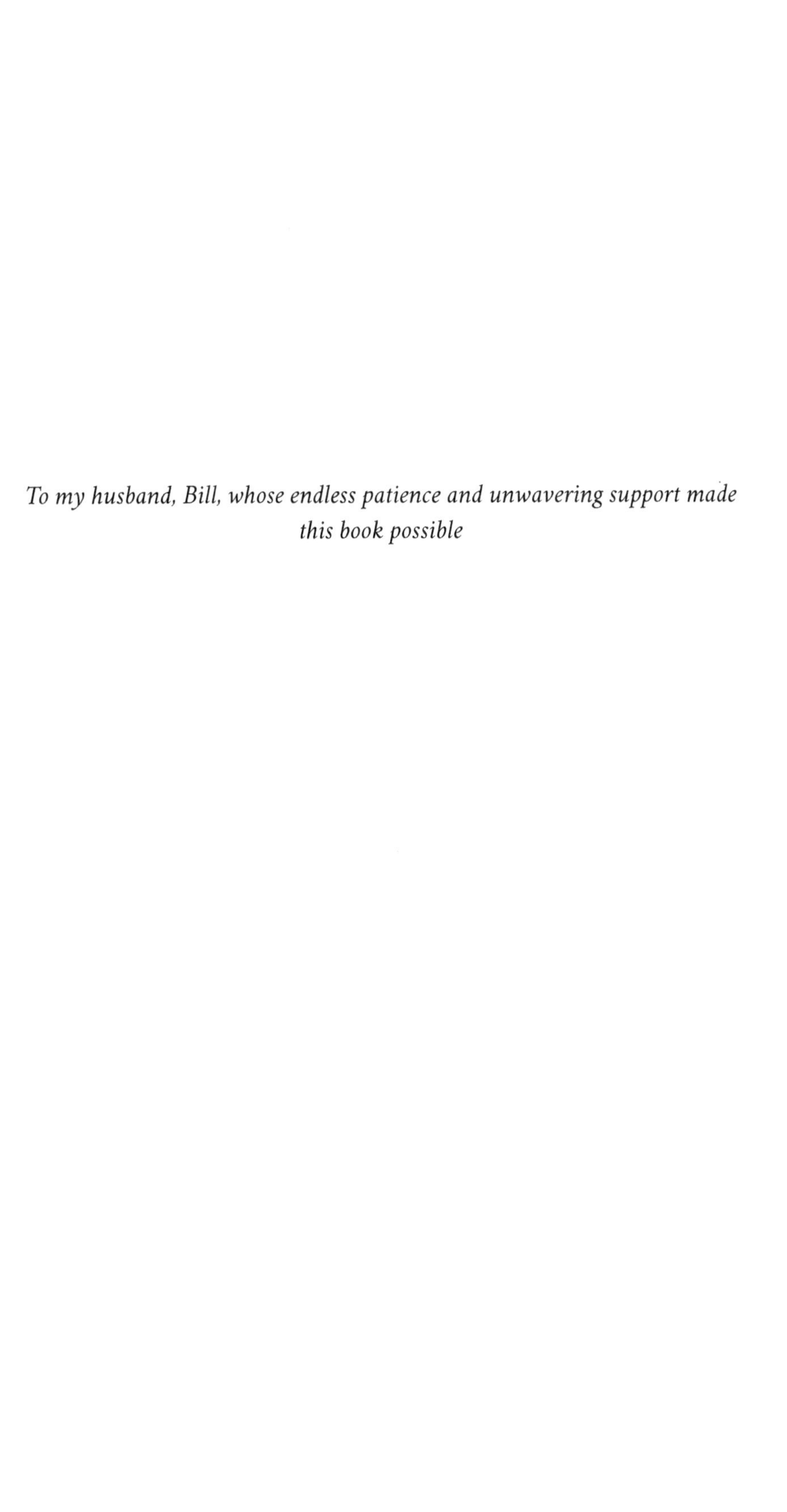

To my husband, Bill, whose endless patience and unwavering support made this book possible

PROLOGUE

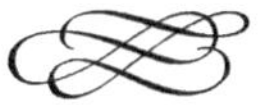

 *000 B.C.*
It was a Hell of a party.

Samael, Demon of Pride, couldn't remember a better one. Along the back wall of his apartment, a quartet of demons yodeled disharmonies while their audience yelled insults and pelted them with rotten figs. In the middle of the room, at a bar consisting of a slab of granite balanced on stalagmites, a bartender boiled wormwood with anise for an endless line of takers. They shuddered as they slugged back the bubbling concoction and immediately got in line for more.

Near the front of the apartment, still more demons roasted wild boar sausages over an open fire while others, drunk on wormwood cocktails, tried to pee on the sausages. Here and there fights broke out when one of them was successful.

Like every apartment in Hell, Sam's was fashioned from hardened lava, but it contained one feature no other demon's apartment had. A thousand years ago, as an anniversary gift, his wife, Lilith, had arranged to have a skylight carved into their ceiling. Sunlight streamed in during the day and when the moon was full, as it was tonight, the skylight all but eliminated the need for the torches that billowed sulfurous smoke throughout the rest of Hell. Their skylight was the envy of every demon Below.

As if summoned by his thought of her, Lilith appeared at his side, finger-combing her unruly hair back from her face. He put his arm around her waist, breathing in her signature scent of anise and sesame. She lifted her face for a kiss and he obliged.

Lilith had been born human. Some might say that her nose was a smidgen too long or her lips a fraction too full. Her dark hair, instead of flowing over her shoulders in glossy waves, tumbled down her back in rebellious curls, but none of those defects made her any less beautiful in his eyes. She might not possess the beauty of a fallen angel, but Sam loved everything about her. If she lacked the flawless features of a fallen angel, her vitality and ferocious intelligence made her once-celestial counterparts seem pale and uninteresting.

A short, skinny figure with skin the color of rancid cherries and a pair of onyx horns poking from the top of his head pushed his way through the crowd, snarling at the drunken demons in his path.

"I'm leaving," Lucifer announced like he was making a proclamation. In the three thousand years since he had founded Hell, he had shriveled like a grape left in the sun, losing all resemblance to the bright morning star he'd once been.

"Thanks for dropping by." Sam slapped him on the back. He kept his touch light, but Lucifer staggered and would have fallen if not for the horde of toadies that swarmed so close—within fart-smelling distance, as Lilith, termed it—he didn't have room to drop.

Lucifer's eyes swept the room.

"Fools," he sneered. "The Enemy must be congratulating himself on unloading these idiots."

"They're just blowing off steam," Sam said. "They work hard."

"Not as hard as you." Lilith said. She smiled at Lucifer. "I hope you had a good time?"

"I've had better." He spat on the ground, the tips of his forked tongue flickering into view for an instant.

"Boring," one of his toadies said.

"Weak," another chimed in.

"Lousy food," said the third.

Within the circle of Sam's arm, Lilith went rigid. He tightened his arm around her waist. "Glad you enjoyed it."

Lucifer scowled but Sam's smile didn't waver. The boss could enjoy the party or stay home or go fuck himself. It was all the same to Sam. After a long moment, Lucifer hitched his chin. "Come see me tomorrow morning. I have something to discuss with you."

Two a.m. had come and gone and the party showed no sign of winding down. "Is ten o'clock okay?"

"Make it nine." Lucifer's expression said he wasn't feeling reasonable.

"See you in the throne room at nine, then," Sam said.

"The throne room at nine," the toadies chorused.

"Not the throne room." Lucifer aimed a kick at the closest one. "Meet me in the Vestibule. What I have to show you lies Aboveworld."

"Not the throne room," the toadies chorused. "Tomorrow we go Aboveworld."

Lucifer loosed another kick, connecting this time. "Not you. Just Sam."

The first toady kicked the second one. "Not you. Just Sam." The second toady kicked the third. "Not you. Just Sam."

Lucifer stomped away, disappearing into the dark corridor of Ring One, his entourage limping in his wake like a school of impaired minnows.

Lilith frowned after them. "What's his problem?"

Sam leaned down to whisper against her ear. "He's jealous of how happy we are."

She shivered, melting against him. "You gave me chills."

"Get rid of these rowdies and I'll give you more than that."

She purred a low laugh that made him consider ordering their remaining guests out the door. Other demons changed partners as often as they changed clothing—in some cases, more often—but he and Lilith had achieved a most un-Hellish accomplishment, long-term happiness together.

It didn't bother him that Lilith had been married before. She hadn't chosen her ex-husband, Adam. They were the Enemy's first experiment with humankind. Adam hadn't known how to please her —not in the ways Sam had done for the past two thousand years.

"Do you think he's upset with us?" Her gaze returned to the darkened hallway.

"For what? Inviting him to a great party?"

"For throwing a party that drew ten times as many demons as his last gathering."

"What else should we have done? Left him off the guest list?"

She rubbed her arms. "Maybe we should have gone with a smaller list. You know how touchy he is."

He put his hands over hers to still them. "Do you honestly think Lucifer will dare to penalize me for giving better parties than he does?"

"He wants us to call him Satan now. And no, but I do think he might punish you for being better liked than he is."

Sam shrugged. "There's nothing he can do to me. In Heaven, I was a seraph while he was a mere cherub."

She frowned. "You're not in Heaven anymore."

And he had no desire to be. The work he did in Hell was far more interesting. In Heaven, his only task had been to worship the Enemy, all day, every day. Was it any wonder he'd grown bored?

"The hierarchy still prevails," he said. "No angel can hold dominion over an angel of higher rank." Lucifer's signature move, placing a demon in thrall and operating him like a puppet, didn't work on Sam. He was the only demon in Hell who could make that claim.

She squeezed the arm wrapped around her waist. "I know he can't enthrall you but that doesn't mean he can't punish you in other ways."

Sam dropped his arm. "You worry too much."

The next morning Sam winced at the sunshine pouring through the skylight when Lilith woke him at eight a.m. His head pounded and his tongue tasted like mildewed straw.

She offered him a cup of ginger tea. "You need to get up. You're meeting Satan at nine."

He dragged the antelope-hide blanket over his head. "There's no point in arriving early. He keeps everyone waiting so we'll realize how important he is."

Ruthlessly, she yanked the hide from his hands. "But he knows through his spies whether you're on time or not."

Groaning, he sat up and drank the tea. Almost immediately, he felt better. He looked around the apartment for something to eat but the previous night's guests had been a swarm of locusts, consuming everything in their path.

Lilith scavenged a shriveled sausage from behind the bar and offered it to him. "He seemed really angry last night."

"He's always angry." Sam swallowed a bite of the sausage. His stomach threatened to send it back. He handed it back to Lilith.

"You're not eating." Her eyes narrowed. "Do you have heartburn?"

She believed he got heartburn from keeping secrets from her, though nothing could be further from the truth. "I'm fine."

"His anger felt more focused than usual." She caught her lower lip between her teeth. "Couldn't you, just this once, try appeasing him a little?"

"Everyone else down here appeases him. It's made him insufferable." Sam wiped his fingers on the antelope hide. "I don't have to, and I won't."

Lilith's jaw tightened. "One of these days, your pride will be your destruction."

"Never happen," he said. "I'm indestructible, remember?" And he headed off to the waterfall to shower.

Sam arrived at the Vestibule nearly ten minutes early. When Lucifer finally showed up, he headed up the narrow path that led from the Vestibule to the surface without so much as a word of greeting. Could Lilith be right? Was he genuinely upset about the party?

A few minutes later they exited Hell into sunshine and a cloudless sky. Sam stood for a moment, breathing in fresh air and enjoying the view. Rolling fields of barley and wild wheat spread out before them in a golden vista. Nearby, lush vines sagged under the weight of fat purple grapes.

Lucifer's lip curled. It infuriated him that the Enemy had created all this beauty for mere mortals. He would have claimed this territory for Hell if it hadn't meant full-scale war with Heaven.

"I've been thinking about creating a new position in Hell," he said abruptly.

"What sort of position?" And why had they needed to leave Hell to discuss it?

"I'm calling it 'Devil's Advocate.'"

Sam snagged a bunch of grapes from a nearby vine. "And what will this Devil's Advocate do, exactly?"

"Look behind you."

Sam turned. In this direction, the view was completely different. Perhaps a mile from where they stood, all the greenery had been stripped away and a thousand-foot circle dug into the earth. Within that circle, smaller circles of stone pillars reached for the sky. He counted twenty of the smaller circles, each comprised of ten pillars. The amount of work involved in cutting two hundred pillars from stone with hammers and chisels and then raising them upright boggled his mind.

"What is that?" The last time he'd come through here, with Lilith, there had been nothing manmade in this valley.

"They call it Gobekli Tepe. It's a temple."

"Their building skills have progressed a long way." Perhaps Lil's complaints about how long it had been since they'd taken a vacation were valid after all.

"As have their communication skills." Lucifer's words expressed admiration but his tone did not. "And this is only the beginning. In the coming centuries, projects like this will teach them to collaborate."

Sam heard what he didn't say. Without interference, humanity would move closer to the Enemy's vision of amity and cooperation and away from Hell's goal of turmoil and misery.

Lucifer's tone became brisk. "Fortunately, that will require them to make rules for interacting with each other. That's why I brought you here today. We need to ensure the laws they create move things in our direction."

In the valley below them, tiny figures scurried like ants.

Sam lifted one eyebrow. "So, an actual job." Over the years, he had tried to interest Lucifer in creating an organizational structure similar to the one in Heaven, but the boss preferred chaos.

"An actual job." Geniality sat awkwardly on Lucifer's narrow face, which had always seemed more designed for resentment.

"With a primary task of undermining humanity's quest to improve itself?" It sounded like a stimulating job, one that would grow in complexity as human civilization evolved.

"Precisely."

"What are the qualifications?"

"A legalistic frame of mind is a good starting point."

Lilith often described him that way, though she didn't mean it as a compliment. Was Lucifer toying with him, pretending to offer him his heart's desire just so he could rip the prize away? He seemed perfectly serious.

"The ideal candidate also needs the ability to work with other demons in a supervisory capacity," Lucifer continued.

Sam plucked a fat grape from the bunch in his hand. Since the day they arrived in Hell, after their vicious but ultimately undecided battle with the angel forces, he'd been supervising lesser demons, but only informally. With this job, he would be the first demon with a clearly defined role in Hell. He liked that; he liked that a lot.

He popped the grape into his mouth. It tasted sweet on his tongue. "This job sounds custom-made for me."

"You have only one drawback that I can see, and it's a small one. One tiny adjustment and you'll be a perfect fit." Lucifer smiled agreeably. It was even more unnatural looking than his earlier geniality.

Sam pictured the bowing and scraping that would result from this promotion. Other demons respected him, but this role would make it clear he was their superior. "What adjustment would that be?"

"You need to break things off with Lilith."

The grape went sour in Sam's mouth. "What?"

"You need to divorce her. I can see how, as the first human to join our team, she was a novelty in the beginning, but why are you still with her?"

Sam searched for words to explain the pleasure he received from his relationship with Lilith. Lucifer had known love in Heaven, but he'd rejected it in favor of lust, envy, greed and anger. In the end, Sam settled for asking, "Why would I want to divorce Lilith?"

"She's a human." All of Lucifer's resentment of the Enemy's favored beings came through in his tone.

How to make him understand Lilith was more than a mere human? "We're compatible."

Gray smoke issued from Lucifer's horns. "You were once a seraph, from the highest sphere in Heaven. Now you ally yourself with the lowliest of the low, a barren dust wench. She's not worthy of you."

"She's my wife." It was as close as Sam could come to expressing the bond he felt with her.

The smoke from Lucifer's horns thickened. "Your marriage is an embarrassment to every demon in Hell."

"Every demon in Hell can mind his own business." *You included.*

But Lucifer's face didn't lighten and the smoke didn't thin. "I cannot put you in a leadership position when your personal life is an outrage. Demons are complaining."

"None of the demons at the party last night seemed to have any objections."

A shadow materialized overhead, blocking the sun and spreading gloom across the land. Around them, the wheat flattened as though beset by a strong wind, though the air remained calm. Sam scanned the skies. High above their heads, a meteor streaked earthward.

The falling star slowed as it descended. As it grew nearer, it took on the shape of an angel wearing a white robe, wings tight against its body. Closer still and Sam could see that the angel's hair was red as fire. Twenty feet above the earth, he spread his wings, slowing his descent even more. Sam didn't recognize him, but his robe and human-like appearance placed him in the lowest tier of angels, the class used as couriers. Did he bear a message from the Enemy?

Lucifer's eyes flickered in what looked like recognition, but he didn't greet the angel.

The angel's feet touched down but his wings remained open, blocking the sunlight. Sam and Lucifer had forfeited their wings when they'd rebelled against the Enemy but if this angel expected envy, he would be disappointed. With Hell's low ceilings and narrow passages, wings wouldn't be of much use Below. Sam had traded the ability to fly for a more interesting job and a life with a beautiful partner. He would gladly make that trade again.

Lucifer folded his arms across his skinny chest. "What brings you here?"

They definitely knew each other.

The angel inclined his head. "I saw you admiring the world's first temple and flew down to accept your compliments."

Sam bristled at his air of superiority. "That's a temple? We mistook it for a garbage dump."

The angel scowled. His coppery locks lifted like coral snakes gathering themselves to strike. "This is mankind's first attempt to build something lasting."

"It looks like a first attempt."

His hair writhed a little faster. "We think it a marvel. Yahweh is greatly pleased."

"He is easily satisfied where humans are concerned," Lucifer said.

The snakes writhed so fast they looked like they would tie themselves in knots. The angel took a deep breath, calming them. His piercing gaze turned on Sam. "What of you, Samael? Are you still happy with the choice you made of evil over good?"

The choice had never seemed quite that clear cut—more like a choice of honesty over hypocrisy. "I am."

"And are you still married to Lilith Firstwoman?" The angel

attempted to sound casual, but his hair started moving again and a vein throbbed in his temple.

"I am. She is the source of my contentment Below." Sam aimed that last bit at Lucifer.

Without appearing to move, the angel closed the gap between them. He stood so close his breath ruffled the neck of Sam's tunic. "Has she borne you children?"

Like a blade concealed in a pile of feathers, his question was as sharp as it was unexpected. Sam and Lilith's childlessness had been a source of disappointment for the past two thousand years. Lilith desperately wanted a child and having offspring would demonstrate his superiority to other demons.

Where had this question come from? Not from the Enemy. He already knew Lilith had borne Sam no children. "Not yet."

The angel's answering smirk was like a thorn in Sam's pride. This winged messenger would not get the upper hand. "But now that you mention it, having a child might be amusing."

The angel's smirk disappeared as if it had never been and his hair burst into flame. Whirling to face Lucifer, he intoned, "Hear my words and beware, Lucifer Morningstar. If the demon Samael begets a child with Lilith Firstwoman, you will lose your empire."

Sam listened, stunned. Lucifer grew as still as marble. "What mean you?"

The angel spread his wings, making him seem more imposing. "Heed what I say, Morningstar. If Samael and Lilith spawn a child, that child will rip your domain from your fingers."

A muscle ticked in Lucifer's jaw. Sam stifled a groan. That thrice-blessed angel had tapped into the boss's worst nightmare. He resented Sam and Lilith's happiness, but it was more than that. Together, they constituted a threat to his supremacy. He feared their popularity would allow them to wrest the leadership of Hell from his grasp, though Sam had no interest in leading the chaos that was Hell.

Lucifer's paranoia, never very well-contained, burst forth. His face darkened and his horns puffed black smoke. "This will not happen. I will not allow it."

But Sam had spent thousands of years listening to the Enemy's every utterance. The angel's prophecy didn't sound like anything the Enemy would say. "Who sent this message?"

The angel ignored him. "Disregard me at your peril, Morningstar." With that, he flew away.

Lucifer stood silent as the winged form disappeared into the sky. When the angel was no longer visible, he said, "You and Lilith must separate."

Sam snorted. "Nonsense. A child of mine and Lilith's would be half human. It would be far too weak to challenge you for leadership of Hell."

Lucifer's face didn't lighten. "You heard his prediction."

"I heard it but I don't believe it."

Smoke from Lucifer's horns hung over their heads in a dense cloud. "Making a false prophecy is grounds for being evicted from Heaven. He wouldn't risk that."

It was clear they knew each other. "Who was he?"

"I haven't seen him before."

Lucifer was lying. Sam would bet his skylight on it. He tried another tack. "Lilith and I have been together for two thousand years without conceiving. If she was going to bear me a child, she'd have done so by now."

"That's not what you told our visitor."

Because he'd been too proud to admit the truth.

Lucifer waited a moment for him to answer. When he didn't, the boss's voice hardened. "I will not risk my empire being stolen from me. You must separate from Lilith immediately."

This was the confrontation Sam had been avoiding since they'd founded Hell. Now that it was here, he couldn't back away. "I will not."

Lucifer's pupils squared off. Filthy smoke clouded the air above his head. "I say you will."

Lilith was the greatest joy in Sam's life. He was the center of her universe and her adoration made him feel appreciated in a way nothing else did. "And if I refuse? You hold no dominion over me."

It was the wrong thing to say.

"I may not have any power over you," Lucifer snarled, "but I have the power of life and death over the dust wench. I made her immortal. Leave her, or I will revoke that immortality. Without my gift, she'll crumble into the pile of dirt she should have been two millennia ago."

Shock froze Sam in place. "You can't do that."

Lucifer bared his teeth in a ferocious grimace that had nothing to do with smiling. "Watch me."

Sam had no fear for himself, but Lilith was another matter. She was human, with all the frailty that entailed. After she'd left Adam, Lucifer had offered her immortality in exchange for abandoning Earth and joining Hell while she was still alive. She was his first human recruit. Later humans, rejected by the Enemy after their deaths and consigned to Hell, were tortured accordingly, but she was different.

Over the past two thousand years, Lilith had picked up some demon traits—she could deploy her scent to distract people and her pupils turned rectangular when she was angry—but she had started out as a human, and Satan never let her forget it. Without his gift of immortality, her body would disintegrate. She would become a wraith, like all the other damned souls in Hell.

"You made an agreement with her," Sam said.

Lucifer shrugged. "Satan giveth and Satan taketh away. She won't be the first to discover it's a mistake to make a deal with the devil."

"You didn't have a problem with our being together two thousand years ago."

"I didn't know about the child two thousand years ago."

"There *is* no child." Sweat popped up on Sam's forehead. "Lilith is barren."

"She gave her first husband a child."

"She was a lot younger then. What is the likelihood she'll conceive after all this time?"

"Enough," Satan said. "It's your choice. Leave her or I will end her."

Perhaps if their popularity hadn't already felt like a threat, Lucifer would have been more willing to listen to reason. As things stood, it was clear that if Sam didn't agree to separate from Lilith, Lucifer would reduce her to a pile of dust. Leaving her would be painful, but it was better than watching her die.

He licked his lips. "If I agree, will you swear never to revoke her immortality?"

Lucifer's color lightened. "I don't want to destroy her. I've always had a soft spot for her. That's why I lured her to Hell to begin with. As long as you stay apart, I'll let her live."

What choice did he have?

"Understand me." He looked his boss directly in the eye. "This is one contract you cannot break. I have no desire to rule Hell, but if you destroy Lilith, I will take your throne and exile you to the desert for all eternity." As a seraph, he could do that right now, but it wouldn't save Lilith. Lucifer alone held the power of life and death over her.

Lucifer's complexion darkened again. "I will hear no treasonous talk."

"You need hear none, as long as you honor your word."

Lucifer stuck out his chin. "Stay away from the dust wench and she'll be fine."

No one must know of Lucifer's threat. As the only demon in Hell who wasn't subject to Thrall, Sam commanded a lot of respect. If they discovered Lucifer had coerced him into leaving Lilith, he would lose that respect.

"It would be best if Lilith believes you gave me a choice between her and this new position and I chose the job," he said. "Otherwise, she'll badger you endlessly."

Lucifer shrugged. "Tell her whatever you like. Do we have a deal?"

"Yes, we have a deal," Sam said. A lowly messenger angel had just cost him the only woman he had ever loved.

The next time they met, it was the angel who would lose.

CHAPTER 1

ugust 2022

Lilith stepped off the elevator onto Ring Four and shook the last maggot from her hair. At least, she hoped it was the last one. She shuddered as the tiny white body dropped to the rock floor, writhing sightlessly.

She'd spent the past month swimming in larvae and she reeked of ammonia. It would be great if she could shower before answering Satan's summons, but she couldn't afford to keep him waiting. Not if she didn't want to wind up back among the tiny white worms. She broke into a trot.

Whatever the boss had in store for her, whatever disagreeable task he wanted her to perform, no matter how onerous, humiliating, or downright disgusting, she needed to keep that in mind. Otherwise, she'd be back in the maggot pit faster than a fallen angel could claim credit for work he didn't do. So, no smarting off. No being difficult. Today would be all "Yes, my lord," and "Of course, my lord."

Now, where in Hell was conference room 4H? She pictured the layout of the fourth ring in her head. Was 4H the one with the stalagmites on either side of the door? That sounded right.

A pair of limestone columns flanking a metal door came into view. At the sight of it, she slowed to a stroll. Survival in Hell required catering to Satan's whims but self-respect demanded not letting it be too obvious.

In the middle of the door was a small window made of wire mesh sandwiched between thick panes of glass. She checked her reflection in the greenish glass. Her hair was in good order, but the lapels of her crimson silk suit were rumpled and stained. Grimacing, she awarded herself a C+. Not bad for someone who had spent the past three weeks up to her armpits in fly larvae.

The only demon she could see through the window was Satan. He appeared to be talking to someone—some over-rewarded and underperforming member of the old demons' network, no doubt. The boss's face was darker than normal and a haze of smoke hung in the air above him.

Apparently, it was not a good day in Hell.

She took a deep breath. Respectful, she reminded herself. Accommodating. She opened the door and stepped inside.

"You wanted to see me?" She tried to strike the right note—polite but not boot-licking.

Satan scowled. "What took you so long?"

Jeez Louise, who peed on his Pop Tart? It was tempting to remind him that the maggot pit was seven levels below Ring Four, but all she said was, "I got here as quickly as I could."

He grunted. "I have a mission for you. If you're successful, I'm prepared to be very generous."

Despite a hundred centuries of experience warning her not to get excited, a tiny bud of hope sprouted inside her. Was this the mission that would finally prove her worth to Satan and elevate her to the position she coveted—Director of Demon Resources?

She inclined her head gracefully. "Whatever I can do to further the cause of Hell."

"At least someone down here is a team player." He shot a nasty look at the demon sitting across the table from him.

Who had pissed him off this time? She followed his gaze and her pulse spiked. The object of his ire was her ex-husband, Samael, Demon of Pride, Devil's Advocate and Hell's chief counsel.

For a moment she couldn't stop herself from drinking in the sight of him. He wore a charcoal suit and a snowy white shirt with a red silk tie. His beautifully tailored jacket showcased his shoulders to perfection. No doubt the pants did the same for his tight little tush, a tush that was perfect for gripping when… She banished the image. He was also a soulless jerk.

What was he doing here, anyway? He hadn't dirtied his hands with operational work in a thousand years. Maybe longer. Then she registered the identities of the remaining six demons in the room. They were the Deadlies, so-called because they headed up Hell's deadly sin divisions. Whatever was going on must be something big.

"I'm willing to do what you ask." Sam folded his arms across his broad chest, his body language at odds with his statement. His gaze focused on Satan like she wasn't even in the room. "All I'm requesting is time to finish up the acquisition I've been working on."

She breathed in but she was too far away to smell his signature scent of leather and lime. Then she realized what she was doing. Her face heated and she stopped inhaling. After ten thousand years, why did he still have this power over her?

"What's the job?" she asked.

"It's a great opportunity," Satan said.

It must be a real stinker. On the other hand, it couldn't be any worse than finishing out her sentence in the maggot pit. A truck carrying a new load of fly larvae had pulled up just as she left. That truckload would bring the depth to chin level.

"This is the one you've been waiting for," Satan said. "Make a success of this mission and I'll give you that promotion to D.R. director you've been pestering me about."

She couldn't believe her ears. As Director of Demon Resources, she would finally have some influence down here. She could set up personnel policies to enforce some accountability on the wingless slackers that lounged around Hell doing nothing to earn their keep.

"What's up?" she asked. And what, exactly, constituted success?

"Heaven has requested trade talks."

Interesting. Open warfare hadn't broken out between the spheres in centuries though there were constant squabbles. Angels and demons were immortal, but when they fought, humans sometimes got killed in the crossfire. "On which front?"

"Global warming, the increase in gun violence, the rise of social media, the future of space, the status of women—the whole shebang."

The status of women. As a human, she was the logical representative on that topic. She couldn't repress a smile. For the first time in her very long history down here, Satan had asked her to join a delegation representing Hell. Maybe he really was grooming her for that directorship. "Who else will be part of the delegation?"

Satan swept one skinny arm to encompass the room. "All my division heads."

This was a major deal, then. Maybe, just maybe, his offer was the real deal this time. It wouldn't do to seem too eager, though. She needed to play it cool. "How long will the conference last?"

It was apparently the right question because Satan beamed at her. "Three weeks."

Hosanna, it was really going to happen this time. She tilted her head and smiled. "And what will my role be?"

"Administrative." Satan pronounced the hated word like he was conferring an honor.

Her lips flattened. She should have known it was too good to be true.

Satan smiled his smarmiest smile. "You'll make all the arrangements—reserve hotel rooms, plan meals, interface with the staff at the conference venue and so forth. The last time we got together for a trade summit, Heaven hosted and we met in a monastery." The curl of his lip made his thoughts on that clear. Then he rubbed his hands together. "I'll give you the budget to do it up right. I want to blow their wings off."

She swallowed and forced the next words out, all too aware of Sam watching and listening. "And once the conference begins?"

He beamed like he was doing her a favor. "You'll keep things running smoothly."

In other words, she'd be a go-fer. There was no direct line from this assignment to her dream job. Satan was dangling the directorship in front of her as bait so she would do what he wanted. Which meant he expected her to resist, which meant he thought she'd view this assignment as worse than returning to the maggot pit. But why? What could be worse than the maggot pit? With a sinking feeling, she asked, "Who is the mission lead?"

"Sam."

Her gaze flew to her ex-husband's face. It was as calm as it had been on the day he'd told her he had accepted a promotion in exchange for divorcing her. Three weeks later she was working as a succubus and he was dating a she-demon with red hair and breasts higher than her IQ.

She couldn't do it. She just couldn't. "No way in heaven."

Satan's face, which had lightened to an affable shade of rose, darkened again. "You'll do as you're told."

"You can't put her on this mission." Sam's voice was devoid of emotion.

Satan whirled on him. "Why not?

She tensed, waiting to hear Sam's objection. As Satan was her witness, if Sam insulted her, she would yank off her shoe and drive its stiletto heel straight through his eyeball.

"She can't be part of a cosmic summit," Sam said. "She's human."

Satan shrugged that off. "She's immortal. That makes her as good as demon."

Not to Sam, who knew to which heavenly order each and every demon had once belonged. Humans were a rung beneath even the lowest of them. When they met he had nicknamed her "dust wench." At the time it had seemed like a term of endearment. It was only after their split she realized it described how he really felt about her. How in Hell had she lived with him for two thousand years without realizing how much he despised her?

"You said you needed a competent admin." Satan raised his skinny eyebrows at Sam. "Are you saying she's not competent?"

She eased her heel out of her shoe.

"She's a brilliant operative." Sam's tone remained flat and unreadable. "Everyone knows that."

Somewhat appeased, she settled her heel back into her shoe. Sam considered her brilliant. He'd never told her that, not even when they were a couple. Of course, she'd had little opportunity to display brilliance back then, keeping house in what was essentially a cave. As bad as their breakup had been, at least it had gotten her off her duff and onto an actual career path.

"She's very emotional," Sam said. "The trait appears to be a result of her humanity. It makes her the most difficult demon to deal with in all of Hell."

Around the room, the other division heads murmured their agreement. She raked them with a scorching glare. They needn't think she'd forget this. The next time Lust wanted a wingman while seducing a Hollywood starlet, or Gluttony was on the hunt for barbecue made from some endangered species, or Greed wanted the inside scoop on a pyramid scheme, they were on their own. Under her baleful eye, they slouched in their chairs. The murmur died away.

"It's not going to work, Luce." Sam used Satan's nickname from their Heaven days. He was reminding everyone how far back their alliance went. "If you coerce her into doing this against her will, she'll sabotage the talks."

Satan stiffened. "She wouldn't dare."

So that was what Sam really thought of her these days: brilliant, but thorny, deceptive and vengeful. And he was absolutely right. If she took this gig, she would use the opportunity to earn Sam some quality time in the maggot pit. The thought of him wading chest-deep into smelly fly larvae in his immaculately tailored suit filled her with glee. It wouldn't do to appear too eager, though.

"Forget it." She turned toward the door but Satan's claw-like hand shot out and grasped her elbow, stopping her in her tracks.

"You will work on this mission." His tone was low and deadly. "You will cooperate with Sam and you will do your best to make the negotiation a success for Hell."

His talon dug into her arm, puncturing the skin. The wound burned like acid.

What was going on here? Ten thousand years ago, he'd bribed Sam to split up with her but now he wanted them to work together? Even as she framed the question, she knew the answer. The central goal of Satan's existence was to best the Enemy. This trade summit was one such opportunity. She was the best tactician down here and Sam was the best strategist. Together they were unbeatable. That was why he'd split them up in the first place.

She yanked her elbow from his grasp. "Or what? Back to the maggot pit? Do you really think that scares me? I've spent so much time down there I have my own coffee cup."

Satan's face darkened to the color of a pinot noir. His horns streamed filthy smoke and his pupils squared into goat-like rectangles. Uh-oh.

"Have I become too predictable?" His silky purr sent a shiver down her spine. "Perhaps we should change things up. Instead of returning to the maggot pit, which you find so dull, how about if I send you to Bolgia Five for a while?"

Well, that went from zero to sixty in no time. In Bolgia Five, the damned swam in pools of boiling pitch. If they tried to climb out, guards prodded them back into the bubbling tar with pitchforks—and they weren't careful about where the tines landed, either.

Sam made no attempt to intervene on her behalf. No surprise there. When Satan had ordered them to separate ten thousand years earlier, Sam had made no effort to resist, choosing a promotion to Devil's Advocate over her. Prideful bastard.

Had he intended to get her into trouble today? Or would he say this outcome was a product of her own choices, as he'd claimed about their breakup so long ago? One thing was clear—he was as reluctant to have her on this mission as she was to go.

She couldn't be seen to give in too easily, though. She waited for another beat, until Satan's grasp on her elbow became unbearable. As well as giving her a shot at undermining Sam, it might also let her finally achieve her dream job.

"Fine," she said. "I'll do it."

CHAPTER 2

*L*ilith exited the room still bristling like a porcupine. Sam would take a thousand quills for a chance to be with her again, but Satan would never allow it.

Over the years, Sam had quietly run interference for her whenever he could, but it wasn't easy. Satan was constantly on the lookout for signs they were secretly communicating. After their split, he had assigned her to the Lust division to work as a succubus. With her history, it was the worst possible assignment. Sam had been livid but Satan's surveillance made it impossible to get it changed without putting her at risk.

It had taken him nearly a century of quiet work behind the scenes to get her transferred to Envy. A few other times, a confidential exchange of favors had saved her from punishment, or gotten her released from the maggot pit early, but that was all he could do for her. The boss had never relaxed his vigilance. On the contrary, the longer he ruled Hell, the more paranoid he grew about losing his throne.

So why was he throwing them together now? Did he hope they would hook up while they were Above and give him an excuse to end

Lilith for once and for all? In spite of the heat, a cold shiver traveled down Sam's back.

The other six division heads filed from the room, but Satan signaled him to stay behind.

"I know she's a pain in the ass," Satan said, "but she's the best there is at dealing with human bureaucracy."

Sam eyed him warily. It would be safest if the boss believed Sam's reason for not wanting Lilith on the mission was professional, rather than personal.

"I don't care how good she is at winding petty clerks around her little finger. She'll happily spend the next millennium in the maggot pit if she thinks there's a chance she can drag me down there with her. Let me use my admin instead. Estelle can easily handle the arrangements."

Satan shook his head. "Estelle hasn't been above since 1665. She'd have no idea how to arrange a conference in the modern world."

"How about Gomory?" Sam named his co-worker and current girlfriend. "She's bright and willing."

Satan shook his head again. "We tried her as an operative before she joined Legal. She was a disaster. She didn't compromise a single soul and I had to pull two of our best demons off mission work for decades while we waited for the hysteria to die down."

If Satan insisted on putting Lilith on this mission, they would have to work together to plan the conference. He'd have to breathe her anise and sesame scent every day. His fingertips would graze her smooth skin each time she handed him paperwork to sign. It would be exquisite torture, but worse would follow. Once they went Above, he'd have to watch her head for her hotel room every night, unable to follow.

In the meeting just now, the craving to touch her had nearly overwhelmed him, but being with her meant signing her death warrant. Aware of Satan's watchful eye, he'd hidden his feelings behind a cloak of professionalism. "Surely there's someone else who would be more effective than a dust wench."

Satan shook his head. "There's no one in her league."

"Doesn't Greed have someone on staff that can set up a conference? He runs the Travel department, for Hell's sake."

Satan's face darkened to the burgundy hue that warned his temper was fraying. "They're morons. All they know how to do is save money. Not an ounce of imagination in the lot."

"How much imagination does it take to set up a trade conference?"

Smoke, pale gray but smoke nevertheless, seeped from Satan's left horn. "This is more than a trade conference. I want the venue to be so sensational Heaven is humiliated by their pathetic offering last time. I want the most delicious food those manna-eaters have ever tasted. I want music that makes their harpists sound like tone-deaf organ grinders." His voice rose in pitch with each item. "I want this summit to make them realize they chose the wrong side."

Sam watched him dispassionately. "Even if that's true, they won't admit it."

Satan's eyelids slitted till he looked like a snake. "You'd better hope at least one of them does. That's the measure of success for this mission."

Sam frowned. "What is?"

"I want an angel to defect to our side."

Satan had finally lost his mind. Sam had been expecting it for centuries and it had finally occurred.

"That's not going to happen. Not one single angel has joined Hell since the Great Rebellion." Sam thought for a moment. "Is that the real purpose of this conference? To entice an angel into joining Hell?"

"Think of it more like the icing on the cake. I want concessions *and* I want an angel to defect."

There was no way to pursue both objectives simultaneously. If Heaven's delegation realized Hell was trying to recruit an angel they would retreat back to their cloud kingdom in an instant.

"Do you have someone specific in mind, or will any angel do?" he asked.

"I understand the angel Gibeon is very dissatisfied." Satan's leathery eyelids descended again, masking his thoughts. "He's Heaven's administrator for the conference."

No wonder this Gibeon wasn't happy. Look at how Lilith had responded to being offered that role.

"What order is he?" There were nine orders of angels. Seraphs were the highest.

"He's a messenger."

The lowest order. Sam's mind flew back to the messenger whose prophecy had cost him his marriage all those millennia ago. Could this be the same fellow? No, that was ridiculous. Heaven had thousands upon thousands of angels—twice as many as there were demons in Hell. "How did you learn that he wants to come down here?"

"I've run into him a few times when I've been out and about." Satan's face took on a crafty look. "Don't tell anyone. Stealth is your best chance of success."

His best chance of success would be a boss with realistic expectations but, apparently, that wasn't an option.

"Take me off the mission." He tensed in anticipation of gale force blowback. Satan couldn't torture him as he did other demons—Sam's origin as a higher order angel ensured that—but he could make life unpleasant. "Or give me the trade talks but assign another Deadly to do the recruiting. Leviathan is a great recruiter and envy is universal."

"That may be, but pride is Gibeon's besetting sin."

Reluctantly, Sam nodded. A demon that shared his prospect's besetting sin was more likely to succeed in recruiting him. That still didn't address Sam's overload problem, though. "Then let me choose someone from my organization to entice him. Naberius has successfully enlisted a number of challenging prospects over the years."

Satan flicked his fingers dismissively. "Those were humans."

"He's the most persuasive demon on my staff."

Satan shook his head. "Naberius was only a Principality. Gibeon won't be impressed by a mere Principality."

Sam blinked. "Gibeon is a ninth-tier angel. You think being approached by a former seventh-tier angel won't impress him?"

"Not like being approached by a former first-tier."

That was true but Sam wasn't ready to give up. "You're not looking at the big picture. Adjusted boundaries with Heaven will have a much more profound impact on Hell's success rates than adding a single angel to our ranks." Gibeon was a trophy, nothing more.

"He has a lot of promise," Satan said stubbornly.

He was thinking about the Enemy's reaction when he learned an angel had defected. Satan had founded Hell with the intention of competing directly with Heaven for control of Earth. It was only after the Fall that he realized he lacked the Enemy's ability to spark life. Without that power, he'd fallen back on the talents he did have—temptation, destruction and division.

Sam spread his hands. "Regardless of how much promise he shows, there's no way I can balance two opposing goals and do justice to either of them."

To his surprise, Satan's face didn't darken further but actually lightened. The smoke issuing from his horns thinned out. "What if I sweeten the pot?"

"Sweeten the pot in what way?" The boss had already promised him a choice promotion if the negotiations were successful. Wrath and Envy would report up through Sam, creating a whole new branch in the org structure with him at the top. There was no way Satan would hand over more power than that. Not for a single angelic recruit, even if he was the first since the Fall.

"What if I said that, while you're on this mission, you can have a hall pass to hook up with Lilith?"

He opened his mouth to deny any interest in being with Lilith but Satan cut him off. "I watched you as she walked out the door. You'd like nothing better than to hit that again."

Was Satan truly offering him an opportunity to be with Lilith again without condemning her to death? The thought was alluring. Was he serious? "What about the prophecy?"

Satan smirked. "It turns out there's a loophole."

A loophole? Why hadn't he heard about this before? "What loophole?"

"I don't have to kill her to stop her child from taking my throne."

Sam stilled. "You don't?" Did that mean he and Lilith could resume their marriage?

"No," Satan said. "I'd just have to kill the kid."

Sam was caught between shock and fury. "You do realize the infant you speak so casually of murdering would be mine as well as Lilith's?"

Satan shrugged. "So don't knock her up."

She hadn't gotten pregnant in two thousand years of actively trying. Assuming she'd even agree to be with him again—and she had held a grudge with remarkable tenacity for a very long time—the chances that she'd conceive in three short weeks were slim, but they weren't zero.

"You don't have to rely on chance." Satan seemed to read his mind. "Humans have mastered contraception. No woman has a baby these days unless she wants one."

Sam suspected this was an exaggeration, if not an outright lie, but it contained a kernel of truth. With human technology, they could essentially eliminate the minuscule chance of Lilith conceiving.

He should refuse this offer, but the opportunity to hold her again, even for a very short time, was irresistible. But how would he persuade her to partake of this offer? He could tell her the truth—that he hadn't wanted to give her up, that he'd done so only to save her life.

No, it was too risky. Angry as she was, she might spread the news throughout Hell that Sam, the untouchable seraph, had been bullied by Satan. He'd become a laughingstock. No, he'd have to think of something else.

"I'll do it," he said.

After the meeting, Lilith caught the elevator down to her apartment on Ring Eight. She still felt scummy from her larvae immersion, and the puncture wound on her arm throbbed. Because of her immortality, most injuries healed almost instantly, but supernatural wounds tended to fester. She'd need to clean it out when she got home.

As the elevator plunged downward, she considered her situation. Most of the denizens in this den of sin would be thrilled to spend three weeks Above, hobnobbing with Hell's highest-ranking demons and their angelic counterparts, but she wasn't most demons. She'd only ever had one interaction with angels and one was plenty.

After she left her first husband, three angels had visited the cave where she'd just given birth to her beautiful little daughter, Ayelet. They had commanded her to return to Adam. One had threatened Ayelet with death if Lilith didn't do as he ordered. She'd obeyed, but her tiny daughter had perished on the return journey to Eden. Twelve thousand years had passed, but her heart still ached at the recollection. She rubbed her arms, trying to erase the memory.

What if that angel was part of the heavenly delegation? The thought made her bones go cold even though the temperature around her warmed steadily as the elevator drew closer to the center of The Earth.

Given the number of angels in Heaven, the likelihood of that particular angel being assigned to this particular diplomatic mission was negligible. After killing her baby, he'd probably been promoted to seraph for a job well done. According to Sam, seraphs rarely left the heavenly throne room.

When the elevator arrived at Ring Eight. she stepped into murky darkness. The neighborhood where she'd lived with Sam, in Ring One, was the most prestigious in Hell. Adjacent to Aboveworld, it had access to sky and sun and fresh air. Sam set the rules in Ring One and enforced them with an iron fist. Anyone could walk safely there, night or day.

After he dumped her, Housing had assigned her an apartment in Judecca, in Ring Eight. Satan supervised Ring Eight and he let chaos reign. Judecca was a bad neighborhood, even by Hell's standards.

She crossed the stone bridge over the Phlegethon River. A hellrat skittered across the toe of her shoe, startling her before it disappeared beneath the bridge. An instant later, a wiry tail raked her shins as a hellcat raced by, chasing the rat. Thank hell she'd been wearing a pantsuit when she got hauled off to the maggot pit this time. The scratch of a hellcat's tail on bare skin left a fiery rash that took days to heal.

On the far side of the bridge, she paused for an instant. Were those footsteps behind her? Squeals and yowls emanating from beneath the bridge made it impossible to tell. She palmed her keys, fanning them out between her fingers. The yowls ceased as the hellcat emerged, the rat's limp body between its teeth. She listened carefully. If there had been footsteps, they were gone.

Her street, Atrocity Way, lay two blocks from the bridge, in one of the thousands of tunnels that honeycombed Hell. A series of heavy wooden doors, each opening to a small apartment, lined the streets here.

Hades, the tribe of miners and metalworkers that had peopled Hell before Lucifer arrived with his horde of fallen angels, had built her apartment. Because of course they had. It wasn't like fallen angels would do a day's work. They considered themselves above manual labor. Whatever bad things she might have to say about Sam since their breakup—and there were many—at least he wasn't a lazy, privileged idler like most former angels.

When she turned onto her street, it was even darker than usual. The imps that lived on Abomination Avenue must have snuffed out the torches again. Keys splayed through her fingers, she hurried toward her door. She didn't hear footsteps, but she couldn't shake the sense of being followed. Fortunately, the torch beside her front door still burned, so she had no trouble fitting her key into the lock.

Breathing a sigh of relief, she turned the key but before she could open the door, hands reached out of the darkness. She whirled to jab the key into her attacker's eyes but, at the last second, she caught the scent of leather and lime. She halted her hand.

Reaction exaggerated her annoyance. "You idiot! What are you doing?"

Even though she wore six-inch stilettos, Sam towered over her. His sculpted face was calm in the flickering light as he stared at her searchingly. What, exactly, was he looking for? Not forgiveness, surely. She had none of that to offer. Then he grinned. The murky corridor brightened, as if the torches blazed brighter because he smiled.

"Let's collaborate on this mission and get you promoted to your dream job." His voice was a sweetfall of persuasion as his scent wrapped itself around her.

"What do you know about that?" She stepped back, scowling. It wasn't wise to linger within scent distance of a demon. Their fragrances were designed to weaken human resistance and, despite her immortality, she was only human.

"I saw the way your face lit up when Satan mentioned it."

There didn't seem to be much point in denying it. His hands slid off her shoulders, stroking down her sleeves to her wrists. "What do you say?"

She pulled away, removing her arms from his hands. "Let me think about it." She tilted her head and tapped her chin.

He redoubled the wattage on his smile. "This is an opportunity for both of us to shine."

Since their breakup, Sam had done nothing but move ahead while she was stuck doing one-off missions. Although her successes outnumbered her failures, and far exceeded any other operative's total, she also spent more time in the maggot pit than any demon down here. Was it a bias against humans? Against women? Or did Satan simply enjoy torturing her? He treated her more like a client than an employee sometimes.

"What did he promise you if the negotiations are successful?" she asked.

Sam hesitated, so briefly that, if she hadn't known him well, she might not have noticed. She waited.

"More responsibility," he said finally.

He was hedging. There had to be a reason for that. "What kind of responsibility?"

This time the pause lasted longer. "If we're successful, Wrath and Envy will report up through me."

Rage worthy of Wrath himself detonated inside her skull. Having two divisions report to Sam represented a giant step up the ladder.

She had brought more souls into Hell than he had—more than any demon down here, for that matter—but it was the former angels who garnered all the perks and promotions.

"So happy for a chance to contribute to your meteoric rise." Her voice was as dry as volcanic ash.

He folded his arms across his chest. "He offered you Director of Demon Resources."

"He's promised me that job a dozen times, but it's never materialized," she said. "He always finds an excuse, some tiny misstep, to use as a justification to pass me over."

"That's not my fault."

No, but the callous way Sam had tossed her aside had not been without consequences. His abandonment had left her prey to the degenerates and dung-eaters who inhabited Hell. Opportunists had sensed in her, an unattached human female, an easy target. She'd spent every day since their split fending off unwanted advances, acquiring a reputation as a ball-buster in the process. It had taken all her strength, all her cunning, and a fair amount of ruthlessness to convince Satan's minions she wasn't their plaything.

"I'm a professional," she said. "I don't let personal feelings get in the way of doing my job."

Sam snorted. "Lil, be real. You're hoping to use this as an opportunity to get even with me for our breakup."

Humiliation set her face on fire. "Don't flatter yourself. I got over that long ago."

Under the flickering torchlight, the twist of his lips said he didn't believe a word of it. "Then come by my office this afternoon so we can plan this conference."

He had just summoned her to his office like a junior stenographer. She didn't like it, but Satan had left her little choice. "What time?"

"Two."

Now that he had gotten what he wanted, she expected him to leave but he lingered, gazing down at her with a look she couldn't interpret. It caught her off guard when he slipped his hands inside the cuffs of her suit jacket, stroking the bare skin of her forearms. Instantly, her mind filled with images of the way they'd been back in the day—of him smoothing her hair aside to kiss the back of her neck; of the two of them stealing plump grapes from the vineyards in Carmel, laughing like children and racing away when the vintner caught them; of him pouring wine into the valley between her breasts and slowly licking it off. The images were so rich she could taste the grapes, smell the wine and feel the stroke of his tongue on her flesh.

It was a demon gift, this ability to swamp a human's mind with implanted images. Thank Hell she knew how to fight it. She dragged up an image from the day he'd abandoned her. Remembered anguish nearly brought her to her knees but the visions he'd planted shattered like glass. Gritting her teeth, she knocked his hands away. "What are you doing?

"We'll be Above for three weeks." His voice was so low it sent a shiver through her. She could feel the heat coming off his body. The scent of leather and lime filled her nostrils like a narcotic.

"So?" She was a fool for not walking through her door and slamming it in his face, but she wanted to hear what he had to say.

"What happens Above stays Above." Leaning down, he nipped at the spot where her neck met her shoulder. The warmth of his lips on her skin made her back arch. Her pelvis pressed against his. He was already as hard as the rock that surrounded them.

For an instant, desire bent reality, promising they could be together again. When they were a couple, the air had smelled sweeter, food had tasted better, colors had been richer. Even Satan's cacophonous symphony had sounded more harmonious from the shelter of Sam's arms. With him, she'd felt cherished, safe.

His lips brushed her jaw and then took her mouth with a hunger that said being apart had been as hard for him as it had for her.

Except it hadn't. None of that was true. She hadn't been safe, only blind to the danger. In the centuries since they'd split, he'd dated a parade of she-demons, each more lovely than the last. He was currently seeing a blonde she-demon who worked in his office.

The thought of Gomory stiffened her spine. She shoved at his chest and the feel of his pectoral muscles against her palms almost undid her. It had been so long since she'd felt his body pressed against her, reveled in his lips on hers.

Dragging her mouth free, she drew in a breath and forced her tone to lightness. "Tsk, tsk. What would Gomory think?"

"I don't care about her," he said.

Her heart sang but she wasn't about to let him off the hook so easily. "What about Satan? What will he think about a demon of your stature consorting with a mere human?"

"What happens Above stays Above," he said again. "We'll have three weeks." His voice promised bliss. "Twenty-one glorious nights together."

He dragged her hands above her head and pinned her against the rock wall with his hips. Lowering his head, he kissed his way toward her breasts. Traitors that they were, they tightened in anticipation.

If she agreed, she would spend three weeks in his arms, but on their return to Hell, they would go their separate ways. She weighed the pleasures of what he offered against the desolation that would surely follow.

Twenty-one nights could form a cool oasis in the parched desert of her life without him. They would give her limpid memories from which to sip when the drought returned. She raised her knee, rubbing the inside of her thigh along the outside of his leg. Touching him, even with layers of fabric separating skin from skin, was so intoxicating her bones wanted to melt. His scent wrapped around her, as sensuous as Salome's dance. He reached inside her jacket to rub his thumb over a taut nipple. Her treasonous body urged her to give in.

As if he sensed her imminent surrender, he smiled. His teeth were a triumphant slash of white in the flickering darkness.

That slash of white brought reality flooding back. After their breakup, the other demons had been like jackals, their predatory teeth on dazzling display as she fought them off. When they finally stumbled away to lick their wounds, there came a time of black days and endless nights, when Satan's grant of immortality had felt more like a curse than a gift. If the Lake of Fire had existed back then, she would have thrown herself into it.

It had taken centuries for her to pave over the destruction of their parting. For Sam, the three weeks Above would be a fling—an affair he could resume and then end again with no regrets. But for her, the devastation would far outweigh the short-term gratification.

She lifted her knee higher, opening herself to him a little more. His smile grew wider. Then she stomped her foot down, jamming the heel of her stiletto into his instep.

Howling in pain, he sprang away from her. "What the heaven, Lilith?"

Jubilation filled her as he hopped on his good foot. Finally, there was some pain on his plate, even though it was only a morsel of what he'd served her. Before he could recover, she whisked herself inside her apartment. With shaking hands that didn't want to obey, she locked the door.

If only she could lock him out of her mind as easily.

CHAPTER 3

Sam headed back to his office, walking gingerly on his wounded foot. Lilith had grown a lot more spirited over the past ten thousand years. He cursed the hunger that had made him misplay things with her so badly.

When he'd said, "What happens Above stays Above," he'd meant it would be safe to be together but she hadn't known there was ever any danger. Consequently, she'd interpreted his words to indicate he was trying to deceive Gomory. She didn't realize there was no need to do that. He hadn't promised Gomory, or any woman he'd dated since Lilith, monogamy.

He'd wanted to be clear that what he offered was temporary, a fling that could only last for the duration of the conference. That was just fair. He didn't want to hurt her more than he already had, Should he tell her Satan had given them a hall pass? No. She would think that he only wanted to be with her because there would be no cost to his career.

There had to be some way to convince her. The way her body had reacted to his said it was possible. She might think she hated him but the fire still burned as hot for her as it did for him. He just needed to slip past her guard. And once he did… He let himself fantasize for a few minutes.

"A package arrived for thee from Peru." A voice like gravel broke into his erotic dream as his admin set a bakery box on the corner of his desk.

Before dying of the bubonic plague, Estelle had worked in a solicitor's office in London. Rumor had it that when Hell's intake counselor informed her that her afterlife assignment was to work in Hell's legal department, she'd snorted. "Be that the best thou canst do?" Sam didn't know if that was true but no matter what he asked of her, she never batted an eye. In return, he ignored intermittent orders to send her to mandatory torture sessions in Ring Eight.

"What be this?" she asked, sniffing at the box. "It smells of anise and"— she took another sniff, "—sesame."

"Never you mind what it is."

She tilted her head, causing her tightly curled ringlets to fall away from her face. "Thou hast never ordered pastries for a client before."

"She's not a client." According to Lilith's DemSec profile, rosquitas were her favorite treat. DemSec was the department charged with outfitting demons for Aboveworld assignments. Over the centuries, their scope had grown to encompass all technology in Hell and they kept profiles on every being in the universe, demon, angel and human.

"She?" Estelle might be a cranky old bat, but she was as sharp as the thorns on a Sidr tree. When Lilith arrived for their meeting, she was sure to put the pastries together with Lil's scent and realize who they were for. On the other hand, she had proven herself loyal to him. She had never, to his knowledge, revealed anything she'd seen or heard in the office.

"What do you know about human contraception?" he asked abruptly.

Her eyes widened and she cast a swift glance sideways, toward Gomory's office before looking at the pastry box again. "'Tis said that if the woman doth place half a lemon rind over the entrance to her womb, a child may thus be prevented."

Sam surveyed her skeptically. "Who says that?"

"The women in the marketplace."

And that was the downside of asking her for help. Estelle's knowledge dated from when she'd lived Above. Maybe Satan was right that she wouldn't have been a good choice to arrange the conference. "Do you have any more recent knowledge?"

"If thou wishest to know of modern methods, thou should'st consult with DemSec." She returned to her desk in the reception area, her long skirts swishing across the lava floor.

She was right, of course. If anyone knew the most advanced way to prevent a pregnancy, it would be DemSec. On the downside, they weren't nearly as careful about confidentiality as Estelle. They treated every nugget of information that came their way as potential fodder for blackmail.

Setting the box aside, he tried to pull up Gibeon's profile, but the database came back "Record Unavailable." He glared at the screen. The quality of the DemSec's work had gone steadily downhill ever since the previous division head left and Ornias took over Sloth. Sam picked up the phone only to replace the handset without dialing. If he was going to ask about contraception, it would be better to do it in person.

Fifteen minutes later he arrived at the DemSec suite in Ring Six, a cavern filled with modular workstations and workers that appeared to be a mix of Hades and former humans. They all wore jeans and hoodies and hiking boots. The only way to tell them apart was the horns that curled from the foreheads of the Hades.

He walked straight through to Ornias's office at the back of the suite, where he found the Demon of Sloth slumped over his desk, napping. Sam shook his head. Before taking over Sloth, Ornias had been a workout freak, with muscle on top of muscle. After only a few years in the job, his body looked like scoops of ice cream that had been left to melt in the sun.

Sam picked up a thick technical manual and slammed it on the desk. Ornias jolted awake.

"Who? What?" He looked around, blinking like an owl.

"Two things," Sam said. "I tried to look at the profile for a messenger angel named Gibeon but I got "Record Not Found."

Yawning, Ornias tapped some keys and peered at his screen. "I don't see anything on a 'Gibeon.'"

"Your predecessor claimed he had profiles on every demon and angel in the universe."

"Bad was prone to exaggeration. What was your other question?" Ornias's eyelids were already starting to drift closed again.

"What's the safest method of human contraception?"

"That's easy—abstinence." With that, Ornias's head fell forward and he relaxed back into slumber.

Abstaining was precisely what Sam didn't plan to do.

At 12:30 Gomory popped her head into Sam's office. The long brown face of Vual, her camel, hung over her shoulder, eyeing him balefully beneath its long eyelashes. Gomory and the camel were almost inseparable. At least he'd managed to banish it from their bedroom. A noise like the sounding of the last trump issued from its behind.

"Satan have mercy." Out at her desk, Estelle wheezed a long, gagging cough. "I believe the beast's vapors have singed my eyebrows off."

"Take me to lunch," Gomory ordered. "I want to hear about your new project." It was clear from her expression that she wouldn't rest until she'd had a chance to cross-examine him about his assignment.

He enabled a curse on his computer and got to his feet. "Where do you want to go?"

"Let's do Bel's Bistro."

Bel's Bistro had outside seating, which meant Vual could hunker down near his mistress. It also meant they'd have to depend on the overhead awning to protect them from the mix of snow and freezing rain that fell constantly in Ring Three. On the plus side, the stink from the gigantic garbage dump in the center of the ring would disguise the smell of Vual's farts.

From the menu, Sam selected a crispy-skinned salmon curry with lentils and carrots. The high volume of protein would help him stay on his toes this afternoon with Lilith. This Lilith was a lot more challenging than the girl that had once been his wife. Any discussion with her would be a debate, a matching of wits like the kind he enjoyed in a courtroom.

After considering each dish, Gomory settled on a mung bean salad. He suppressed an irritated frown. Why did she bother to read the menu? She didn't eat anything but salad, and not much of that. Unlike Lilith, who plowed through whatever was in front of her with gusto.

"What did Satan want?" she asked after the waiter took their order.

Sam's jaw tightened. She knew perfectly well what Satan had wanted—she was a primary branch of Hell's grapevine—but it was her circuitous way to pretend ignorance. Briefly, he told her about the trade summit.

"Why didn't you ask me to help?" Her delicate features pinched with hurt.

He held his water glass up to a nearby torch and inspected it for debris. "Did that waiter look like a spitter to you?"

"They're all spitters. That's why they're in Hell."

His water looked as good as water in Hell ever looked. He took a sip. "Setting up a conference is grunt work. You're far too talented to waste your time doing brainless clerical tasks."

Preening a little at the compliment, she picked up her napkin and shook it out. "Who did he give you as an admin?"

He checked her face and saw genuine curiosity. She truly didn't know. This wasn't going to go over well. He took a deep breath. "Lilith."

Her slender fingers crushed the napkin. "You mean your ex, Lilith?" Outrage fought with disbelief.

"That ended thousands of years ago."

The waiter brought their orders. Overhead, sleet pelted the metal awning that protected the café. An icy breeze blew through. He shivered. How much did it cost to maintain these frigid temperatures in the middle of Hell? And why had he agreed to come here?

After the waiter left, Gomory said, "I thought Satan didn't want the two of you working together?"

"That is evidently less of a priority than making a success of this trade summit." And by trade summit, he meant recruiting effort.

Eyeing him the same way she eyed lying witnesses in the dock, Gomory cut off a tiny piece of lettuce with her knife. "How does Lilith feel about the assignment?"

"She was not pleased."

Her eyes narrowed. "How do *you* feel about it?"

He took a bite of salmon and told the truth—or at least part of it. "Lilith is a giant pain in the ass."

That cleared a little of the storm from her brow. "Ask him to assign someone else."

"I tried," he said. "She tried. He wouldn't budge."

Gomory patted her golden hair. "Let me talk to him. I'll tell him I want to help you make this a big success for Hell."

Gomory was bright, but she tended to be narrow in her outlook and somewhat rigid. Lilith was famous for her ability to improvise when things didn't go as planned.

"I suggested it," he said. "He refused."

She opened her mouth to argue, but he cut her off. "I can't very well send in my girlfriend to plead my case. That's not the approach Satan expects from the demon who will soon direct Wrath and Envy."

He hoped that dangling his promotion in front of her would serve as a distraction but her delicate jaw went surprisingly square and her cornflower blue eyes hardened until they were like sapphires. "I want to go to Above."

If he allowed Gomory to accompany him, he'd have no opportunity to lure Lilith into his arms. She was like a mosquito bite deep inside him. Finally, after all these centuries, he had an opportunity to scratch that ceaseless itch. He wasn't about to give it up.

He arranged his face into earnest lines. "I need you here, helping Estelle finish up the Centauran acquisition. It's critical to the future of Hell. That's why I gave it to you in the first place."

She tossed her head, setting her golden hair rippling. "There's no firm deadline on that. A few weeks won't make any difference."

"I'll be tied up with the conference. You'll be bored up there by yourself."

"We'll have the weekends."

"I'll be working through the weekends."

Her nostrils flared. "You never take me Aboveworld."

He hadn't been Aboveworld, except for work, since the last time he and Lilith went to play in the vineyards of Carmel. "We've discussed this. We both work in Legal. If Satan thinks we're settling into something exclusive, he'll reassign one of us."

And it wouldn't be Sam.

The desire to argue was written all over Gomory's face but something in his own expression must have told her it was useless.

"When you get back, can we take a business trip to Alpha Centauri to see how things are going there?" she asked.

If this mission went exceptionally well, maybe he could convince Satan to let him take Lilith there. He smiled. "Alpha Centauri sounds great."

CHAPTER 4

*L*ilith arrived at Sam's office promptly at two p.m. She'd dressed carefully, in a skirt that barely covered her ass and a figure-hugging red silk jacket with a lacy black shell underneath. Six-inch black stilettos completed her outfit. She had no intention of sleeping with Sam but could still enjoy baiting him.

"I have a two o'clock appointment with Samael," she told his admin. Like all damned humans, Estelle wore the clothes she had died in—a long gray skirt draped over a bum roll and layers of voluminous petticoats, with a peach-colored bodice constructed of whalebone stays. The bodice squeezed her waist to tiny dimensions and held her back rigidly straight. That alone should have been punishment enough for whatever bad things she had done in life.

"He be expecting thee." Estelle waved her toward Sam's office door, an elaborately carved slab of mahogany set into a rock wall.

Sam was head of Hell's legal department. It didn't surprise her that he'd proven to be a brilliant lawyer. His mind was built for legal chicanery. The legend in Hell was that he'd only ever lost one case, when he'd defended the trio of traitors who'd tried to leave Hell. Sam hadn't enjoyed the experience of losing. After that, he changed the law so that traitors could be executed without a trial.

Gomory appeared in the doorway next to Sam's office. Jealousy crackled in her blue eyes. It was misplaced but still satisfying. Her blonde hair curled damply over her shoulders. Lilith frowned. Why was her hair wet? Had they gone home for a nooner that got so heated she had to shower afterwards? Lilith's hands curled into claws.

Vual hung his head over Gomory's shoulder, glaring at Lilith balefully. Gomory reached up to stroke his broad nose, murmuring to him under her breath. As Lilith passed by, Vual spat at her, barely missing her jacket sleeve.

She stopped dead and stared straight into his bulbous eyes. "Try that again, Quasimodo, and I'll turn you into a carpet."

Gomory dragged him back into her office and slammed the door.

Estelle cackled. "If you do, mistress, I have need of an area rug."

Lilith grinned. "I'll keep that in mind." She opened Sam's door without knocking and sauntered in.

Like most offices in Hell, Sam's had rock walls, heavy furniture, and an underlying stink of sulfur, but it differed from all the others in one significant way. It had a skylight that allowed sunlight to flow in. He had her to thank for that. She'd had it installed, along with the one in their apartment, when they were together. Not that she'd gotten to enjoy either one for very long.

Sam's desk had rich leather insets embossed with golden scrollwork. Trophies lined the front edge of the desk. The most impressive was a crystal spike with a brass plate proclaiming him "Demon of the Millennium 1000 - 2000 A.D."

He pointed to a guest chair. His hair was damp, too. Lilith's fists clenched so hard that her nails cut into her palms. She couldn't do this. She could not do this.

Then a smell like wet garbage reached her. Her hands relaxed. They hadn't gone home for a nooner after all. She made a show of sniffing the air. "Did you have lunch at Bel's Bistro?"

His only response was to growl under his breath. She threw back her head and laughed, relief adding extra joy to her chuckles.

He picked up a white paper box from the corner of his desk and offered it to her. "Perhaps these will offset the stench."

She opened the box. Inside were a dozen rosquitas. Rosquitas hadn't been invented until centuries after their split. "How did you know that I like these?"

"A little bird told me."

"A little bird named DemSec?"

He grinned. "Maybe."

He'd made an effort to find out what she liked. It wasn't much, but it was more than she'd expected. He leaned toward her, a lazy smile lifting the corners of his mouth, reminding her what that mouth had felt like pressed against hers a few hours before.

She loved rosquitas and they were tough to get down here, but she set the box back on his desk. "No, thanks."

His face fell and she mentally high-fived herself. Opening her laptop, she spoke briskly. "To do any planning, I'll need numbers. How many will be attending this summit?"

He sat back in his chair. "Each Deadly will bring ten subordinates. Heaven will match our numbers."

"So we need to accommodate one hundred and forty-four delegates, plus two admins." She made a note. "A conference that small should be easy."

"Before the summit, Satan wants to hold a sales kickoff for the rank and file."

She deleted what she'd typed. "How many for the kickoff?"

"Each Deadly will choose his top two hundred performers."

She rolled her eyes. To reach those numbers, they would have to drag along every demon who'd ever corrupted someone. "And how long will this pep rally last?"

"We'll send the grunts home after the first day. Leadership will remain behind and Heaven's delegation will join us to hammer out new agreements."

She raised her eyebrows. "And you found a venue large enough to hold fourteen hundred demons but cozy enough to facilitate small workgroups?"

"Not yet. Where do you suggest?"

Her fingers stilled on her keyboard. "You don't have a venue reserved?"

"No." He lifted his chin, a sure sign he was uncomfortable, not that he'd ever admit it. "I learned about this summit yesterday, just before you did."

"But you plan to hold it next month?" Despite her determination to keep things professional, amusement slipped into her voice.

"I didn't plan anything." He looked irritated. "Is it a problem that we don't have a venue selected yet?"

Her lips twitched. "It might be. Humans have a nasty habit of using the buildings they construct for their own purposes."

"I'll deal with the humans."

She was enjoying herself far more than she'd expected. "When was the last time you actually did an Aboveworld mission?"

His chin came up again. "I triggered the Great Schism of 1054."

Her grin widened. "You haven't been to Earth in a thousand years?"

"I've been busy. Earth isn't the only planet where we have interests, you know."

She tilted her head, savoring his discomfort. "Things may have changed a little since you were last there."

He brushed that off. "Humans never change. The most recent cohort we brought in isn't substantially different from you." He was clearly determined not to let her get the upper hand. "Pick a location and I'll make it happen."

"Can you narrow it down a little?"

"It doesn't matter." He dragged his fingers through his hair. Her hands itched with the urge to reach out and feel the crisp texture against her palms, as she'd done almost every night for two thousand years.

"Can you at least give me a continent?" She needled him to distract herself from the near-irresistible temptation. "Maybe draw straws? Throw a dart at a map?"

"Fine. How about that abbey where we met last time?"

She checked her notes. "I see two problems with that location. First, Satan already said he wants somewhere flashier this time."

Sam waved that away. "I can talk him out of that."

"Also, it was destroyed by Henry the Eighth in 1538."

Sam scowled. "You might have led with that." After a moment, his brow cleared. "How about if we return to where we held it last time Hell hosted?"

"The Coliseum in Rome?"

He nodded, his enthusiasm growing. "It's a beautiful place with a lot of great history."

"But, sadly, no roof. I suggest looking for a place that's a little more weather-tight."

He inhaled audibly through his nose. "Such as?"

She considered. "Again, I don't think it's likely we're going to find a spot the humans will let us use on such short notice—"

"I told you I'd handle that. Where's the best place for this kind of meeting? If you could choose anywhere in the world, where would you pick?"

Where did humans hold global summits? Geneva. Buenos Aires. London. Tokyo. Or her favorite city in all Above, New York.

"The United Nations Conference Center," she said. It really was the optimum location. It got bonus points for being impossible to attain.

"Very good." He picked up his phone. "Who should I talk to?"

His utter, unshakeable belief in himself had attracted her the first time they met. While they were together, it had made her proud to be with him. After their breakup, though, it had come to infuriate her. He needed to be taken down a peg or five. "Start with the Secretary-General."

He pressed the intercom button. "Estelle, get me the Secretary-General of the United Nations on the phone." He set the phone in its cradle with a crisp nod. "Assume the U.N. conference center as the venue."

It was tempting to let this play out, but for the good of the mission, she had to stop toying with him. "You won't be able to reach him."

"Why not?"

"Because he's a busy, important man and you're not on his radar."

Sam gave her a condescending smile. "You underestimate my powers of persuasion."

"It's not about that. You don't understand what his position represents Above."

She might as well have thrown a chunk of raw meat in front of a ravening wolf. His jaw lifted. "Would you like to make a wager on it?"

"What would you like to bet?" Belatedly, she realized she might have just gambled her body. Sam had made it crystal clear that morning what he was after.

"If I'm able to secure the U.N. for our conference, you'll stop trying to undermine me."

Well, that put her firmly in her place. He was far less interested in sleeping with her than he was in climbing the corporate ladder.

"For the duration of the conference," she stipulated. "But what if I'm right?"

He opened his hands. "Set your terms."

If he could make this all about business, so could she. "If I win, you convince Satan to make good on his promise to promote me."

"Done." Sam held out his hand. She shook it, trying to ignore the zip of electricity that shot up her arm.

The intercom buzzed.

"Secretary-General Kudar won't take thy call," Estelle said.

Lilith couldn't stop the smirk that spread across her face.

"Why not?" Sam asked.

"He is much occupied," Estelle said. "Also, his secretary hath never heard of you."

Sam cut off the intercom. "Blessit."

Lilith could think of at least a dozen ways to get in to see Kudar but Sam was too rusty to come up with anything. She had this one in the bag. Sam would force Satan to make good on his promise this time and she would be free to harpoon Sam whenever she got the chance.

But he wasn't ready to throw in the towel. "What do we know about the Secretary-General?"

She pulled up Kudar's dossier. "He grew up on the island nation of Archiepelagro. Married, has two kids."

Sam shook his head irritably. "No, what do we *know* about him?"

He was looking for a weakness they could exploit. Every human had one. For many it was a vice, some sin they found irresistible. For others, it was a love object, a person, an animal, or even an inanimate object they would do anything to hold and protect.

"There's not much in here," she said.

"Let me see." Sam waved his fingers. Reluctantly, she handed over her laptop.

He skimmed the entry. "He was a child soldier, adopted by the former Prime Minister and his wife. They got him into therapy and he went on to graduate from college with a degree in international affairs. His life appears to be fueled by good deeds."

He leaned back in his chair and pursed his lips. Far above the skylight, a cloud scudded in front of the sun, throwing shadows over his sculpted cheekbones and chiseled lips. His nose reminded her of a hawk.

Abruptly, he sat up. "Good deeds or no, that stint as a child soldier will have scarred him. If we can get in, we can work with that."

He handed back her laptop and dragged the big Rolodex toward him, flipping through it. "Ah, here she is: Abezethibou."

There was a name Lilith hadn't heard in a long time. After the Fall, Abezethibou had been trapped in a pillar of water until Satan freed her. "Where is she these days?"

"She is currently the Minister of Foreign Affairs for Archiepelagro."

"Kudar's adopted country."

"Exactly." Sam dialed the phone and put her on speaker. "Abez, Samael here."

"Sam." The she-demon's voice was low and sultry. "Good to hear from you. Are you thinking about coming up my way?"

Jealousy stabbed Lilith's gut like a dagger. Abez's greeting suggested she'd had some kind of liaison with Sam in the past and would be more than happy to pick things up where they'd left off.

"I may be." Sam's lazy smile could be heard in his voice.

Lilith clenched her teeth, only to realize Sam was watching her closely. She relaxed her jaw and adjusted her expression to indifference.

"I've got Lilith here with me," he said.

"Bring her along," Abez said. "I always enjoy a good threesome."

Heat swarmed up Lilith's throat and face. No way in Heaven that was happening.

Sam laughed. "I'll keep that in mind. Right now, we're trying to set up a trade summit with the angel crowd. Lil thought the U.N. Conference Center would be a good venue but I haven't had any luck getting through to the Secretary-General."

"It won't do you any good. He is the straightest of straight arrows."

"I'll deal with Kudar. I merely need to get in front of him. Surely you have some leverage there."

"He hates me." She made it sound like a point of pride.

"What if you show up at his office and drop in?" Lilith couldn't resist asking. That was what she'd do.

"He'll say he's too busy to see me," Abez said.

Lilith pulled up Kudar's calendar via a hack into the U.N. office computer system, courtesy of DemSec. "He has an opening tomorrow around eleven a.m."

"It's an eighteen-hour flight from here to New York." Abez's voice took on a whine that set Lilith's teeth on edge. Demons were so blessed lazy. It was a wonder Hell ever accomplished anything. "There's no way I could get there in time."

"Use the portal system."

"There's no portal on Archiepelagro," Abez said. "The closest station is in Melbourne. That's six hours away."

"Then you'd better get moving," Sam said. "We'll meet you—" He mouthed, "where?"

"The lobby of the Conference Center." The words were out before Lilith could question why she was helping him.

"In the lobby of the U.N. Conference Center at 10:45 local time tomorrow morning," Sam said.

"But—" Before Abez could object further, Sam hung up.

It would be fun to watch him fall flat on his face.

CHAPTER 5

The next morning Sam met Lilith at the portal station at the bottom of Ring Nine. Her skirt was a breath above her knees, unusually conservative for her, and her heels were a mere four inches in height. Her nails were pale pink. Over a short-sleeved cream-colored sweater she wore a tailored gray jacket that molded her curves, but not too closely.

From her behavior yesterday and the way she was dressed today, she appeared to have given up on sabotaging the mission. He smiled with satisfaction. Making that wager with her might be the smartest thing he'd ever done.

He'd managed to defang Lilith, but the question of how to recruit this unknown angel to the dark side remained unanswered. His stomach, which had been on fire ever since Satan had saddled him with this unwanted recruiting assignment, sent a spurt of acid shooting upward. He stifled a belch.

Lilith shot him a suspicious look. "Do you have heartburn?"

"No, Lilith, I'm not keeping secrets from you."

Her gaze didn't waver. "Because that always gave you heartburn."

"What gave me heartburn was you badgering me about keeping secrets."

She glowered, but, thankfully, didn't follow up. They stood in silence for a moment. Then Lilith glanced at him out of the corner of her eye. "You truly haven't been Above since 1054?" she asked.

He heard the amusement in her voice but decided to ignore it. "I have not. Once I started the argument that split the Roman and Byzantine branches of the church, Satan finally recognized what a strong contribution I could make down here."

A smile flickered at the corners of her lips. "It's changed since you were last Above."

He waved that away. Most technological developments on Earth originated in Hell, so they would be familiar to him. If anything, he would be ahead of his time Above. "I monitored humankind's progress for eleven thousand years. They discovered wheels and fire and metal eons ago but they didn't do much with them. I can't imagine that another thousand years has made any real difference."

The flicker grew into a full-fledged grin. "Hold that thought."

Her amusement nettled him. "I'm not completely out of touch, you know. I sit on the Hellish Scientific Council. I help decide which technologies get released Above. Let's face it: humans aren't all that smart. Whatever I don't know I can catch up on in a day or two."

"Whatever you say."

The elevator arrived. He followed her aboard, still irritated. After pressing the button marked, "New York." she slid down the wall and sat on the floor. Her skirt hiked up a little, revealing her tanned thighs. Even though thousands of years had passed, he could still remember what they felt like wrapped around his waist.

He lifted one eyebrow. "What are you doing?"

She tilted her head to look up at him. "You've never taken the portal before?"

"It wasn't yet completed when I last went Above."

"It accelerates at three meters per second squared," she said, but the words meant nothing to him. She rummaged in her bag and extracted two sticks of chewing gum. She offered him one.

"Don't be ridiculous." Chewing gum was as undignified as sitting on the floor of an elevator. What if an angel was there when the doors opened and they saw him lolling on the floor like a dog and chomping like a cow?

An instant later the portal car shot upward. Massive hands seemed to press down on Sam's shoulders. As it gained speed, his knees and ankles locked as the bones in his legs tried to jam their way through the floor. If Lilith had been the woman he remembered, he would have taken a seat beside her but, under the circumstances, it would encourage her to think she'd been right and he wrong. It would be unwise to let the balance of power tilt too far in her direction.

The car continued upward at breakneck speed. Pressure mounted in his ears until the pain was excruciating. He touched the side of his neck, expecting to find blood flowing from his ear canals, but his skin was dry. He dropped his hand to his side and felt a tap on his fingertips. It was Lilith, once again offering him gum. He ignored her.

"Take it, you imbecile," she said. "Before your eardrums burst." Her voice sounded muffled, as though it was coming from underwater. Pain radiated from his ears out to his jawbone. He snatched the gum from her hands, unwrapped it and put it in his mouth. After a few chews, the agonizing pain subsided.

They continued upward. The temperature dropped until gooseflesh ridged his arms and legs. A moment later, the elevator slammed to a halt, lifting his feet off the floor and then dropping him back down so hard his knees buckled.

Lilith got to her feet, supple as a cat. She brushed off her skirt as the doors slid open to reveal a cavernous room filled with arched brass tubes on wheels.

"Where are we?" he asked.

"In the basement of the Putnam Hotel."

"Hotel?"

"It's like an inn, only much larger."

He pointed at the brass conveyances. "What are those?"

"Luggage carts. They're used to transport guests' belongings to their rooms."

He was astounded. "How many belongings do people take with them when they travel these days?" The last time he'd been Above, people brought no more than they could carry on their backs. Carts were reserved for sellable goods.

She detoured around the luggage carts with the expertise of long practice, her laughter rippling behind her. This new Lilith had nothing in common with his adoring, supportive wife of long ago. He tried to tell himself she'd changed so much he didn't even want her anymore, but the fact that he couldn't stop looking at her rounded ass said he was deluding himself.

In the hallway, she summoned another elevator, which carried them upward, more slowly this time, to another huge room. This one was quite beautiful, with a marble floor and crystal chandeliers. It reminded him of Heaven. Off to his right lay still another big room. Paneled in a dark wood, it was dotted with sumptuous leather chairs and glowing brass lamps.

"They have moved forward a bit in the last thousand years, haven't they?" he said.

Lilith's eyes sparkled. "Hang onto your hat. You ain't seen nothin' yet." She crossed the lobby, her hips swaying. Every head turned to watch as her heels rat-tat-tatted on the marble floor. He followed her through a pair of brass-trimmed doors into the most cacophonous, horrifying world he had ever seen—and he lived in Hell.

Outside the inn, buildings rose like canyon walls. Far above his head, the sky was blue and presumably, the sun shone, but only a tiny vestige of that sunlight successfully made the trip down those man-made cliffs to street level. Through the center of the canyon ran a sleek black road. Vehicles roared by at stunning speeds, fouling the air with fumes and noise.

He'd seen cars before, of course. Operatives who spent a lot of time Above sometimes drove them back to Hell but, with the possible exception of the armored vehicles, humans used in their wars, man-made cars weren't practical on the jagged roads of Hell.

He followed Lilith onto a path made from an unyielding white substance. It was as hard as the lava streets of Hell beneath the soles of his wingtips.

"What is this?" He tapped the path with the toe of his shoe.

"It's called a sidewalk." She said the last word with exaggerated slowness. She was enjoying this far too much. He should have taken more time to acquaint himself with the changes he might expect to see Above.

Around them, the canyon reverberated with honking horns and shrill whistles, along with oscillating tones she informed him were called sirens. Stray bits of music assaulted his ears from all directions. Saxophones, guitars, violins and clarinets all vied for his attention. And everywhere, there was human speech.

Mortals of every size, shape and color jammed the sidewalk, speaking a dozen different languages. Along the edge of the black road, vendors hawked their goods, shouting for attention. The racket made him long for the peace and quiet of Hell but Lilith took it all in stride. In fact, she seemed to revel in it.

"Do you actually like this maelstrom?" he asked, astonished.

She grinned. "As they say, New York is a helluva town."

"I can certainly see the resemblance to Hell." He surveyed the people surrounding them. "Do you know what this reminds me of?"

"Babel?"

He nodded and she threw back her head and laughed. The Tower of Babel was one of Satan's best pranks, made even better because the Enemy had reaped the blame. For a moment they were in perfect amity. It was just like the old days. He smiled down at her.

Abruptly, Lilith stopped smiling. She checked her watch. "It's ten-thirty. We need to hurry."

Setting a pace that left him breathless, she strode through the canyon, not pausing until they came to a crossroads. The surrounding crowd of humans jostled them. Offended, he released a blast of negative energy. The people nearest him backed away, but only half a step. He frowned. Back in the day, a blast like that would have cleared a battlefield.

"What are we waiting for?" He raised his voice so Lil could hear him over the din.

She pointed at a yellow metal box suspended from a pole across the street. The box had a small black screen that displayed a ghostly orange hand. As he watched, numbers appeared beside the hand, counting backward from ten. When they reached zero, the orange hand disappeared, replaced by a ghostly figure of a man walking. The crowd surged forward, carrying him along on the tide. He sent out another blast of negative energy but this time it had no discernible effect.

"Is there no other mode of transportation?" he asked at the third corner.

She considered that. "We could take an Uber but this is probably faster."

He had no idea what an Uber was but it was true that the wheeled vehicles on the road beside them weren't progressing much quicker than they did on foot. After ten minutes, his shins burned with the unaccustomed exercise. If it bothered Lil in her high heels, she didn't show it.

When they reached the next corner, the ghostly orange numbers counted down in the little yellow box. Sam halted behind a pregnant young woman.

As they waited, a taxi roared up to the intersection, clearly determined to make it through before the light changed. Simultaneously, someone jostled the expectant mother, who lurched off the curb.

So quickly Sam didn't see it coming, Lilith dove in front of the taxi. She grasped the mom-to-be by the shoulders and pushed her at Sam. The taxi's brakes squealed as the bumper rammed Lilith's legs, flinging her onto the hood.

Thanks to his angel reflexes, Sam caught the pregnant woman and stood her back on her feet on the curb. She burst into tears but he had no time for her. He lunged toward Lilith. "Are you all right?"

Her left leg was bent at an impossible angle.

The taxi driver jumped out. "This is not my fault. Those women jumped in front of me."

Sam scorched him with a look. "If you are very quiet, and don't annoy me, or cause any more damage, you may escape this without a lawsuit."

The driver crawled back into his taxi.

Meanwhile, a bystander snapped pictures of Lilith's leg with his cell phone. "That doesn't look good. Do you want me to call 911?"

Sam had no idea what that was.

"Not necessary," Lilith gasped, but the bystander had already punched in numbers.

She sat on the hood, a sheen of sweat on her forehead. Her immortality prevented death, but it was no protection against injury and pain.

"Is the girl okay?" she asked through white lips.

"She's fine," Sam said. Lilith's leg would heal on its own, but he could speed up the process. Demon first aid was something every fallen angel had learned. "Do you want me to—?"

"Yes, please."

He put his hands on either side of her knee and wrenched it back into place. Her face went paper white but she whispered, "Thanks."

"Are you crazy?" It was the bystander with the cell phone camera. "You should wait for the paramedics."

In the distance, a wailing sound rose.

"No need." Lilith's grin was a little flaky around the edges, but she slid off the tax hood and onto her stiletto-clad feet. "See? Good as new."

The man goggled. "How is that even possible?"

Sam took her arm. For once she seemed content to lean on him. The yellow box gave them the okay to walk and they moved forward. With each step, she leaned a little less, until she drew away. He was pleased to see her recover but missed the excuse to touch her.

"You shouldn't have done that," he said. For as long as he'd known her, she'd had a weak spot for children and pregnant women. "It's up to the Enemy to protect the innocent."

She shook off his hand. "Maybe she wasn't so innocent. She still needed protecting."

Twenty minutes later, a fifty-story glass building came into view across a broad avenue. Behind it, a river flowed. From the pictures in the DemSec dossier, he recognized it as the U.N. Secretariat building.

In front lay a low white building flanked by a long row of flags fluttering on tall poles. The flags celebrated a brave attempt at human cooperation. That attempt would ultimately fail, of course. Tribalism, bigotry and selfishness were baked too deeply into the human psyche for cooperation to prevail. Hell had seen to that.

Sam moved to cross the street but Lilith opened the door of a glass storefront and waved him inside.

He halted, wishing he could rub his burning shins. "Do you take me for a fool? I can see the U.N. Secretariat building across the street with my own eyes."

She laughed, as she had so many times this morning. In the old days, he had been the one who understood how things worked, she the eager student. He didn't enjoy the role reversal, but there wasn't much he could do about it. Once again, he blessed himself for failing to adequately prepare.

"We get security stickers here that will allow us entry into the U.N. building as tourists," she said.

He drew himself up. "I am not a tourist."

"We'll pass as tourists to get inside the building."

That made sense. "Proceed," he said graciously.

She obtained the stickers, which she pressed onto their lapels. They left the shop, crossed the street and entered the one-story glass-fronted building, where a guard checked their stickers and waved them through. From there, they passed into a huge, vaulted room dotted with sculptures and paintings. There was no sign of Abez.

Sam pulled out his phone and texted her. WHERE ARE YOU? For the first time, he was grateful that Satan was a texting addict. At least his skills in this area were up to par.

UNDER THE STAIRCASE came the response. And there, beneath the massive arch that supported the stairs, stood a crooked figure with a brightly colored cloth twined around her body and a matching turban on her head. When Lucifer's followers had left Heaven and the Enemy had confiscated their wings, Abez had somehow retained one of hers. Satan wasn't about to allow any of his demons to have something he lacked, so he amputated her remaining wing. The surgery had left one shoulder higher than the other.

Although she was beautiful, Sam had no desire to sleep with her. Her blatant sexuality didn't appeal to him. He preferred to be the hunter, rather than the hunted.

She led them down a series of corridors, past a sign that read, "The U.N. was not created to take mankind to heaven, but to save humanity from hell."

"Good luck with that." He and Lilith spoke at the same moment, in the same wry tone.

Abez shook her head indulgently. "You always were two peas in a pod."

Lil's smile disappeared, just as it had when he'd made the Babel reference. She clearly didn't like being reminded of their time together. If he had told her the truth about why he was divorcing her, would she have felt differently? He thrust the thought away. He'd done what he had to do.

At the end of the corridor, they boarded still another elevator. It was faster than the hotel elevator, though not nearly as fast as the portal, thank Satan.

"If you want to get inside Kudar's head, use his experiences as a child soldier," Abez said. "I spent a lot of time in the jungles back then, visiting terror on the recruits. One time I convinced them their tents were filled with snakes. They ran screaming into the night. One of them got bitten by a real snake and died." She chuckled reminiscently. "Good times."

Lilith's lips tightened. She had always had a soft spot where children were concerned.

In a spacious office suite on the twentieth floor, they presented themselves to Kudar's administrative assistant, a woman dressed in a turban and brightly patterned cloth, similar to Abez's clothing. Her nameplate read, "Rita Ajuntar." Uniformed guards stood on either side of Kudar's door.

Abez strolled up to the desk. "I have some important visitors, Rita. Can the Secretary-General spare a few minutes to see them?"

Rita started to refuse but Sam stepped closer to her. She inhaled in his scent and her posture softened. Her eyes grew drowsy and a tiny smile lifted the corners of her lips. She waved at the door. "Go right in."

The guards tensed, unsure how to react. Abez sidled up to one, Lilith to the other. The guards breathed in and their rigid stances relaxed, just as Rita's had. They backed away from the door, smiling sleepily.

Sam opened the door and strode into Kudar's office with Abez and Lilith right behind him. The Secretary-General looked up. At the sight of Abez, he scowled. "Who let you in?"

Sam closed the door. Abez repeated her line about visitors. Kudar's scowl didn't lighten. "What do you want?"

Sam produced a business card and offered it to him.

"I come as an emissary from Hell." Sam spoke in his most honeyed tones. "Lord Satan wishes to use the conference center next month to host a summit with Heaven."

Kudar didn't take the card. Instead, he picked up his phone. In a flash, Abez was at his side. She removed the handset from his grip. "You really want to listen to him."

"You are the last person in the world I would ever take advice from." Kudar's face was rigid with dislike. "You are up to your neck in every kind of corruption. Whenever something bad happens in Archiepelagro, you are in the middle of it."

Abez smiled modestly. "Thank you." She did not release her grip on the handset.

Kudar bellowed, "Rita, get in here."

The door flew open. Rita, appeared, the guards hovering behind her.

"Is something wrong, sir?" she asked.

Sam moved to her side, propelling his scent toward her. Abez and Lilith positioned themselves close to the guards.

"Everything is fine," Sam said.

"Everything is fine." Rita's eyelids drooped again.

"Everything is not fine," Kudar barked.

The guards stiffened. Abez and Lilith redoubled their efforts until the room was a veritable cesspool of pheromones. Rita's forehead furrowed in confusion.

"Now would be a good time to take a coffee break," Sam said.

Her frown cleared. "I'd like to take my coffee break now."

If Lilith and Abez had done their jobs, the young guards should be equally suggestible.

"Coffee would taste good right now," he said. The guards nodded sleepily.

Rita looked at Kudar. "We're going for coffee. Can I get you anything, sir?"

"You can get these people out of my office!"

Rita and the guards tried to react to his distress but they moved like bees in a smoke-bombed hive, dozy and aimless.

"Everything is fine," Sam said. "You won't be back for at least a half hour."

"We'll be back in a half hour," Rita told Kudar and walked out the door. The guards followed her.

Now to convince him that demons were real.

CHAPTER 6

Kudar's face morphed from frustration to fury as his secretary ambled from the office with his guards in tow.

"How did you do that?" Perhaps because of his background as a soldier, he seemed more annoyed than fearful.

"That's what demons do," Sam said. "We persuade people."

Kudar huffed. "There are no such things as demons."

"And yet, here we are." Sam gestured gracefully. "And there they go."

"You must have used hypnosis." Kudar's face twisted into a grimace. "Or perhaps you drugged them before you came in here."

Sam turned to face Lilith, his head cocked to the side. "He doesn't believe in demons. Is that common these days?"

"It usually works to my advantage. It's easier to influence people if they don't know they'd be wiser to resist you. Once in a while, though, it can be a hindrance."

"How do you get past it?"

"Parlor tricks." She curved her lips into a syrupy smile. "Let him stab you with his letter opener and see how quickly you heal. That will convince him."

"I was afraid you'd say that." Sam removed his jacket and hung it over the back of Kudar's visitor chair. He picked up a letter opener from Kudar's desk. "If I may?"

Kudar wheeled his chair back, his small eyes bulging. "What do you plan to do with that?"

"A demonstration that doesn't involve you, except as a spectator." Handing the letter opener to Abez, Sam took a snowy white handkerchief from his pocket.

"Where?" Abez asked.

"Forearm." He rolled back his sleeve and held up his arm for easier access.

She stabbed the letter opener into his arm. Sam yelped as the blade penetrated skin and muscle. Yelping was undemonly, but expressions of pain were useful in convincing mortals. With the hankie, he caught the blood that squirted from his arm before it could stain the carpet.

After a moment, the bleeding slowed and the wound sealed itself. He displayed the unmarred skin on his forearm to Kudar.

Kudar snorted. "A cheap trick."

Sam pressed his lips together. He held out the blood-soaked hankie for closer inspection but the Secretary-General waved it away. "Corn syrup and food coloring."

Sam looked at Lilith. "What is he saying?"

"Humans make very convincing fake blood from corn syrup and food dye."

He stared at her, bemused. "They've grown clever, haven't they?"

"I've seen more convincing stabbings in amateur plays." Kudar crossed his arms. "You used a fake blade."

Sam took a deep breath and counted to five. When he spoke, his tone was mild. "It was your own letter opener."

"Sleight of hand. You replaced it with a retractable stage prop."

"Humans have taken the craft of creating illusions to the level of artistry," Lilith said. "It's a lot harder to convince them these days." She was enjoying this far too much.

"I see that." He stroked his chin. If Kudar wouldn't believe the proof of his own eyes, what would convince him? Perhaps his other senses. A more tactile experience might work. Taking the letter opener by the blade, Sam offered the handle to the Secretary-General. "Inspect it."

Kudar pressed the tip of the letter opener against his palm. The blade didn't retract. His lips set into a stubborn line. "You must have switched them back."

"Stab me." Sam spread his arms. "You were once a soldier. You have experience in hand-to-hand combat."

"I have left that part of my life behind." Despite his words, the skin around Kudar's eyes tightened. Violence experienced as a child never left a person.

"What do you have to lose?" Lilith's voice was a seductive purr. "Either he's a demon and he'll heal, or it's a ruse and you won't hurt him anyway. Go ahead. Stab him."

She sounded far too enthusiastic. Abez unwound her turban in preparation.

Letter opener in hand, Kudar rounded the desk. With one swift motion, he rammed it into Sam's gut.

Both men yelled "Gaaahh!" Kudar's was a shout of horror while Sam's was a shriek of pain.

Stepping forward, Lilith tore open Sam's shirt. Buttons flew everywhere. The gash in his abdomen was impossible to miss. Blood spurted from the open wound. Swiftly, Abez wrapped her turban around him, staunching the blood flow as the room whirled around his head like a millwheel in a fast stream.

When the world came back into focus again, all the color had left Kudar's cheeks. His shoulders hunched with guilt. "Should I call for an ambulance?"

"I'm fine," As Sam spoke, the edges of the wound knitted themselves together, though his ears continued to ring. Lilith dragged his shirt open again to reveal a thin white scar.

Kudar looked haunted. "I have prayed on my knees never to do such a thing again."

"No harm, no foul," Lilith reassured him in a chipper tone. As she spoke, even the scar disappeared.

"Do you see?" Sam used every ounce of his self-control to sound calm and in control. His belly still burned like fire and the room continued to rotate, though more slowly, as the ringing in his ears slowly subsided.

Kudar's lips were still ashen. "You are all right? Truly?"

Sam lifted his chin. "Of course. I'm a demon. Do you need further proof?" Please, Satan, let him not require further proof.

Kudar backed away. "No, no. I believe you are a demon."

"So you'll let us borrow this facility?"

Kudar's jaw tightened stubbornly. "Since you are demons, I see no positive outcome for Earth in letting you utilize this campus."

"Without these trade talks, there's a risk of open warfare between Heaven and Hell," Sam said.

Kudar folded his arms. "Earth would, of course, take a neutral stance in such an event."

"Unfortunately, that's not an option. Hell will use proxies." When Kudar's face remained closed, Sam added, "Like a paranoid world leader who commands a nuclear stockpile."

He let the threat hang in the air. Several candidates would fill that bill.

Kudar swallowed. "You leave me no choice."

He didn't look happy, but the Secretary-General's happiness wasn't Sam's goal.

"What do you need to make loaning us your campus happen?" Lilith asked.

It was clever of her to leave it open. She could be asking what type of assistance Kudar needed, or she could be offering a bribe. The Secretary-General could take it in whichever direction he preferred.

Kudar shook his head. "It will be impossible to clear the complex of other meetings on such short notice."

"Hold them virtually," she said. "You've done it before."

"There must be a good reason to make such an accommodation."

"Say that you have an insect infestation," Sam suggested.

"I'm not sure anyone will believe that without proof."

"We can provide proof. Which would you prefer? Locusts? Spiders? Bees?"

Kudar recoiled. "That's all right. I'll figure something out."

"If you need any help—"

"No, thank you. I'll manage."

"The place needs to be empty, other than essential maintenance personnel," Lilith said.

Kudar nodded resentfully.

"Very good," Sam said. "Is there anything else?"

Kudar was still a little pale. "How do you plan to explain your presence here to the world?"

"I don't," Sam said. "Your cover story will need to allow us to come and go discreetly without humanity becoming aware of us."

Kudar scowled. "See that you stay out of the spotlight."

"Of course." Sam inclined his head. "Lilith will be in touch about the details."

Outside Kudar's office, Lilith walked away while Abez and Sam were still high-fiving each other. She should have known he'd pull off obtaining the U.N. He was almost as clever as he prided himself on being. Now she was stuck with making the conference a success. The thought filled her with frustration, but it wasn't smart to welsh on a demonic wager. The last demon who tried that wound up with his limbs redistributed. She preferred her legs positioned below her hips and not coming out of her neck.

She arrived in the lobby only to find Sam right behind her. She blessed under her breath. She'd had about all the Pride she could handle for one day. From her phone, she summoned a ride back to the Putnam.

"Great work with Kudar." Sam tried to clap her on the shoulder but she ducked away before he could make contact. He slid his hand into his pocket as though that was what he'd planned to do all along. How very Sam.

"How's your stomach?" she asked.

"Fine."

"Liar."

He shot her a look out of the corner of his eye. "It's nothing."

"You got heartburn when you tried to keep things from me."

"That's what you believed, anyway."

She still did. Even if she'd been less sure, that sideways glance was a giveaway. Sam was hiding something. But what? Before she could ask any more questions, her phone chimed and a black SUV pulled up to the curb.

She opened the rear door and motioned him inside. "This will return you to the Putnam."

"You're not going back with me?"

"I have things I need to do up here." Like, coming up with a strategy to figure out what he was hiding.

"I'll go with you," he said. "You've convinced me I need to learn more about Above."

No way in Heaven was that happening. She gestured at his button-less shirt. "You're really not dressed appropriately.

"I'd forgotten about that. " He got into the car. "Schedule time with me tomorrow to finish nailing things down. Estelle has my calendar."

She gave a mock salute. "Will do."

She closed the door and the car pulled into the flow of traffic. She needed inspiration and she knew just what would do the trick. When the going got tough, the tough got a mani-pedi.

At one o'clock the next day, Sam heard the tap of stilettos on the hardened lava floor outside his door.

"Is he ready for me?" he heard her ask Estelle.

"I know not, mistress," Estelle replied, "but it looks like thou'rt ready for him." Then she cackled like the crone she was.

Just as he'd expected. She would do everything in her power to ferret out his secret. Grinning, he took a deep breath. This battle of the sexes might well be the most enjoyable he'd ever waged.

An instant later Lilith appeared in his doorway wearing a microscopic miniskirt and a sweater that was tighter than Mammon's purse strings. Gone was her pretty pink manicure from the day before. Her shoes displayed scarlet toenails that exactly matched her scarlet claws. The scent of sesame and anise engulfed him in a sensual wave. Then she sat down, knees primly together, and opened her laptop. The message might be mixed but it was still perfectly clear: *I'm hot, but you can't have me.* His cock stretched toward her like a dowsing rod.

"Now that we have the venue secured, I can get to work on the details. Do you have a copy of the agenda?" She sounded brisk, professional and helpful.

Those were all things she was capable of being, but none were likely under the circumstances.

"The first day is the sales event," he said. "We'll need prizes to pump up enthusiasm. Let's do one prize for the best salesman from each division and a grand prize to the demon who has brought in the most souls this decade."

"That would be me," she said.

"Conference personnel aren't eligible."

She smiled drily. "Of course, they aren't. For the prizes—are you thinking vacations, or something more concrete?"

"Consult with the Deadlies and find out what works for each of their divisions."

"Will do." She made no effort to argue. Challenging her to that wager yesterday may have been the smartest thing he'd ever done.

"The second day, I'll give a welcome. Then keynote speakers, St. Peter, then Charon."

"Satan isn't speaking?"

That had been its own battle. "Heaven made that a ground rule for the conference, that he would not come Above for the duration. He's recording an address to be shown. After the keynotes, we'll break into workgroups by division."

Pursing her lips, she typed a note into her laptop. Her cheeks went hollow, bringing back memories. He knew she was doing it intentionally but his cock pressed painfully against the fabric of his trousers. He shifted position, trying to relieve the pressure, and his chair creaked.

She looked up from her computer, watching him unwaveringly. Deliberately, she bit her bottom lip, then ran the pink tip of her tongue across it. He swallowed a groan.

She returned her gaze to her screen. "What's the theme for the conference?"

In the old days, she had been available whenever the whim took him, enthusiastic in her responses and gleeful in her orgasms. Where had she learned to tease like this? From Belial? When he was still in Hell, all the she-demons had vied for a turn in his bed. Lilith had had an affair with him three thousand years earlier. To the best of Sam's knowledge, Belial was the only demon she'd ever slept with besides him. Jealousy flared, making his heartburn seem like a guttering candle in comparison. "Theme?"

"Yes, a theme, a tagline." She crossed her legs, drawing his gaze to the shadowed vee inside her tiny skirt. "Like 'Peace through Cooperation' or 'Destroying Humanity One Soul at a Time.'"

He knew he was a fool, but he couldn't drag his eyes away from the shadowy location between her thighs. His balls were electric blue by now. "Satan didn't say anything about a theme."

She settled one smooth thigh on the other. Her skirt rode up another inch. He swallowed.

"Let's think about it another way," she said. "What's his end goal?"

He knew what she was doing. She had driven all the blood from his brain and now she was going to interrogate him until he gave away his secret. He forced his lust-clouded brain to focus.

"Heaven wants fewer human casualties from our recruitment efforts. Our stance is that fewer restrictions and less interference from guardian angels are the way to make that happen."

"Also, a great way to increase our success rate."

"Exactly."

Her charcoal-shaded eyelids swept down, veiling her eyes. "What else?"

"Why does there need to be something else?"

"It's important to get the theme right. It will drive all the other decisions. What else can you tell me about Satan's goals for this conference?"

He might be distracted, but he wasn't stupid. "Let's go with 'Peace through Cooperation.'"

She arched a brow. "That doesn't sound very satanic."

"It will do."

Her shoulders dropped. The movement was so tiny he wouldn't have noticed if he hadn't been looking for it. The sight allowed him to step back, just a millimeter, from the web she'd been weaving around him. "What else do you need?"

"Colors. What colors do you want to use?" She leaned forward so that her breasts jutted inside her tight sweater.

He could remember, as clearly as if it were yesterday, the weight of them in his hands, the way her nipples tightened at the slightest bit of attention. His mouth went dry. "Colors?"

"For the banner and the gift bags. Do you want a heavenly blue and gold? Or an incendiary red and black?"

Her voice had deepened, gone sultry, bringing back the way she had sounded when they made love. He swallowed. "It doesn't matter."

"Of course it matters. If we're trying to appease them, we use their colors. If the intention is to challenge them, we go with ours."

He dragged his eyes away from her breasts. "Let's use our black and their gold." He hoped those were among the colors she'd mentioned.

Again, her shoulders dropped. He almost laughed out loud. She lifted her chin. "Unless you want to approve every purchase I make, I need to understand the end goal of this summit."

"I've outlined the goal in general terms. If you want to know the details of what each division is responsible for accomplishing, talk to the Deadlies individually."

There were exactly two things Lilith was proud of from her succubus days. The first was that in a hundred years of working the loathsome assignment she'd never once allowed a man to force her to be on the bottom. The second was that she'd learned to use men's desire for her as a tool to get what she wanted, instead of being a sad little victim.

So it was disappointing that her strategy today—to distract Sam until he said something he didn't intend to—wasn't working. There was no question he wanted her. When she'd walked into his office in the shortest skirt and tightest sweater she owned, his eyes had practically popped out of his head. She was willing to bet that behind his imposing mahogany desk, his dick was even harder than the desk. But he'd resisted talking out of turn. If lust wouldn't make him careless, maybe anger would do the trick.

She raised her eyes, gazing at him squarely for the first time since she'd come into his office that morning. "I may have believed every word that came out of your mouth back in the old days, but I'm not that child anymore. Your stomach was burning up with secrets yesterday. What's really going on?"

He folded his hands. "I can't tell you."

So there was something more going on here. "Why not?"

"Because Satan asked to keep it confidential."

"Still his lapdog, I see."

He flushed. "You only want to know so you can thwart me."

She closed her computer with a snap. "In the past two days, you've groped me, insulted me and badmouthed me to my boss in front of all his division heads."

His jaw went rigid. For a moment she thought she'd provoked him enough to make him lose his temper and say something unplanned. Then he exhaled out noisily through his nose. "What else do we need to cover?"

Blessit. She ticked off her list on her fingers. "Set up a schedule of events. Arrange catering. Order gift bags and seminar packets."

"That's a short list." He looked pleased.

"Those are bullet points. Each of those is hours, even days, of work."

His smile faded. "You always were one for over-planning."

"Careful planning was why our parties were so popular."

"All it takes to throw a good party is good food, good music and plenty of booze."

"A, that's not true. B, even if it were true, that approach won't work for this conference. The cloud crowd will have all their defenses up. They won't be softened by food and wine."

"Then there's no point in spending a lot of time on menu planning."

"They may not admit it, but they will enjoy it, and the memory of it will haunt their dreams when they get home."

She expected him to argue, but he threw up his hands. "I accept your approach. What do you need from me?"

"The agenda will drive all the other preparations," she said. "You do have an agenda, right?"

Growling, he took a scroll from his center desk drawer and slapped it into her hand. "This should give you everything you need."

She unfurled the scroll. It contained a list of events and the contact demon for each.

"Anything else?" he asked.

"What do we know about this Gibeon who will be my counterpart?"

"Nothing." Sam's eyelid twitched as he spoke.

That was interesting. Whatever was going on, this Gibeon was involved. She tried to call up his DemSec profile. "I'm getting a Record Not Found."

"I ran into the same thing when I tried to look him up." This time, Sam's eyelid remained smooth. He was telling the truth. "Ornias says we don't have a profile for him."

"Do we even know what level he is?" she asked.

"He's a messenger angel. He works for Gabriel."

Before she could drill down, Sam's desk phone squawked.

"Thy two o'clock waiteth," Estelle's voice said.

"I have another appointment." Sam stood and walked to the door.

Lilith stayed put. She wasn't about to leave when she was finally getting somewhere.

"Just a moment," Sam said to whoever was outside the door. He turned back to her. "I'm afraid that's all the time I have. If you need more guidance, ask Estelle to schedule additional time."

She could get by without him looking over her shoulder, second-guessing all her decisions. She slammed her laptop closed and stomped to the door.

"One more thing," Sam called after her. "Greed has asked that we handle the room reservations for our side."

She stopped in her tracks. "That's seventy-seven room reservations."

"Correct."

"To make in New York City, near the U.N., with less than a month's notice?"

"Correct."

Was this the secret he'd been keeping? "Why can't everyone make their own arrangements?"

"The last time Greed let individuals book their own rooms, we didn't get the corporate rate. I gather he's still having flashbacks."

Sam's face was calm. Eye-to-eye contact with no tics and no fidgeting. Far different than how he'd behaved when they were talking about Gibeon. Despite the extra work he'd just dumped on her, she was pleased with the progress she'd made. There was more than one way to skin a fiend. She'd ask around and see if anyone knew this Gibeon.

She was less pleased when Gomory breezed past her into Sam's office carrying a vacation brochure for Alpha Centauri in her hands. That stupid camel was right behind her. As Vual's hindquarters moved past Lilith, he released a loud, smelly stream of flatulence. She slammed the door to Sam's office, trapping the gas inside.

Beyond the door, Sam yelled, "Blessit, Gomory, what have you been feeding him?"

Estelle waved a hand in front of her face. "I thank thee for that, mistress."

"Anytime," Lilith said.

The next morning Lilith visited the Travel office, where row upon row of men and women sat at cramped desks, arranging for various demonic missions. Their chairs were bolted to the floor two feet from their desks, forcing them to lean forward to reach their keyboards and phones. After a few minutes, their backs burned with the strain and they worked twenty-hour days. If she pissed Satan off, it could be her reaching for one of those desks.

Focalor opened and closed his wings as she walked in the door. Leaning his leonine body against the counter, he squawked a greeting. The griffin had run Travel since the first demon made the first trip Aboveworld to corrupt a Neanderthal. Behind him, a sheet of paper lifted and sailed across the room. A worker jumped up from his chair and gave chase, only to have the paper land in a smudge pot and burst into flames before he could reach it.

"Oh, man." Feet dragging, he walked back to his desk and dialed the phone. "Could you give me your travel dates and locations again? I seem to have lost my notes." A blast of fire issued from the receiver, setting his hair aflame and blistering his ear. Yelping, he slapped out the flames with the handset while he took notes with his other hand.

Focalor hopped down from his stool and came to the counter. "What's up, Lil?"

"I need hotel rooms in the Turtle Bay area of Manhattan for seventy-six demons and a suite for myself." Sam could fend for himself.

"When?"

"Four weeks from Sunday."

"Seventy-six rooms?" Focalor's wings fluttered again, sending paperwork flying. "Less than a month from now?"

"Yes, please." A pair of feathers drifted onto the counter. A couple more followed them.

"Stress makes me molt." Above his curved beak, the griffin's beady eyes bugged out. For being half lion, half eagle, he got upset easily.

"Whatever you can find," she said soothingly.

His wings settled into a closed position again. "Are you looking to book everyone together in a large hotel, or to spread them across smaller boutique hotels?"

Sam would have a harder time controlling his demon delegation if they were spread apart.

"Let's go with the boutiques," she said.

CHAPTER 7

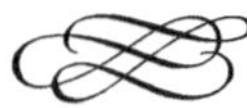

ne month later

The uniformed bellhop opened the door to Lilith's suite at the Ferguson Hotel with the air of a magician producing an especially impressive rabbit from a top hat.

His pride was justified. The hotel was five-star and, in return for booking two dozen rooms in the hotel, the management had given her one of their best suites. Maybe there were advantages to handling Sam's administrivia after all.

The main room of the suite was large and furnished with a serpentine red leather sofa. Lilith instantly fell in love with it. When she got back to Hell, she'd have to think about getting one for her own apartment. It was perfectly on brand for her.

On the right, separated by a half-wall, lay a kitchenette. On the left, a paneled door opened to a marble-lined bath. Another led to a bedroom.

The most impressive feature, though, was a balcony overlooking the East River. The trees along the East River were the red and gold of early October. The balcony held a wrought-iron table and a pair of chairs and her imagination painted her and Sam sharing coffee and chatting as they watched joggers trot by twenty floors below. She quickly shut down those thoughts. If Sam had a balcony, he'd be sharing it with Gomory.

But he had no balcony. He didn't even have a room. She grinned as she checked her watch. Six-thirty p.m. Sometime in the next hour, he would arrive in New York and discover he was homeless. A smile lifted her lips. He was going to be so pissed.

The bellhop dragged a luggage cart piled high with suitcases into the room. "Where do you want this stuff?"

She slipped out of her stilettos, sighing with pleasure as her feet sank into the deep pile of the carpet. "The bedroom, please."

He unloaded her two largest suitcases onto wooden folding stands before setting the three smaller ones on the paisley duvet cover. She gave him a big tip in appreciation and closed the door behind him.

In the bedroom, she hung her suits in the closet so the wrinkles could fall out. She had just finished putting her lingerie in the drawers when her phone rang. Grinning in anticipation, she pressed the answer button.

"Lil, this is Sam." He sounded annoyed.

Her grin widened. "Yes?"

"I called to let you know something's come down. I won't arrive in New York till tomorrow morning."

Blessit! She took a deep breath. She needed to be patient. Her little payback wasn't canceled, just delayed. "Thanks for letting me know."

Before she could hit the disconnect button, he said, "What needs to be done at the conference center before everyone starts arriving tomorrow?"

He had given her no help since snagging the U.N. conference center for the summit, just cursory status checks. There was no way he was going to second-guess her preparations at this late stage.

"I've got it covered," she said.

"Did the name badges arrive?"

She'd arranged to have them sent to the U.N. mail room, but she had no idea if they'd actually arrived. "Yes."

"And you checked them? Everyone's name is spelled right?"

She dragged her foot across the lush carpet. The thick fibers massaged her sole. "Every single one."

"Good work. I've told the divisions to stagger their arrival times so you won't be swamped. Envy should be there at nine-fifteen."

"Sounds good."

"Expect me around eight," he added.

She hung up before he could think of something else to micromanage.

After putting her empty suitcases in the closet, she wandered around the suite, checking everything out again. She'd expected to spend the evening arguing with Sam about his lack of accommodations. With that confrontation on hold, she was left with no plans.

She strolled out onto the balcony, watching the traffic far below and listening to the occasional honk of an angry driver. Should she go for a mani-pedi? She checked her nails. Her signature crimson polish was still flawless. A room service menu lay on the Queen Anne desk but it was too early for dinner.

She could head to her favorite hole-in-the-wall bar in the East Village. The bartender was the great-grandson of the original owner. She liked to sit at the bar and drink white wine while she regaled him with stories of his ancestor, claiming to have heard them from her grandmother. Judging by the way he smiled at her, he was interested, but tonight the thought of toying with him held no appeal.

On her phone, she scrolled through a list of the current off-off-Broadway shows but none caught her interest. She could have visited a museum, but even in New York none would be open on a Sunday evening.

In the end, she ordered a salad from room service and turned on the Hallmark channel. She watched three movies in a row with paper-white characters and paper-thin plots, rolling her eyes when they inevitably wound up happily matched up despite the odds against them. What a complete and total fantasy. There was no such thing as true love.

At eleven o'clock she gave up and went to bed, feeling vaguely irritable. She punched her pillow, trying to get comfortable. Tomorrow, she promised herself, would start her revenge.

Lilith might resist his advances Below, but Sam was confident she'd give in once they were Above, so contraception was a necessity, so the next morning he took the Portal to Manhattan, armed with knowledge gleaned from the human internet. According to the web, condoms were good for preventing pregnancy and were easily purchased at any Aboveworld pharmacy

On his way to the U.N. Conference Center, he stopped at a pharmacy with a blue and white sign over the door. Once inside, though, he was unable to locate the contraceptives. The variety of products on display was astounding. Foodstuffs, cosmetics, medicines, sweets and even brightly-colored toys for children lined the shelves. As he canvassed his third aisle, a shifty-eyed individual began following him. Perhaps he knew where the condoms were located.

"Can you point me to the contraceptive aisle?" Sam asked.

The man's gaze ricocheted around the aisle, landing everywhere without ever connecting with Sam's.

"Yes," Sam said. "I'm speaking to you."

"Uh, aisle six."

"Thank you."

He made his way to aisle six, but the sheer number of options overwhelmed him. They were available in latex, plastic or lambskin. They came smooth, ribbed or even studded. They could be purchased lubricated or coated with a substance that would kill sperm.

"Which of these are preferred?" he asked his shadow, who was still skulking behind him.

The man startled, then pointed out a purple box. "Your lady will like those."

Sam plucked the box from the shelf. It promised to deliver

stimulation "where she needs it most." He glared at the man. "I'll provide all the pleasure she requires."

The man held out his hands. "Sorry, buddy. No offense intended." He retreated, disappearing at the end of the aisle.

How would he explain the need for them to Lilith? As a demon, he was immune to disease and, unless Lilith's feelings had changed over the centuries, she wouldn't want to prevent pregnancy. In fact, she would be overjoyed.

Grimacing, he picked up the ribbed condoms the shifty-eyed man had recommended. He would tell Lilith he'd bought them to increase her enjoyment. Satan willing, she would accept something he said without an argument for once. He carried it to the front of the store, where the shopkeeper waited.

"Fifteen dollars and forty-seven cents," the shopkeeper announced.

He dug into his pockets only to realize Estelle had neglected to provide him with currency. It wasn't needed in Hell, where goods were acquired by barter or theft.

"Well?" the shopkeeper demanded. "Are you going to buy them or not?"

He lifted his chin. "I seem to be without currency."

"Do you have a credit card?"

Estelle had given him a small leather folder, saying it replaced the drawstring purse he'd carried the last time he came Above. Removing the folder from his inside jacket pocket, he opened it and selected a yellow card with blue lettering. "Here you go."

The shopkeeper made no move to take it. "That's a Metro card. Try again."

This time he selected a silver card featuring a picture of a warrior. To his relief, the shopkeeper took it without further argument.

He left the store with the condoms in his briefcase. Now all he had to do was seduce Lilith into using them.

Lilith arrived at the General Assembly building on the United Nations campus at seven-thirty. If Sam still had questions about what humans had managed to achieve in the last thousand years, this building should answer them. Built in the shape of a shallow U, its front wall was five stories high and consisted of columns of rectangular windows. Inside, gray and white rectangular marble tiles on the floor echoed the design of the windows. The white railings of the second, third and fourth-floor lobbies soared overhead.

The first floor was devoid of furniture. Where were the registration tables she'd been promised? She looked up the cell number of Kudar's secretary but before she could dial it, the elevator dinged. A man in denim coveralls got off, pushing a cart loaded with a pair of long tables. He hitched his chin at her. "Where d'ya want 'em, lady?"

She stifled a grin. New Yorkers were so direct. It was one of the reasons she liked this city so much. She pointed to a spot facing the row of outside doors. "Put them right here."

No sooner had he set up the tables and disappeared back into the elevator than it dinged again, this time with a delivery from the mailroom. She directed the young woman pushing the cart to stack the boxes next to the tables. In addition to the cartons, there was a long cardboard tube. It contained a banner that read "Peace Through Cooperation" in red letters on a blue background.

She attached the banner to the tables and stepped back. It looked great. She'd been right to ignore Sam's input.

Next, she opened one of the two smaller boxes. It contained turquoise badges with gold lettering. The one beneath it held onyx badges with red jasper letters. They wouldn't need those until tomorrow. She shoved both boxes beneath the table.

This morning's focus needed to be on the cheap plastic badges she'd purchased for today's crowd. She tore open the largest carton. Inside were seven bags, each holding badges in different colors. She dumped out the one containing Gluttony's orange badges and began alphabetizing. After Gluttony came Greed's yellow and then Envy's green.

She'd finished sorting green badges when Sam pushed through one of the revolving doors. The dress guidelines she'd sent out specified "mortal business casual" but Sam wore a charcoal gray suit, a crisp white shirt and a scarlet tie. His black brows were slashes above green eyes so dark they looked black, too. He gazed around the huge lobby with its massive windowed wall and soaring upper floors and gave a silent whistle.

"Impressed?" she asked.

He smiled. "No more than I'd expect from Hell's first Director of Demon Resources."

She kissed two fingertips and pointed them downward. "From your lips to Satan's ears."

Then he saw what she was doing. "I thought you told me this was already done."

She crossed her arms, annoyed at his criticism. "I make it a point to lie to micromanagers."

"Touché." His grin faded. "Why isn't anyone assisting you?"

"I don't have the luxury of staff."

His brows rose. "You mean, you've done all of the preparation by yourself?"

"What can I say? My fairy godmother's been swamped."

"You might have mentioned your lack of staff in one of your status updates."

"See my earlier comment about micromanagers."

"What can I do to help?" Without waiting for an answer, he stepped behind the table and pulled the bag of purple Pride badges out of the box "Tell me again why we're giving badges to demons who have worked together for thirteen thousand years?"

"It makes them feel special. Plus, it's an easy way to identify anyone who skipped out of showing up."

"Spoken like a true D.R. director." He grabbed a handful of badges and laid them out on the table alphabetically.

A demon of Sam's stature doing grunt work? Would wonders never cease? She placed Abezethibou's badge between "Aasvi" and "Allocen" in the Lust section.

"How about if we make this a competition?" Sam said.

"Superhuman being versus an ordinary human?" she said. "That's hardly a fair contest."

"And you're hardly an ordinary human." He said it so smoothly it took her a minute to hear the compliment. When she did, she smiled in spite of herself.

"I'll sort Wrath and Sloth while you finish Lust," he offered.

"What stakes are you proposing?" She couldn't match his demon speed, but she only had half a dozen badges left to sort. He wasn't three times faster.

He met her gaze and held it. The room seemed too warm. "One night of passion."

Heat clenched low in her belly but she smiled sweetly. "We don't have to compete for that to happen. I already loathe you with every fiber of my being."

Fire seemed to smolder behind his dark eyes. "Love and hate are two sides of the same coin." He was pumping out the pheromones, too.

She turned her head to suck in some fresh air. "That currency isn't accepted here."

"Disappointing." He tilted his head, doing that smolder thing with his eyes again. "Given the U.N.'s charter, I expected a little more inclusivity."

"I don't think it's part of their mission to facilitate one-night stands."

"I'm more than willing to extend our arrangement to include the entire three weeks we're up here." His tone promised a wonderland of delights if she'd give in. He did not, she noticed, make any promises about what would happen after they returned to Hell.

"Pass. What other stakes can you offer me?"

He shrugged philosophically. "Loser buys dinner?"

Even dinner with him was probably unwise, but she had only six Lust badges left to place while he still had the rest of Wrath and all of Sloth to sort. As the winner, she could choose where they'd have dinner. There was a sushi restaurant in the Village with great wines, excellent appetizers and sky-high prices. It would be worth spending an evening in his company to stick him with the astronomical bill.

"Deal." As soon as she agreed, he shifted into high gear. His hands moved so fast they blurred. Each placement was precise. Despite her huge lead, his speed rattled her. As she moved to set her last badge in its proper spot, she knocked it under the table. By the time she retrieved it, Sam was putting his last badge in place.

He smiled at her. "I'll let you know where I want to go."

Blessit. Now she'd have to endure an evening in his company *and* foot the bill. A little frisson of excitement shivered down her spine despite herself.

Sam's phone buzzed. "It's Satan, I have to take this." He strode to the far end of the lobby.

Right. Satan would always come first with Sam.

She had just placed Leviathan's badge at the top of Envy when the caterer arrived. She directed him to set up the coffee bar near the doors to the assembly hall. Soon, the smell of fresh coffee filled the air. As the caterer was leaving, Gluttony strolled in, accompanied by his department heads. He scanned the lobby. "Where's breakfast?"

The conference didn't start till ten. She'd scheduled it that way to give everyone time to eat before they arrived. "Just coffee and tea this morning."

His plump lips pouted. "The brochure said there would be a breakfast buffet." Behind him, his team grumbled.

"That starts tomorrow." Despite Satan's promise to fund the conference lavishly, Greed had authorized barely enough to cover meals for the actual trade summit. "This morning's offering is limited to coffee and tea."

"You might have told us that ahead of time." Gluttony's whine reminded her of a mosquito.

Her palm itched to whack him, but she kept her patience. "It was clearly stated in the schedule."

The mutterings grew louder. She gritted her teeth. Pampered, privileged...

Gluttony's round face brightened. He snapped his fingers. "You could order something to be delivered." He beamed at his inspiration. "I'd like a croissant with ham and Swiss."

His team quickly followed his lead. "I'll have a bagel with lox." "Ditto, but with cream cheese." "Get me a Danish."

Before she could respond, Sam returned, tucking his phone into his jacket pocket. "What's going on?"

Gluttony explained about breakfast. She steeled herself for criticism but to her surprise, Sam scowled at Gluttony. "I passed a dozen Manhattan bakeries on my way here. Go find one and buy yourself a bagel."

Lilith stared at him in wonder. He'd taken her side.

Grumbling, they stomped out of the assembly hall. She was steeling herself to thank Sam when he turned to her. "I need you to show me how to operate the audio-visual controls in the assembly hall."

"I've never seen the AV controls in the hall." Maybe they shouldn't have been so insistent that Kudar keep only a minimum of staff onsite for the conference.

"Perhaps not," Sam said. "But there's a substantially better chance you'll be able to figure out how to work them than I will."

He had helped her, he had stood up for her and now he had acknowledged her superior expertise. She found herself softening toward him, which was probably what he intended.

"Fine." She followed him up the stairs.

The Assembly Hall was four stories high and decorated in blue, green and gold. Its tiered rows held enough tables to seat delegations from 193 countries. Wedge-shaped, the room narrowed to a series of wooden panels that formed a rotunda, angling upward to a 75-foot ceiling. In the center of the panels was the U.N. emblem—a pair of olive branches curved around a map of the world. A black marble podium stood in front of the emblem.

She hooked Sam's laptop into the system while he stood so close behind her she could feel the heat coming off his body. The scent of leather and lime wrapped itself around her. Gritting her teeth against the ache of desire his nearness created, she showed him how to raise and lower the screen and how to turn on the projector and microphone. When she stepped aside to let him get a feel for the controls, he caught her in his arms. His attraction pulled at her like the full moon pulls at the ocean.

"Don't waste this opportunity," he said softly. "There's no knowing if we'll ever get another." His mouth descended on hers and the rotunda where they stood whirled around them in giddy circles.

Fortunately, the madness didn't last. She pulled away, bumping into the control panel in her haste. The screen lit up and a giant image flickered to life. Although the imposing figure didn't look much like Satan, he sat on Satan's throne in the Ninth Ring and spoke in Satan's voice.

"Good morning, delegates," he said majestically. "Welcome to the fourth quadri-centennial trade summit between the realms of Hell and Heaven." He went on to speak about his hopes for a positive outcome for both sides, though that was a clear impossibility. Heaven and Hell were locked in a zero-sum game—ground gained by one was, by definition, ground lost by the other.

She cocked her head. This Satan was taller and broader and generally less wizened than the Satan she knew.

"Makeup and prosthetics," Sam said. "Don't ask how we got him to look that good."

She didn't have to ask. Hell had a lot of makeup artists. Hollywood was a prime hunting ground for demons. "If I didn't know what he really looks like, I wouldn't question this."

Sam's shoulders relaxed. "Good."

The motion brought her back to reality. Sam's primary focus was pleasing Satan, not her.

"It looks like you've got this." She headed for the door.

"When did you become such a timid little mouse?" he called after her.

She stopped in her tracks and turned to face him. "I am not timid."

"My mistake. It must have been the scurrying for safety that confused me."

She stalked back toward him. "I'm not afraid of you."

"Of course not. Why would you be?"

"And I'm not going to sleep with you."

His eyes did that smoldering thing again. "Why not?"

Because you abandoned me. Because you betrayed me. Because, even now, you're seeing another woman. Impossible to say any of the things she was thinking. "Because I have no desire for you."

He didn't look convinced, but that was no surprise. She hadn't even convinced herself.

"Really?" He moved toward her with the lithe grace that characterized all his movements.

"Really." She fought to control her breathing, aware that her flushed cheeks gave lie to what she said. She put up a hand to forestall him from pulling her into his arms again. Perversely, she was disappointed when he dropped his hands.

"Do you remember how glorious we were together?" he asked.

She had never stopped remembering. It was he who had forgotten. "The operative word is 'were.'"

"It doesn't have to be."

"Because what happens Above stays Above?" She parroted his words from a month ago.

He opened his mouth and then closed it again.

"I thought so," she said drily. "And the best part is if it doesn't stay Above, if you're wrong and someone winds up being punished, it won't be you."

"Neither of us will be punished," he said.

"You can't know that."

"I can. Satan gave us a hall pass for the duration of this mission."

She was so stunned she wasn't sure she'd heard him correctly. "He said that?"

"He did."

"You mean he gave me to you as an incentive to get you to take this assignment?" Humiliation washed over her. She'd been awarded to Sam like some kind of prize.

"A glorious incentive," Sam said. "The thing he knew I desired above all others."

She turned her head, pretending to check the console again. When she had her emotions under control, she said, "What about Gomory? Did she also give you a hall pass to fuck me while we're up here?"

Color crawled up his neck, as if he'd finally realized how insulting this all was, but he didn't let it go. "We have a chance to be together and you're refusing to take advantage of it out of pride."

She unclenched her fists. "Well, what do you know? It turns out I learned something from you after all." She walked out of the Assembly Hall without looking back.

Now all she had to do was hold on to that attitude for the next nineteen days.

CHAPTER 8

"What do we want?" Satan screamed. Black smoke poured from his horns and his face was practically purple. The figure on screen looked like the real Satan, and not the altered image he had created for the angels.

"More souls!" the demon crowd roared back.

"When do we want them?"

"Now!"

"Whose ass are we going to kick?"

"The Enemy's!"

Sam listened with half an ear, his thoughts focused on Lilith. Why was she so determined to avoid him? She wanted him as much as he wanted her. Her signature scent of anise and sesame grew more potent when she was around him. This morning the aroma had poured off her.

The more time he spent with her, the more he realized how much she'd changed from the sweet little human who had been his wife so long ago. That Lilith had adored him. This Lilith challenged everything he said or did.

It was incredibly stimulating.

He had yearned for the old Lilith for ten thousand years, but the new one excited him in ways her softer self hadn't. This new Lilith was proud and strong. She wouldn't allow herself to be taken advantage of. He respected and admired that, but he had less than three weeks to connect with her. Unless something changed, that wouldn't be long enough to get past the barriers she had erected against him.

A flash of light caught his eye. At the back of the room stood a small figure, backlit by the lights in the hall. She listened to Satan screaming for about half a minute before backing out and closing the door.

He wished he could do the same.

Lilith slipped away from the General Assembly Hall with the shouts of fourteen hundred demons ringing in her ears. Thirty seconds was as much pep rally as she could take.

She returned to the registration table, debating whether to go ahead and set out tomorrow's badges and gift bags. Better not while there were Envy demons in the house. Those guys would pilfer a lead penny, much less badges made from gold and gemstones.

As she bent to put the boxes back under the table, one of the front doors opened. Although they'd requested Kudar leave only a skeleton staff onsite, she expected to see a security guard or a janitor, but the being that came through the doors had wings. This must be Gibeon, here to set up Heaven's registration.

She tried to see his face but he was talking on his phone and his hand blocked her view. His skin was so pale it was practically translucent and coppery red curls haloed his head. Her breath caught in her throat. The angel who had predicted Ayelet's death had been red-haired.

Like Sam, Gibeon had ignored the suggested dress code, going with a navy suit, a light blue shirt and a white tie. As he drew nearer, his wings furled, disappearing into his jacket. The strap of a leather messenger bag crossed his chest diagonally.

"Yes, sir. I'll see to it." He slipped his phone into his bag and his face came into view. At the same instant, The smell of burnt sugar invaded her nose. Her stomach dropped. It was him—the messenger who had condemned her darling Ayelet to death.

A feeling of disconnect came over her, so strong it was like vertigo. The last time she'd seen this angel was twelve thousand years ago, in the opening to the airy cave where she'd just given birth. Two other angels had accompanied him, but he'd done most of the talking. All three had been dressed in flowing white robes. He'd glared down at her, a naked teenager sitting cross-legged on the floor of a cave amid piles of blood-soaked straw and afterbirth, cradling her infant daughter.

He had delivered a message from the Enemy: "Return and submit to your husband or you will lose every child you ever birth."

She'd had no desire to go back to Adam, with his clumsy hands and domineering ways, but fear for her child had made her do as the angel bade her. She had followed the angel's order, but the Enemy had killed her baby anyway.

Thousands of years had passed but her heart ached like it was yesterday. There were some things you could never get over.

"Lilith Firstwoman." His voice vibrated with loathing. "What are you doing here?" His wings emerged again and the smell of burnt sugar filled the air. He was definitely the angel who had followed her to that cave. She flinched and his eyes gleamed with triumph.

That brought her up short. She was no longer a scared adolescent to be browbeaten by a terrifying supernatural being. She was one of Satan's best operatives, with ten thousand years of experience under her belt.

"I'm assisting with the summit," she said coolly. "What are you doing here?"

"I represent Heaven." His shoulders were stiff, his mouth tight. He had the same job she did and he hated admitting it.

"Well, what about that?" she drawled. "Who would have thought that all these years later we'd both wind up as gofers?"

The air surrounding him crackled. "I am here to provide support to Heaven's delegation."

Her eyes dropped to his brown leather bag. "You mean, like delivering messages?"

He made a noise that was anything but angelic. Fingers curling, he advanced on her. Despite her six-inch heels, he towered over her. Her heart pounded but she stood her ground.

"Begone, demon," he ordered. His red curls lifted like tiny adders.

"No can do." She eyed the snakes warily. "The boss assigned me to be here."

His face reddened and his hair burst into flames. He pointed at her with a long pale finger. "Return to Hell, from whence you came, strumpet, or the wrath of Heaven will fall upon you."

His hair had blazed exactly like this when he'd prophesied Ayelet's death. She swallowed.

"I don't take my orders from you," she said but her voice was weaker than she liked.

Lightning streaked across his eyes. Her heartbeat sped up but she fought the urge to retreat. She would not let him intimidate her.

He advanced on her. "By the power of Heaven, I order you to abandon this mission and return to Hell!" he shouted.

She couldn't meet his eyes so she fell back on her usual defense, being a wise-ass. "A lot of people want a lot of things but wantin' ain't gettin', sweetie."

Veins pulsed in his forehead. He spread his wings wider so that he loomed even larger. "If you stay, bawd, the wrath of Heaven will fall upon you."

Her heart slammed against her ribs. Then she realized he'd already said that. With repetition, his threat became less terrifying. Her lips twisted. "Been there, done that."

He danced with fury, his feet barely touching the ground. She thanked Satan for the immortality that meant bullies like this could no longer threaten her life.

He grabbed her arm, his fingers biting into the muscle until it ached. "Do as you're bid, hussy, or lions will rend your bowels and vultures will tear at your entrails."

That was new. She swallowed. Just because he couldn't kill her didn't mean he couldn't maim her. She'd heal, but it would still hurt. A lot. Before she could respond, a snarling lion sprang from the empty air behind him. Simultaneously, a pair of vultures swooped from the ceiling. She screamed as the lion's claws tore at her belly and the birds' beaks ripped at her face.

She tried to curl up to protect her soft middle, but Gibeon's hand was an iron manacle holding her in place. She expected to see her vivisected bowels pile up on the floor in front of her but the carpet there remained a soft shade of sea foam green, unmarred by human intestines.

That brought her back to reality. The attacks weren't real. He was using his angelic abilities to implant images and sensations in her mind. She yanked her arm free. Instantly, the lion and the vultures melted away.

She straightened her suit jacket. "Well, that sounds like quite the party but I'm afraid I have to decline your invitation."

The dancing flames rose higher. Directly above his head, she noticed a small silver gadget extending down from the ceiling. Uh-oh.

"You might want to dial it back a notch with the fireworks. You're going to set off—"

"Silence!" he roared. The flames climbed over each other in a race for the ceiling. Lilith moved out of range as, with a hiss, the sprinkler over his head came on, squirting water everywhere. Beneath the spray, the flames sputtered and died but the sprinkler continued to spew water. Wet curls straggled down his forehead and over his ears. Water drenched his jacket and pants. He looked so bedraggled a snort of laughter escaped her.

"Harlot," he screamed, side-stepping the still-active sprinkler head. "You will pay for this." With both hands, he reached for her throat.

Without warning, Sam appeared, scowling. "What's all this commotion?"

His gaze took in the water still spouting from the sprinkler head and Gibeon's sodden state. He strode forward but the slick soles of his wingtips slipped on the wet carpet. If he'd been any less graceful, he would have fallen. Being Sam, he recovered his balance as though he still had wings. "What in Satan's name is going on here?"

The angel pointed his pasty little finger at her. "This Jezebel called forth torrents of water from the heavens to drown me."

Sam stared at the angel. His eyes lit with recognition and his nostrils flared. He not only knew this angel, he also didn't like him. Good. He'd side with her.

"Would someone care to explain what's going on here?" he asked instead.

Gibeon squeegeed water from his brow. "The slut doused me with the waters of Hell."

That was it. Lilith curled her fingers into claws. "Call me a whore one more time and your morning shower will be the least of your worries."

Sam took her arm, his hand like iron. "Give me a moment to chat with my associate," he told Gibeon.

"What are you doing?" he demanded in a furious whisper as he dragged her away. Under the overhead lights, his pupils had gone rectangular. "You know how important this negotiation is to Satan. This is no time for your pranks."

Did he genuinely believe she'd soaked Gibeon as some kind of practical joke?

"I didn't do squat," she said flatly. "The Cosmic Torch over there doesn't want me here. When I refused to leave, he got so pissed his hair caught fire and set off the sprinkler system."

It was the angel that had cost them their marriage. Sam recognized him the instant he set eyes on him. He was a troublemaker. If Sam had been reacting based on his own feelings, he would have applauded Lilith for dousing the fool. Unfortunately, if he didn't pacify the angel,

Gibeon would refuse to join them in Hell and Lilith would wind up in the tar pits.

"What did you do to annoy him?" Sam asked.

She yanked her arm away. "Nothing. He showed up and started making threats."

Sam snorted.

She glared at him. "Do you really think I'm stupid enough to undermine a negotiation in a way that could be tied back to me? If Satan found out I sabotaged this mission I'd have a lock on the gold medal for tar pit breaststroke."

She was right, of course. "You need to smooth things over with him."

She folded her arms. "Can't happen."

"Why not?"

"He doesn't want me here."

"Why doesn't he want you here?"

"How would I know? Maybe he doesn't like women."

They glared at each other, at an impasse. Down the hall, a human in blue coveralls appeared. From a safe distance, he inspected the gadget squirting water.

"Take care of the sprinkler," Sam said. "I'll talk to Gibeon."

He followed her down the hall, trying to come up with a way out of this situation that didn't involve tearing Gibeon's wings off and feeding them to him one feather at a time.

For the rest of the day, Lilith made it a point to keep her distance from Gibeon. It was clear that Sam was on his side. If there were any more incidents she could wind up in the tar pool.

Why was there no DemSec profile for Gibeon? She'd asked around but none of her colleagues had heard of an angel by that name. The boss certainly knew of his existence. Satan, in the form of a snake, had been there when Gibeon had sent her and her newborn out into the desert to die. What game was he playing?

Maybe he was trying to keep Sam from being influenced by her hatred of Gibeon. If so, it was a wasted effort. For Sam, work came first. If he knew what Gibeon had done, he might regret what had happened, but that wouldn't affect his ability to work with the angel for the duration of the conference. Something else was going on and she was pretty sure it connected back to the secret Sam was keeping.

Over dinner tonight, he would renew his attempt to seduce her. It might be fun to match wits with him but she'd be a fool to succumb. No matter how good he smelled or how wonderful his lips felt on hers, she was a distant second to his first love—his career.

At four-thirty she texted him: "WHERE ARE WE GOING FOR DINNER?"

Fifteen minutes dragged by before he responded. "TAKING GIBEON OUT TO DINNER TO SMOOTH THINGS OVER. LET'S MAKE IT TOMORROW NIGHT INSTEAD."

Tomorrow the angel delegation would arrive and Sam would be busy. She was off the hook for dinner. The thought pleased her less than she expected.

Once again, Sam's career had come first.

CHAPTER 9

The air inside The Lion and the Lamb was redolent with the twin scents of cumin and cardamom. Sam had chosen the restaurant because they served Middle Eastern food, hoping it would make Gibeon feel at home. Owned by Muslims, the restaurant didn't serve alcohol but he suspected the angel would have refused a drink anyway.

He gave Gibeon a friendly smile. "I understand you're interested in joining us."

"That's a lie!" Gibeon's gaze darted around the room, his eyes panicked. "Where did you get that idea?"

What? It took Sam a minute to figure out what was going on. Gibeon feared the Enemy would find out he was job-shopping and there would be Heaven to pay. He was probably right, but that wasn't Sam's problem.

"Relax," he said. "God doesn't spy on his angels."

Gibeon looked around uneasily. "You can't know that."

"I spent thousands of years in his presence. To be honest, he's not that into angels. His real interest is humanity."

Gibeon's mouth tightened into a rosette of resentment. Like Satan, he was bitter about the lack of attention the Enemy paid to his staff. Excellent. Bitterness made a great lever.

"You were a messenger when we met long ago," he said. "You're still in the same job classification. Why haven't you been promoted?"

Color surged up Gibeon's throat. He glared at Sam. Hmm. This was apparently a touchy subject.

"There was an incident," Gibeon said, finally. The tight skin around his eyes made it clear he did not want to discuss it further.

Was this related to his prophecy about Sam and Lilith's potential child?

"What kind of incident?"

"I was sent to deliver a message." Gibeon's sharp tone said he resented Sam's questions. Satan must have led him to believe there would be no interview, that all he had to do to get the job was to ask for it. "When the recipient refused to follow my directive, I took the initiative to ensure Yahweh's orders were followed. My supervisor said I exceeded my brief."

Their conversation at Gobekli Tepe had contained no directives from the Enemy. Whatever misstep was holding Gibeon back, it wasn't related to his prophecy to Satan about Sam and Lilith's progeny. Satisfied, Sam took a sip of water and changed the subject. "This seems like a plum assignment."

To his surprise, Gibeon flushed even darker and his eyes sparked with anger. "I was excited when I was told I got to participate in a diplomatic mission. Then I arrived and found *her* in charge."

"She's not in charge," Sam said. "I am."

Gibeon leaned toward him. "Then send her back to Hell."

What had triggered his squabble with Lilith this afternoon? She claimed she hadn't done anything to prompt it. She was probably telling the truth. He'd seen for himself how touchy Gibeon was. He tried for a soothing tone. "Lilith can be a little abrasive, but she is a very competent administrator."

The angel folded his arms across his chest. "She shouldn't be part of a cosmic summit."

"Why not?"

"She's human."

"Not really. She's immortal."

"The Almighty created her as a human." Gibeon scowled. "She would have died eons ago if Satan hadn't interfered with the natural order of things."

Sam's fingers tightened on the stem of his water glass. How casually Gibeon discussed Lilith's death. Perhaps he was a good fit for Hell after all.

The waiter arrived with their meals, setting a tabbouleh salad before Gibeon and a plate of kibbeh in front of Sam. Sam plowed into the ground lamb and bulgur with gusto. "Gluttony suggested this place and he was right. The kibbeh is excellent."

Gib tried a tiny nibble of his salad before setting his fork down. "Is all the food this spicy in Hell?"

"There's a lot of variety in Hell," Sam said. It wasn't exactly a lie, though none of the food on this table would earn a place in Hell, where everything was so fiery you couldn't actually taste anything. "It tastes great to me, but I missed lunch."

Gibeon folded his arms. "If the harlot were competent, she would have brought you sustenance. You should replace her."

Sam breathed in through his nose and reminded himself he couldn't walk away without losing his promotion. Even worse, Lilith would be punished for his failure. He needed to discover the root of Gibeon's aversion. "Tell me how things went awry this afternoon."

"She insulted me."

It was a non-answer. Sam's suspicions deepened. "Her manner can be a little direct."

Gibeon poked at his salad. "She called me a ground squirrel."

Sam paused, a forkful of kibbeh halfway to his mouth. "A what?"

"A ground squirrel."

Sam tried to untangle this statement. "Do you mean a gopher?"

"Yes. She called me a gopher."

"That was a joke."

"No." Gibeon shook his head stubbornly. "She meant it as an insult."

He was probably right. "She's been instructed to be polite to you from now on."

Gibeon's jaw hardened. "That is not acceptable. She needs to return to Hell."

"I personally guarantee she'll be courteous to you." Sam hoped he was telling the truth.

Gibeon flushed an unattractive red. "I don't want to be around her."

There had to be a compromise here. Gibeon and Lil had the exact same job, so it would be difficult to keep her out of his orbit, but it was a solution he might accept. "I need her at the registration desk tomorrow morning, but after things are up and running, I'll relocate her so that you don't have to be around her."

The angel shook his head, his curls bobbing hysterically. "She needs to go back to Hell."

Sam had no intention of sending Lilith back to Hell. He wanted her right here, where they could take advantage of Satan's hall pass. "Let me see what I can work out."

At that, Gibeon's entire body relaxed. What was up with him and Lilith? It had been a mistake to bring him to a restaurant that didn't serve alcohol.

"Satan's very interested in having you join us." Sam hoped the change of subject would make the angel relax. "Tell me about the kind of role you're looking for in Hell."

"I want a leadership position." Gibeon's tone was definite. "My own division, at a minimum."

All the divisions currently had heads. Of course, Satan could create a new division. Sam had long thought Whining should be a deadly sin. Gibeon seemed to know a lot about that. "What else?"

"Pleasant accommodations. A place with good airflow and access to fresh air and sunshine."

Did he know nothing about Hell? "Of course. Anything else?"

"I'd want to select my own team, of course."

"That goes without saying." There was no value in disclosing that all the demons that were willing to work were already fully employed.

Gibeon relaxed enough to eat his dinner. Assuming that his list of demands had come to an end, Sam did the same. The atmosphere, if not companionable, was at least neutral. When he finished his salad, Gibeon patted his lips with his napkin. "And, of course, Lilith Firstwoman has to go."

Sam blinked. "What do you mean, 'go?'"

"I won't consider coming Below if she's there."

Where did he think she would go if she weren't in Hell? It wasn't like she'd be welcome to take his place in Heaven.

Sam tried to temper his words. "Lilith spends a lot of her time Aboveworld. I rarely see her." He'd never been able to decide which was worse—the days he caught a glimpse of her across a cavern and his pulse pounded in his ears, or the weeks on end he spent without seeing her, when what little color there was in Hell drained away, leaving the place dull and empty.

Gibeon's face took on the stubborn cast Sam was coming to know and loathe. "That's unacceptable. She needs to be gone."

"Gone?" Perhaps Satan would transfer her to the new Centauran region. If so, Sam could create some acquisition-related complications and spend time there with her, away from Satan's watchful eye.

"Satan needs to end her," Gibeon clarified.

By "gone" he meant "dead." Sam's chin hit his chest. He searched for a reply over the roaring in his head but he didn't find one.

"Make that happen," the angel said, "and I'll entertain Satan's offer."

I'll see you in Heaven first. Sam swallowed the words without speaking them. Aloud he said, "I'll convey your demands to Satan and let you know what he says."

After they left the restaurant, Sam took Gibeon to a nearby bar, where he plied him with liquor until the angel could barely stand up, but Gibeon still refused to say why he disliked Lilith so much. At ten-thirty, he poured Gibeon into a cab and dropped him at his hotel. Once he was rid of his celestial dining companion, he pulled out his phone to give the driver the name of his own hotel, only to realize he didn't have that information. "Let me check with my secretary."

"WHERE AM I STAYING?" he texted Estelle.

"I KNOW NOT," she responded a few minutes later. "THOU SAID LILITH WAS ARRANGING THY ACCOMMODATION."

Sam's eyes narrowed. Lilith was far too organized to have simply overlooked providing the information. "WHERE IS SHE STAYING?"

"GIV'ST ME A MOMENT TO CONSULT MY SOOTHSAYER."

Sam stifled a groan. "Soothsayer" was what Estelle called her desktop computer. Her understanding of technology was about what you'd expect of a woman who died in 1665.

Moments dragged by. The driver glanced over his shoulder. "You want me to circle the block while you're waiting to hear? Because this is a loading zone."

Sam had no idea what that meant. "Yes. Circle the block."

Another ten minutes passed before his phone pinged, during which time he grew steadily more annoyed. "SHE BE AT THE FERGUSON HOTEL, ROOM 1216."

Lilith sat on the couch, drinking wine and surfing through endless channels on TV, waiting for Sam to arrive on her doorstep after he realized he had no room reservation.

It was quite a coincidence that the angel that had doomed her child and the demon that had destroyed her heart had dined together tonight. Something was going on and she intended to find out what it was.

At eleven o'clock, a thunderous knock sounded on the door. Smothering a smile, she set down the remote. "Who is it?" she sang in a lilting voice.

"Open the blessed door, Lilith," Sam snarled from the other side.

She could call hotel security and report an intruder, but that would mean bypassing the chance to taunt him. She opened the door a crack. "What are you doing here? I thought you had a date with an angel."

"I dropped him at his hotel." Sam pushed his way in and set his suitcase on the floor. His breath smelled of whiskey but he seemed completely sober. "Why don't I have a hotel room?"

She gave him her best wide-eyed stare. "I know how picky you are. I figured you'd rather Estelle made your arrangements."

"Did it occur to you to tell her you were taking that approach?"

"It must have slipped my mind. How was dinner?"

He snorted. "It went the way any dinner with an angel goes—lots of bitching and very little useful conversation."

Before she could follow up, he took off his suit jacket and hung it on the back of one of the stools lining the breakfast bar. His shoulders seemed to fill the room. She stared at him in alarm. "What are you doing?"

He unbuttoned a cuff and rolled up his sleeve to reveal muscular forearms sprinkled with dark hair. "Making myself comfortable."

Oh, no. Oh, no, no, no, no. This wasn't supposed to happen. "Shouldn't you be getting in touch with Estelle?"

He rolled up the other sleeve. "Estelle is busy with the acquisition I was putting together before I got drafted to run this clown show. She doesn't have time to track down accommodations."

Lilith stared at him in alarm. Why had it not occurred to her that when he found himself without lodgings he'd simply move in with her? She should have booked him somewhere in Bedford-Stuyvesant with bedbugs and rooms by the hour, where he could listen to johns getting laid next door while he lay there alone.

"If you talk to the front desk, I'm sure they can find something for you."

He sat on a curve of the red leather sofa and removed first one shoe, then the other. "I spoke with them before I came up. They are booked for the duration of the conference."

She'd known that. She'd actually planned for that. What had she been thinking? This suite had only one bedroom.

"There has to be a room available somewhere," she said desperately.

He set his shoes under the coffee table and stretched out his legs. "I'm good."

Sam was many things, but good was not one of them. "I'll call around and see if I can find you something nearby."

He leaned over to pick up his briefcase and extracted his tablet. "Let me know how that goes."

Ten minutes of internet searching and fifteen phone calls later, she admitted defeat. The closest hotel with any vacancy was the Courtney, where the angels were staying. When she suggested it, Sam lifted one eyebrow. "If I wanted to co-habit with angels I would have stayed in Heaven."

"Well, *I* can't stay there. Gibeon would have a stroke." She checked her list. "There's a vacancy at the Putnam."

"The Putnam is ten blocks away from the conference center. I'm not hiking ten blocks every day."

"The Deadlies are staying here. I need to be nearby, to ensure their needs are being met."

"We're operating under a flag of truce. You won't need to cater to their various depravities on his mission."

She folded her arms across her chest. "I'm not leaving."

He shrugged. "Suit yourself."

If he wouldn't leave voluntarily, she'd force him out. She went into the bedroom and closed the door. From the bedside phone, she called Housekeeping and ordered an extra set of sheets and a blanket. "There's a fifty-dollar tip in it for you if you can find a horse blanket."

"Is it okay if it still smells like horses?" he asked.

"If it still smells like horses, I'll make it a hundred."

Twenty minutes later, there was another knock at the door. Sam looked up from his tablet but made no effort to rise.

"I'll get it," she said sardonically.

"It is your room," he pointed out.

At the door, she took the aromatic bedding from the grinning bellboy and handed him a hundred-dollar bill. Then she plopped the sheets and the smelly blanket down on the sofa. "You can sleep out here."

Sam surveyed the sofa out of the corner of his eye. "This sofa is s-shaped."

"Very observant."

"I'd have to sleep—" He stared at the couch like he was trying to work out how to fit his six-foot-two-inch frame to its contours.

"Curved," she said helpfully. "You'll have to sleep curved."

Sam closed his eyes and his lips moved silently. After ten seconds, he reopened them and got to his feet. He picked up the blanket, grimacing as he registered the scratchy texture. Then he wrinkled his nose. "Who last slept under this blanket? Bucephalus?"

It was all Lilith could do not to hug herself. "It's what they had."

"At a five-star hotel?"

She shrugged. "If you're not happy with the accommodations, there's room at the Putnam." She waited hopefully while he considered his options.

He shook his head. "I can tough it out for the duration of the mission."

Her heart plummeted. "But that's three weeks."

He smiled. "It will be like old times."

Oh, no, it wouldn't. She knew exactly what he had in mind and she wanted no part of it.

Sam was a demon who liked his creature comforts. He was only staying here to harass her. After a night on the serpentine couch beneath a horse blanket, he'd order a couple of the Deadlies to buddy up and he'd take the extra room.

He whipped the fitted sheet into the air and let it settle over the sofa. The fabric slipped off the smooth leather and slid to the floor.

"They have great sheets here," she said. "But the high thread count makes them a little slippery on leather."

"I see that," he said. "It's a shame they don't ensure the same level of quality in their blankets." He picked up the sheet again but instead of shaking it out, he took a rounded corner and fitted it around the back corner of the sofa cushion. That left her staring at his ass—his delectable, first-class ass. For a moment she felt like a poor child outside a bakery window, able to see the treats on display, knowing she wouldn't get a chance to enjoy one.

She swallowed. She needed to get a grip. "I don't want you here."

"I'm aware of that." He tucked the sheet behind a curved cushion. His tone was dry as a glass of Muscadet. "You've never been especially subtle."

Her face warmed. "I may not be subtle but I get the job done."

"Yes, you do." He leaned over even further to fit the next corner. She couldn't see his face, but he sounded sincere.

She steeled herself against his charm. "It's twelve kinds of bullshit that I get the hardest assignments and I never get rewarded when I succeed, but I wind up picking maggots out of my ass when I fail."

"No argument from me." He crossed to the far end of the couch. Even though he was a paper pusher in Hell, he moved with the grace of an athlete—or a fallen angel. Longing so strong it was physically painful made her hands shake. She curled them into fists.

"Look, Sam," she said. "You have to see this isn't going to work."

He didn't pretend to misunderstand. "You must have known I'd come here when I found I had nowhere to stay."

"I figured you'd have Estelle find you a place."

"There's nowhere to find—at least, nowhere I'm willing to stay."

It took her a minute to absorb his meaning. When she did, she was outraged. "Why did you have me make all those calls if you already knew there weren't any suitable vacancies?"

He flashed his wickedest smile, all gleaming white teeth and sparkling black eyes. Her heart lurched. "The same reason you didn't book me a room in the first place. To get even."

She supposed she had that coming.

"Anyway, it's just three weeks," he added.

Three weeks sounded like an eternity.

"We can't do this," she said. "The Deadlies are sure to find out and they'll waste no time spreading the news. Every gossip in Hell will think we're sleeping together."

He eyed her the way a lion eyes an impala. "Is that an invitation?"

Her pulse spiked and heat rushed into her face. She wanted to step back, but that was exactly the wrong reaction. She forced a mocking smile to her lips. "Hardly."

He abandoned the sheet and took a step toward her, watching her face closely. "We have a chance to be together for the duration. I can't believe you're not taking it."

For the duration. Meaning, when they got back to Hell, things would return to the way they'd been. When Satan had ordered them to split, Sam had made no effort to sway him. As Satan had torn away the only thing that had ever given either of them any joy in Hell, Sam had simply walked away. And she had watched him go, a giant sinkhole opening where her heart once was. She lifted her chin. She refused to give him the satisfaction of knowing she still missed him.

"Thanks, but I think I'll pass." She was pleased to hear her tone carried only its usual snark and none of the angst she was feeling.

He bent again to push the extra fabric underneath the front of the sofa cushion. Despite her best efforts, her eyes were glued to his ass. She licked her lips nervously.

He straightened suddenly and caught her staring. His slow smile reminded her that he knew every erogenous zone, every sweet spot on her body. Heat curled low in her belly. Bless him, anyway. And bless herself for her weakness where he was concerned.

He was the first to break eye contact, bending to tuck the sheet a little tighter. "Let me know if you change your mind."

"Not going to happen." Calmly and slowly, so that he wouldn't interpret it as escaping, she walked into the bedroom and closed the door.

She considered propping the desk chair beneath the doorknob, like a heroine in a Gothic novel, but it wasn't necessary. Sam might eye her in a way that made it clear exactly what he was thinking, might use his demon powers to implant erotic images in her mind, might even kiss her without her consent, but his pride would never allow him to force her. They'd lived together for nearly three months before she was ready to consummate their relationship. He'd patiently wooed her into trusting him. It wasn't his desire for her that was the problem; the real issue was her desire for him.

So what to do now? If she left the balance of power with him, for the next three weeks she'd live in a constant state of arousal and he would know it. Even worse, there was a good chance that somewhere along the way she'd give in. Part of her, the pathetic part that had never fallen out of love with him, applauded that thought, but the rest of her knew it was a bad idea. She knew what the future held if she gave in to him because she'd already experienced it once. To live through that nightmare of loss again was inconceivable.

She gazed at herself in the mirror over the dresser, noting with disapproval her downward-drawn lips and corded neck. Satan's gift of immortality meant the tension would leave no permanent marks on her face or body, but "stressed out" was not an appropriate look for a woman who had survived ten thousand years of working for the Lord of the Underworld.

She had two choices—she could leave the power in Sam's hands or she could take back the night. She was no longer the shy young girl she'd been when they first met. If anyone understood the subtleties of sexual power, it was she.

And there were worthwhile things she could do with that power. Like, discovering why Sam had broken a date with her to take a minor league angel out to dinner. Gibeon might be her personal nemesis, but his admin role at the conference said he wasn't a power player.

When Sam was in Heaven, he wouldn't have given Gibeon the time of day. So why was the Devil's Advocate wining and dining a spear-carrier now? Had he spent the evening pumping the angel for information that would give Hell an advantage in the talks? Or was something more going on? Her instincts said it had to do with the secret Sam was keeping.

From the drawer where she'd stowed her lingerie, she selected a lacy pink camisole with matching satin shorts. She had no intention of sleeping with Sam, but the thought of toying with him brought a smile to her lips. The tendons in her throat and jaw relaxed. A glance in the mirror said she looked like herself again.

Let the games begin.

CHAPTER 10

Sam looked up from his tablet as Lilith came out of the bedroom in a clingy pink thing that showed off every inch of her legs. She'd decided to fight fire with fire. His gaze rested on her trim thighs. He could live with that.

He was less sure he could live with the assignment Satan had given him. The boss had promised that if he successfully recruited Gibeon, Lilith would remain immortal. Unfortunately, it was clear that once Gibeon arrived below, he would bend his efforts toward convincing Satan to end her. Once he joined Hell, he would lose his ability to negotiate, but it didn't take much effort to convince Satan to do what he already wanted to do.

Sam thought—he hoped—that his own threat to retaliate would prevent Satan from acting on Gibeon's request, but the Lord of the Underworld was notoriously fickle. If Gibeon joined Hell, Lilith's life would become substantially less safe.

And the alternative wasn't much better. Satan's one talent lay in devising perfectly tailored punishments. If Sam failed to drag Gibeon down to their level, the boss would punish Lilith to punish him. He wasn't sure which outcome was worse. There had to be a third option that allowed her life to go on, unchanged. If he could figure out why the angel disliked her so much, perhaps he could broker a peace accord between them.

She crossed the room barefoot, looking almost exactly as she had the first time he set eyes on her, stumbling naked down the road of what would become Hell. He had been instantly entranced. Compared to the angels that had been living in the sulfurous air of Below for millennia, she had seemed as fresh as a spring flower.

The moment he saw her, he wanted her. She wasn't beautiful in the faultless way angels were beautiful. Her forehead was a bit too high, her lips a bit too full. Careful scrutiny of her legs when she stood with her ankles together revealed a hint of daylight between her knees. She was, in other words, human, flawed and, to him, totally irresistible.

While the road to Hell might be paved with good intentions, the road through it featured sharp rocks and red-hot embers. He had swung her into his arms, promising to find her clothing and shoes. She had snuggled gratefully against his chest, wide-eyed and trusting as a doe. The heart he thought he'd left behind in Heaven melted in his chest.

Satan had promised her immortality in return for becoming the first human to choose Hell over Heaven, but fifteen years passed before he fulfilled that promise. In Sam's mind, she grew more beautiful with each passing day, but the Enemy had created humans to wither and die. Tiny lines around her eyes and threads of gray in her hair signaled an aging process that would eventually take her life.

He'd reminded Satan of his pledge, timing that reminder to coincide with the opening of Hell's second location, in the Andromeda galaxy. Delighted to see his empire expanding, Satan kept his promise and froze her appearance at around thirty-three in human years. She hadn't changed a jot since that day. Was that why she hadn't been able to conceive? Pregnancy required many changes to a woman's body. Hers was, in a way, petrified.

Sam allowed himself the pleasure of sneaking another look as she poured herself a glass of wine in the kitchenette and carried it into the living room. She settled in a leather chair with an ottoman in front of it. Her breasts strained against the shiny fabric of her camisole as she leaned forward to place a small leather travel kit on the ottoman. His cock hardened. This game of torches they were playing was likely to burn them both to the ground. He rose from the couch and moved toward her, enjoying the little flare of panic in her eyes.

"You can get that thought out of your head." She picked up the leather kit and unzipped it. "I'm not interested."

Everything about her body gave that the lie. Her cheeks were bright pink and inside her flimsy camisole, her nipples were like pebbles.

He sat on the ottoman and settled her feet in his lap. "Those shoes must be painful for your toes." He looped his finger and thumb around her ankle, effectively imprisoning her foot.

She tried to snatch it away. "I've been wearing them so long I don't even notice."

He didn't release it. With his free hand, he rummaged through the travel kit, coming out with a bottle of peppermint-scented oil. He poured a few drops into his palm and began to rub her arch.

She let out a tiny moan that went straight to his groin, but he ignored it. The successful hunter was the patient one. After a few minutes, she relaxed against the chair with a sigh.

He bent her toes until they cracked. "Does that feel better?"

She nodded drowsily, looking much more peaceful than he felt. He stole a peek inside the leg of her satin shorts, looking for the familiar riot of dark curls but all he saw was pale flesh.

"People don't have pubic hair anymore," she said without opening her eyes. "The fashion up here is bare skin."

She sounded bored, as though having a man look at her genitals was a situation too familiar to warrant a reaction. Ignoring a stab of jealousy, he placed his hand on her thigh, his fingertips just below the hem of her shorts. "Doesn't that leave stubble?"

She smiled. "Not if you rip it out by the roots."

He flinched and the corners of her mouth quirked. "I've always thought it must be worse for men."

It was all Sam could do not to cross his legs. "That sounds like something they'd do in Ring Two."

She chuckled. "It does, doesn't it? I've heard Asmodeus tried it but I haven't seen him lately."

Was she saying that she'd been intimate with the Demon of Lust? His hands clenched. This time he couldn't deny his jealousy. Human men were work assignments; fallen angels were completely different.

"Ow." Lilith tugged her foot from his hands. "You're getting a little rough there, Pride."

His logical mind pointed out that they'd been apart for thousands of years, during which time he'd dated hundreds of different she-demons, but his less rational side didn't care. Centuries ago he'd heard she was having an affair with one of Satan's favorite acolytes. The affair hadn't lasted long, but it was one of the best days of his life when that demon left Hell permanently.

Her sleek eyebrows lifted. "Is there a problem?"

"No problem," he said, though the words nearly strangled him. He pulled her other foot into his lap and dripped oil onto it. "I didn't think you cared much for Lust." He was pleased with how casual he sounded.

She laughed, "I've always enjoyed lust. It was Asmodeus I couldn't stand."

What was she telling him? Had she slept with Asmodeus or not?

"Did you get any useful intel from Gibeon?" she asked.

He abandoned the topic of Asmodeus. "I wasn't trying for intel. I was trying to smooth his ruffled feathers."

"Literally or figuratively?"

He awarded her wordplay a brief smile before returning to the hunt. "Is there history between you and Gibeon I should know about?"

"No." She leaned back, sinking lower in the chair. Her shorts rode up a little higher.

His mouth went dry. She was trying to distract him and she nearly succeeded. "Let me rephrase that—have you ever encountered him before?"

She licked her lips, clearly torn about what to tell him.

Before he could press for an answer, his phone tolled Satan's ringtone. Blessit. Just as he was getting somewhere. "It's the boss."

She smiled wryly. "Of course it is."

"I won't be a minute."

She rolled her eyes. "Enjoy your chat. I'm going to bed." She disappeared into the bedroom, her behind swaying enticingly with every step.

Groaning beneath his breath, he pressed the call button.

"How did it go?" Satan asked.

"He seems to have some interest." Sam sent mental thanks to Bad, the former head of DemSec, who had shown him how to disable Satan's snooping devices.

"Did he make any demands?"

There was no way in Heaven he was telling Satan that Gibeon had insisted Lilith must be permanently removed from Hell before he would consider coming on board. He opened his mouth to ask whether Lilith and Gibeon had a history, but stopped short. Satan was determined to lure the angel away from Heaven. Even hinting at Gibeon's aversion to Lilith might put a target on her back. He would wait and follow up with the angel, instead. "He wants his own division, and to pick his own team."

"That shouldn't be a problem. I've thought for a while that we should have an Ambition division."

Annoyingly, that made a lot of sense. Ambition was at the root of many a fall.

After promising to extract a list of demands from Gibeon, Sam got off the phone. He tried Lilith's bedroom door, but it was locked. It took another hour on the uncomfortable sofa beneath the smelly horse blanket before he fell asleep. He finally drifted off to dream of seducing her into his bed only to have her disappear in a cloud of dust.

Lilith lay in bed for an hour, listening to the muffled sound of Sam talking Satan out of his latest brainstorm. The door was thick, a heavy, six-paneled mahogany, and she couldn't make out individual words. Should she get up and press her ear to the door? No, Sam was too cautious to let himself be caught out that easily.

The thought of her with Asmodeus had struck a nerve. Should she drive the nail deeper by flirting with Asmo at the conference? Picturing Sam's jealousy brought a smile to her lips but the idea of encouraging the Demon of Lust was less pleasing. She'd lost count of the times she'd had to knee him in the groin to get him to back off. Flirting with him would also undercut her reputation for being off-limits to demons. Messing with Sam's head wasn't worth being hit on by every Raum, Lix and Haures for the next century.

It was after two a.m. before she finally fell asleep. She groaned when the alarm went off at six the next morning. She'd planned to get dressed before Sam was up but light peeping under the closed door told her he was already awake. She banged on the bathroom door with her fist. "I need to shower."

The door swung open to reveal Sam with a towel tucked around his waist. Above the towel, his torso was shaped like a "Yield" sign. Below, it was barely big enough to cover his—

"Put some clothes on," she snapped.

He pulled the towel off and rubbed it across his jet-black hair before tossing it back into the bathroom.

"Anything for you, dear." He strolled across the living room to his suitcase, totally at ease with his nudity.

She usually was, too, but right now she needed a barrier between herself and Sam's potent sexuality. Preferably something like chain mail. She whisked herself into the bathroom and slammed the door.

Sam's toiletries occupied every square inch of counter space on the vanity. She swept them into the trash can with a satisfying crash.

She spent the first few minutes of her shower fantasizing about killing him, but those fantasies were soon replaced by images of the way he'd looked coming out of the bathroom. His torso was all arcs and grids—the curves of biceps and deltoids and pectorals offset by his lattice of abdominal muscles, all covered by satiny olive skin that stayed tan without ever being exposed to daylight. His body hadn't changed one iota in ten thousand years.

She shut down that train of thought. He didn't want her as his wife, only as a temporary playmate. Well, she could torment him as readily as he tormented her.

By the time she stepped out of the shower, the air in the bathroom was so thick with steam she couldn't see herself in the mirror. She wrapped herself in a towel, just like Sam had done. She opened the bathroom door to air out the room, expecting him to comment. When it didn't come, she poked her head out the door. The suite was empty. He'd gone on ahead to the conference without her. She stood in the doorway for a moment, feeling like she'd been slapped. Then she took a deep breath.

This wasn't the end of it. She wouldn't let it be.

Sam dressed and left the hotel in a hurry. Judging by the vengeful expression on Lilith's face when she went into the bathroom, she would be nude when she came back out. If he were still there, it was entirely possible he would drool on himself. He didn't need to know the extent of the power she had over him.

The demonic delegation arrived at the conference center promptly at eight a.m. and feasted on the lavish breakfast Lilith had arranged, but at eight-thirty, the steam table trays reserved for the angels were still piled with food.

As though reading his mind, Lilith said, "I thought these were supposed to be bilateral talks. Where's the other half of the conversation?"

"They probably got delayed." There was a lot of wiggle room around what could be considered a success for these talks, but having the other party boycott them did not fall into that range.

"Maybe they decided not to come." It was hard to miss the glee on Lil's face.

"If that's true, you should start shopping for a swimsuit suitable for the tar pits."

Her glee disappeared.

Sam walked outside and stood beside the Peace Bell, scanning the sky. A bank of thick gray clouds obscured the underside of Heaven.

"Maybe they're on their way, hidden by the clouds." Lilith had followed him out.

"Possibly." From the direction of the East River came a sound like rushing water. He turned in time to see a tidal wave rise above the retaining wall. The wave washed a wooden skiff onto the esplanade. In the prow of the skiff stood a muscular figure in a loincloth, holding a pole. The water washed back over the retaining wall, leaving the skiff behind.

"Did Charon just create a tidal wave in the East River?" Lilith asked. "Because we promised Kudar we'd keep things on the down-low."

"It's early," Sam said repressively. "Perhaps no one saw him."

"Right. In New York. the city that never sleeps."

"Maybe we got lucky and it was taking a quick nap." He turned to the angular boatman. "How was your trip?"

Charon rested his pole in the crook of his elbow and cracked his knuckles. "Good. I saw a few homeless I may snag on my way back."

"No snagging," Sam said instantly. "We're operating under a flag of truce. You're just here to rally the troops."

Charon's bony face lengthened in disappointment.

Above them, a ray of sunlight pierced the clouds, creating a spotlight on the gray cement surface of the esplanade. A white-robed figure with long silvery hair and a golden staff stepped out of the sunbeam. Sam sighed with relief. If Peter was here, Heaven wasn't boycotting the talks. Unless word hadn't made it to the front gate.

"Welcome, Peter," he said. "So glad you could make it."

Charon bowed. "Peter."

Peter bowed in return. Except for their clothing, the two gatekeepers looked a lot alike.

"Where is the rest of your delegation?" Trust Lilith to cut to the heart of things.

Peter looked around as though he expected to see the other angels. "No idea. They traveled separately."

Tension skittered along Sam's nerve endings. If Heaven stayed away from these talks, Satan would be beside himself.

"Maybe I should take these gentlemen inside and show them where they'll be speaking," Lilith said.

Sam nodded but before she could lead them away, the sky darkened again. A massive cloud blocked the sun like a mid-morning eclipse. The cloud hovered in place for a moment before dropping from the sky like a bullet.

Lilith recoiled. "What is that?"

"Heaven making an entrance," Sam said drily.

The cloud screeched to a halt about twenty feet above the ground. Then, one by one, individual angels peeled away and dropped to earth, landing as lightly as snowflakes in a precise matrix in front of the Peace Bell. They were dressed identically in sparkling white polo shirts, white gabardine pants and white loafers.

"What are they doing?" Lilith whispered.

"Making a show of power." It did not bode well for the success of the talks that they had arrived in formation. They wanted to be seen as an army.

When no cloud remained, the matrix contained seven perfectly aligned rows of eleven angels with their wings unfurled. Sam couldn't help but remember the way Hell's delegation had straggled in the day before. Sloth hadn't shown up until near lunchtime.

Lilith eyed the angels admiringly. "They do have impressive wingspans."

Sam scowled. The cloud crowd displayed their wings for one reason only—to remind Satan's legions of their lost wings. Turning as one, the angels advanced on the building in lockstep, each column led by a muscular celestial that shone like the sun. Jehudiel, Sam's old boss, led the first column. He appeared to be in charge.

"Who are the hotties in the front row?" Lilith asked.

"The archangels. They're the Enemy's warriors." Sam watched their soldierly advance through narrowed eyes. Why had the Enemy sent warrior angels to trade talks? Had he summoned Hell's delegation here under false pretenses, intending to destroy them?

Perhaps it had been a tactical mistake to send the demon delegation into the assembly hall, sequestering them in one place before the angels arrived. If so, it was too late to do anything about it.

"They seemed pissed. Do they have it in for you for some reason?" Lilith seemed more intrigued than worried.

"I am the highest-ranking angel to ever leave Heaven."

"That was a long time ago. I mean, it's not like you're the angel that set up an opposing empire."

Maybe not, but he represented that angel.

Jehudiel marched forward until his shoes bumped up against the toes of Sam's wingtips. Their gazes locked in a staredown.

Sam blessed himself. He knew better than to let that happen, but now that it had, he couldn't afford to let Jehudiel win. A minute went by. Sweat beaded his forehead. He'd won in hand-to-hand combat against Jehudiel the last time they'd engaged, but that was a long time ago. His old boss had grown no less commanding over the centuries. Sam hoped the centuries of living below, doing a desk job with no one to challenge him except Satan, hadn't softened him.

Another moment passed. A bead of perspiration crawled down Sam's cheek. Jehudiel grinned ferociously and leaned in a little closer. His face was cool and dry. Sam scowled and felt more sweat pop out.

Unexpectedly, Lilith pushed between them, elbowing them both hard enough to make them grunt and step back. She gazed up at Jehudiel, apparently unthreatened by his thunderous frown.

"You're late," she said. "You won't have time for breakfast, which means all this food will go to waste. Children are starving in Africa, you know."

Jehudiel seemed taken aback. "We were told there was no breakfast on the first day."

"You were given bad information. In the future, you may want to check with me. Now please pick up your badges and take your seats. The kickoff speeches were supposed to start five minutes ago."

By the time she finished speaking, Jehudiel looked two sizes smaller.

"Yes, ma'am," he mumbled. He spoke over her head. "Angels, pick up your badges and take your seats."

It was all Sam could do not to laugh out loud. When he first met Lilith, she was a beautiful child. In their years apart, she had grown into a formidable woman.

She wasn't done, either. She raised her voice. "Those of you who will be speaking, please sit at the conference tables nearest the podium. The rest of you can sit wherever you can find an open seat. Please remember that we're operating under a flag of truce."

The seven columns filed into the building through the seven entrance doors without breaking formation and marched up to the registration table. The first row picked up their badges from the corresponding row on the table and filed up the stairs in lockstep. The second row followed.

"They should apply to be Rockettes," Lilith said.

"What's a Rockette?" Sam asked.

As the angels entered the Assembly Hall, deep growls rumbled from above.

"Sounds like things are getting a little tense," she said. "Should you go play referee?"

"They know better than to start anything." Sam hoped that was true.

Two minutes later, the last of the angels had their badges and were climbing the stairs in synchronized pairs.

"There's no way demons could ever do that," Lilith said admiringly.

"You didn't need to intervene to save me," Sam said. "The Enemy will have given orders not to strike the first blow."

"I didn't intervene to save you." Her voice was tart but her cheeks turned pink.

He wanted to call her out on what was clearly a lie but the grumbles coming from the Assembly Hall grew to a roar.

She pushed him toward the door. "Get up there before the war of the worlds breaks out."

Lilith let out a sigh of relief as Sam disappeared up the staircase. She didn't think he needed protection from Jehudiel, or that she could protect him if he did. Her intervention had been a knee-jerk reaction. She'd had a bellyful of angel power games.

No sooner was Sam gone than Gibeon came through the front door. He wore sunglasses and appeared even paler than usual, almost green.

"Rough night?" she asked.

He ignored that. "Where are the badges?"

"Your crowd already picked them up. The keynotes are starting."

She waited for him to head up the stairs to the Assembly Hall but he slumped into the chair behind his side of the registration desk, looking like the slime in Ring Six. Sam had refused to tell her why he'd taken Gibeon to dinner. Maybe she should question the horse himself. She hunted around in her bag until she found a bottle of naproxen.

"You look like you're feeling pretty rough. Maybe this will help." She offered him the bottle.

He stared down his nose at her. "Angels don't use drugs."

She put the bottle back in her bag. "Okay, no meds. Try eating some oatmeal. There's plenty on the buffet. And drink lots of water. That's the best thing for a hangover."

"Why would you think I have a hangover?"

"Because you spent the evening with Samael."

Sniffing, he walked over to the buffet and ladled oatmeal into a bowl.

"There's brown sugar and maple syrup and raisins and milk—skim or whole."

He returned to the registration table with just the oatmeal. "It was noisy at the hotel. I couldn't sleep for all the car horns and trucks rumbling down the street."

"Maybe you should move hotels. The Putnam overlooks Central Park. It would be a lot quieter."

She was surprised to see him check that out on his phone. He frowned. "That's over a mile from here."

What a whiner. "It's shorter as the angel flies."

He hunched his shoulders. "You're trying to get me to break the ground rules so I'll be remanded back to Heaven."

Not a bad idea, but given that an entire flock of angels had descended on Manhattan that morning, one more wouldn't be a big deal. After eating the oatmeal he drank water and seemed to perk up a little.

"Look," she said. "We're both here, doing the same job, just for different delegations. Why don't we make things easy on ourselves and work together?"

Unfortunately, as he got to feeling better, he remembered how much he disliked her. He pushed the bowl away and eyed the stairs that led to the assembly hall. He got to his feet.

Being subtle wasn't getting her anywhere. "What did you and Sam talk about last night?"

He stalked over to the stairs. "We talked about him sending you back to Hell."

CHAPTER 11

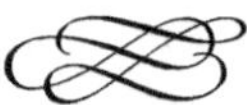

 hen Lilith arrived back at the hotel that evening after the conference, Sam was standing in front of his suitcase in a pair of black silk boxer briefs that revealed his powerful thighs and muscular calves. She clenched her teeth, grateful for her crisp, professional suit. Anything to keep a barrier between her and Sam's potent allure.

As he bent to draw a pair of jeans from his luggage, though, her jacket became too warm. Perspiration beaded her upper lip. It had been a mistake to stay in this one-bedroom suite with him. It was far too intimate.

"Are you ready for dinner?" she asked as he slipped one strong, arched foot into the leg of his jeans. She swallowed. "I made an eight p.m. reservation."

He tucked himself away and zipped his fly. "Where are we eating?"

"Eating?" She was having a little trouble focusing on the conversation.

"That's what you generally do with dinner. Where are we going?"

"Auberge La Grande. Belphegor was raving about it today. He and some of the other Deadlies had dinner there last night."

"Sounds good. I'll buy."

During their marriage, she'd learned to recognize an apology from Sam in gestures like these. "So you realized I was telling the truth and Gibeon really did start things?"

He crossed his arms. "Are we going to dinner or not?"

There was no celestial rule that prevented him from acknowledging that he had been wrong. That was just his pride.

Going to dinner was safer than being stuck in this hotel suite with him. She headed for her room. Two could play at his game. Stepping out of her heels, she stripped off her clothes in front of the floor-length mirror. She lifted her chin proudly. She wasn't the pretty child she'd been when she met him, she was better—a confident, sexy woman.

Back when she and Sam were together, he hadn't been able to resist her. Just a glimpse of her breasts or her high, taut ass was enough to make him hard. How many times had she deliberately teased him past the point of no return? Too many to count, and with delicious results. Tonight would be different. Tonight she'd leave him panting after her.

From the closet, she pulled a burgundy wrap dress and put it on. It plunged between her breasts in front and was so short it barely covered her behind in the back. A single ribbon around the waist held it in place. The fabric was clingy enough to reveal that she wore nothing beneath it but a lacy black thong. She slipped on a pair of strappy black sandals and checked her look one more time.

She looked good, but her appearance made her uncomfortable. During her century as a succubus, she'd mastered using her body to get what she wanted, but since then she'd worked in all the divisions at one time or another. She wasn't a one-trick pony. Discovering Sam's secret would require intelligence and subtlety. She took off the wrap dress.

Instead of appealing to Sam as a nymphet, it would be smarter to appear professional, like a woman who deserved to become Director of Demon Resources. From the closet, she unearthed a sleeveless black linen sheath with a simple, crew neckline. She pulled the dress up over her hips and zipped the back. It was timeless and classic.

She hoped Sam would see it the same way.

Auberge La Grande was narrow but deep, as Manhattan restaurants tended to be. The lighting was dim and the carpet so rich it swallowed the heels of Lilith's stilettos. They followed the maitre d' to a table near the back. It had a snowy white tablecloth, black linen napkins and heavy, ornate silverware.

"What would you like to drink?" the host asked. Sam ordered an anise-flavored vodka. Was that supposed to be a tribute to her?

"Club soda and lime for me," she said.

Sam quirked an eyebrow. "Playing it safe?"

The challenge in his gaze nearly changed her mind, but drinking before going home with him would be an act of idiocy. She'd committed enough of those lately.

"Club soda and lime," she repeated. The host nodded and disappeared.

She waited for Sam's next gambit. Would he drop some innuendo about her choosing to stay sober or plunge into the politics of parleying with angels?

"How did your day go?" he asked.

She blinked. Back in the old days, over dinner each evening, they'd exchange stories of their respective days. Sam's narratives were generally about wins over other demons and confrontations with Satan. Those weren't all wins but he was good at twisting them into at least a partial victory. She had listened with uncritical adoration.

Her own tales were much more homely—problems she encountered cave-keeping or while bargaining with merchants at Aboveworld markets. In the early years, Sam focused his attention on her as though hearing about her day was the most important thing on his agenda. As time went by, though, they were interrupted more and more often by demons from his cadre with issues that needed his immediate attention.

After they split, bad things happened to her. She lost her home. Satan assigned her to work as a succubus. She lost the social capital of being Sam's wife. She had to fight off legions of horny demons who viewed her as easy pickings. The years following their divorce were uniformly terrible, but she sometimes thought the worst part was no longer having anyone to ask, "How did your day go?" and care about the answer.

She looked around, wishing she had her club soda to fiddle with as a distraction. The service was usually better here.

"I spent time with Gibeon this morning," she said. "I'm a little worried about what he might do if I remain on this mission."

"What can he do?" Sam seemed unconcerned. "You're immortal."

"Against all things human, but angels are supernaturally powerful."

"You give our holier-than-us brethren too much credit," he said. "They put their pants on one leg at a time, same as us."

"How would you know? When you left Heaven, everyone still wore dresses."

His lips quirked, but his answer was serious. "They're no more powerful than we are. The Enemy created us all from the same materials."

"Speak for yourself. He made angels from stardust and sunlight. He created me from dirt. What was it you used to call me? A dust wench?"

"Stardust may have a pretty name, but it's still dirt."

But that didn't account for the sunlight that had been left out of her makeup, for the darkness that wouldn't let her bow to him, or to any man. Across the table, Sam studied her face. What did he see?

She reached for her glass again but it still hadn't arrived. She plowed ahead. "Yesterday he set off the sprinklers because he was so angry to find me here. Today he accused me of trying to poison him when I offered him headache medicine. What will he do tomorrow?"

"You're focusing on the wrong thing. Don't let one cranky angel make you take your eyes off the prize. If we're successful in these negotiations, you'll have your own corner office."

"Hell is funnel-shaped. It has no corners."

"Your hemispherical office, then."

She awarded him a brief smile for that. "What, exactly, constitutes success in these negotiations? Has Satan given you a solid definition?" Maybe the answer to that would clue her into the topic of his conversation with Gibeon the previous evening.

"Whatever strikes Satan as getting one over on the Enemy. If we can do that, you'll become Director of Demon Resources and I'll be the first manager of managers in Hell."

Well, that foray had been useless. She knew no more now than she had before. She reached for her non-existent glass. Where was their server?

"I'm so sorry for your wait." A waitress hurried up to the table. She wore a simple white blouse, a straight black skirt and black flats. A lock of hair had worked itself loose from her smooth bun. "I'm Emily. I'll be taking care of you tonight."

The waitress gave Lilith her club soda and lime and then set Sam's glass in front of him. Then she tucked the tray beneath her arm and pulled a tablet from her apron. "What would you like this evening?"

"I'll have the *moules farcies*," Lilith said. Fresh seafood was difficult to find in Hell.

"Make that two," Sam said.

Emily recorded their choices, collected their menus and hurried away. She'd been brusque to the point of near-rudeness, but her harried expression said she was doing the best she could.

"When did you become a woman who would let a waitress off the hook for slow service?" Sam asked.

Lilith lifted her shoulders. "What can I say? She caught me on a good night."

He smiled at her. "I hope so."

If she let him turn this dinner into a seduction, it would make things impossible once they got back to the hotel. Fortunately, there was one surefire way to distract him. "What's your game plan for the talks tomorrow, now that the preliminaries are out of the way?" And where did Gibeon figure in that plan?

It worked like a charm. Sam pulled a miniature scroll from his jacket and unrolled it. "The boss is convinced that since the Enemy approached us, rather than the other way around, we're in a position to demand some things he's wanted for a long time."

"He's never been a big fan of reality."

"He has not." Sam perused the scroll. "Ah, here's a good one. He wants an asteroid strike that creates a dust cloud that causes all the crops in the world to fail and the entire population of Earth to starve."

Lilith thought she'd seen all the craziness Satan had to offer over the last dozen millennia. Clearly, she was wrong. "Is he insane?"

Sam gave her a droll look. "Certifiably."

"The Enemy isn't going to go for that."

"Agreed."

"What are you going to do?"

"You know how much he loves thinking he's an original. I'll tell him it's been done."

"Not since the dinosaurs roamed the Earth."

"A long time for humans, the mere blink of an eye for the Enemy."

She supposed that was true. Sam unwound the scroll a little more. "Ah. Here's another. 'A computer virus that causes the stock market to crash and wipes out all the wealth in the world.'"

"In exchange for—?"

"Removing all our greed demons from Wall Street."

"That would be worse than the greed demons." She took a sip of her drink.

"It would."

"What else is on that list?"

"The usual—war, conquest, pestilence and famine."

"They're not going to go for any of that."

"That's why I'm buying dinner. I thought we could put our heads together and figure out a substitute we can sell to both Heaven and the boss."

And she'd thought it was because he wanted to soften her up for later. Silly girl. When would she learn that work came first with Sam? It was ridiculous to feel disappointed. She should be glad. "We could ask for a damning revelation about a hero."

"Such as?"

"I don't know. Maybe Mother Theresa ran a pedophile ring?"

"Offer them that in exchange for sidelining hundreds of greed demons? You're thinking too small."

"A nuclear meltdown that kills millions?"

"Now you're at the other extreme."

"You are a hard demon to please."

"Not really."

Correction. This was a two-pronged assault, with twin purposes of seduction and work discussion. She gave him points for multi-tasking, but only Sam could think work talk was likely to get a woman all hot and bothered.

Emily arrived at the table. The air filled with the combined fragrances of mussels, tomatoes and cheese. She set their plates on the table and disappeared without another word.

"Is the service always like this?" Sam asked.

Lilith cut into her mussels. "Not at all. Something must be going on."

"Why does Gibeon hate you?" Sam asked.

His question caught her so off-guard she choked on a mussel. It was so like Sam to turn the tables and interrogate her while she was trying to get the goods on him. After she finished coughing into her napkin, she wheezed, "I don't know."

His prosecutorial gaze was back. Most demons couldn't read her, but to Sam she'd always been an open book. "Where have you met him before? On a mission?"

"No." She answered his second question flatly, so he'd know she was telling the truth.

"So, not on a mission." Unfortunately, he was good at parsing out truth from lies. "But you have met him before."

She buried her face in her napkin again and faked a cough, trying to buy time. When she and Sam first met she had told him about the angels who had coerced her into returning to Eden and caused the death of her baby. But she'd also rambled on about everything else in her life—Eden, Adam, her favorite foods, how she sometimes rouged her cheeks with crushed raspberries—as teenage girls do. Thousands of years had passed since then. How likely was he to remember?

"It's clear you two have a history. He makes no secret of his loathing for you," Sam said.

She folded her napkin and set it on the table. "He objects to my immortality. He thinks everlastingness should be granted solely by the Enemy."

"That doesn't explain why your eyes burn with hatred when you look at him."

"An eye for an eye and a tooth for a tooth. I throw back what he sends my way."

She could virtually hear the gears turning as Sam whittled away her evasions.

"He's the angel who foretold your baby's death." He sounded certain.

She stared at him, speechless. Thank Satan, Emily returned at that moment, carrying the dessert tray in one hand and a tray stand in the other. She set the tray on the stand.

Sam declined dessert but requested coffee. Lilith chose crème brûlée and a glass of Sauternes. After the grilling she'd received, she deserved a drink.

"How bad is it—having to work with Gibeon?" Sam asked after Emily left with their orders. "Would you rather I sent you back?"

"To do laps in the tar pits?"

"Now that all the planning is done, we can probably come up with an excuse that would satisfy Satan."

He wasn't threatening her. He was making a genuine offer. She really didn't want to go back, though. She wanted to stay and see how things turned out. "But not one that would still allow me to become Director of Demon Resources."

"That's probably true, but it's up to you."

Warmth flooded her. Over dinner he had treated her as an equal, listening as carefully to her opinions as he'd once listened to her housekeeping stories. It had been surprisingly enjoyable. "I'll stick it out."

"Good." He gave her a brilliant smile and picked up the scroll again. By the time they finished dessert, they'd whittled down Satan's wish list to three objectives that might be achievable: let social media run amok; ignore the acidification of the oceans; allow the wealth gap to continue to grow.

Sam sat back, looking satisfied. "An excellent evening's work. Thank you. Are you ready to return to the hotel?"

The air flooded with Sam's scent. She set her jaw. "Not for that."

Emily chose that moment to return with the check. "I'm so sorry for the delay. We're down a couple of servers tonight."

"We noticed you seemed short-handed and wondered what was going on."

His tone expressed only polite curiosity but Emily had inhaled Sam's scent. "One of our servers attacked another server last night. Justin's in the hospital and Victor's in jail."

It was inappropriate for her to volunteer that, of course, but few humans could resist the compulsion of demon scent.

Sam went still. "Really?" His scent grew even stronger. "What triggered the argument?"

Lilith frowned. Why was he so interested in a trivial human squabble?

"Victor set up a tray jack and then went back into the kitchen to get his order. When he came back out, Justin was using the jack."

"That seems pretty minor to escalate into assault."

"I know, right? Victor was waiting on this table of four guys." For a moment, her gaze lost focus. "They were the most gorgeous guys I've ever seen. Like, they were perfect looking."

"Go on." Sam's tone was clipped.

She shook her head, as though to clear the image. "One of them told Victor he shouldn't put up with that. The next thing I knew, Victor had Justin on the ground, choking him."

If Lilith had poured a glass of ice water over Sam's head at that moment, it would have instantly evaporated into steam. His pupils had gone as rectangular as a goat's. Emily didn't seem to notice but that wasn't surprising. Most humans didn't—or couldn't—see the change.

"It was so unlike him." Emily sniffled and dabbed at her eyes. "I can take your card whenever you're ready."

He handed her his credit card and a few moments later they were headed back to the hotel.

Wrath was about to learn what real wrath looked like.

Sam followed Lilith from the restaurant. She looked like a paper doll posed in front of a two-dimensional storefront, which meant his eyes were still goat. He breathed in deeply through his nose—once, twice, three times. On the third breath, she rounded into three dimensions.

"Summon the Deadlies to a meeting," he said.

Lilith's eyebrows drew together. "A meeting? When?"

He glanced at his watch. "It's nine-thirty now. Set the meeting for ten p.m."

"You're calling a team meeting at ten o'clock at night?"

She went flat again. He breathed in through his nose again, struggling to bring his anger under control. If he couldn't do that, he was no better than Wrath. After a four-count, his surroundings acquired depth again.

"You heard what that waitress said. A godlike customer tells a server not to put up with the actions of another server and the first server puts the second in the hospital. What does that sound like to you?"

"Wrath."

That was another good thing about Lilith—you didn't have to cross every "t" and dot every "i" with her. Still she didn't pull out her phone to summon the Deadlies.

"Where do you plan to hold this meeting?" she asked.

They didn't have access to the U.N. complex at night. There were lots of conference rooms available in Hell but even using the Manhattan portal it would be two a.m. before he had them all assembled. More importantly, if they used the Portal, their coming and going would be logged and Satan would learn what had happened. The last thing he needed was for the boss to decide he didn't have things under control up here.

"Our suite will accommodate all of us." If the Deadlies were in for the night, as they should be, they would have no problem arriving on time. If any were late, it would suggest they were out breaking the truce that was foundational to the negotiating process. He would not tolerate that. Still Lilith made no move to pull out her phone.

"You've got a time and a place," he said. "What are you waiting for?"

"If we meet in the suite, everyone will know we're sharing a room."

"Oh, for the hate of Satan, Lil. While we're standing here chit-chatting, Lust is probably organizing an orgy, Gluttony is encouraging someone to eat until they burst and Envy is pointing out to some poor fool how much better someone else has it." She still didn't get out her phone.

What would it take to convince her? "And Wrath could be inciting more violence—possibly against women or children."

That did it. Jaw tight, she pulled out her phone and typed for a minute. "There, I summoned them. Happy?"

"Delighted."

Then she proceeded to dawdle along, messing with her phone until he wanted to grab the thing and toss it into traffic. When they reached the hotel, he turned toward the elevators, but Lilith blocked his way.

"What are you doing?" He strove for patience.

"I told them to meet us in the lobby."

"Why?' he asked, with exaggerated patience.

"So we can direct them to the conference room I arranged."

So that's why she'd been fiddling with her phone. "Fine."

She pointed at a set of double doors. "It's through there and to the left. I'll stay here and point them in the right direction."

"Fine." He stomped through the doors.

It had taken Lilith five millennia to establish that she wasn't an easy lay. She wasn't about to let that rumor get started again.

Over the next fifteen minutes, the Deadlies straggled into the lobby, with Wrath bringing up the rear. He pushed through the revolving door at a minute before ten, amped and ready to rumble.

"I love this town." He bounced on the balls of his feet, jabbing at the air with his fists. "Where's the conference room?"

He'd just broken the truce again. She would be willing to bet on it. The only thing that wound a demon up like this was bad behavior. She pointed the way and he pushed through the doors.

Should she go up to the suite and stay out of the blast radius? Because there was bound to be an explosion when Sam confronted him. After a moment she decided to join them. Better to know what went down than try to guess afterward. She slipped inside the back door of the meeting room. Sam stood at the front, an imposing figure, even in jeans and a casual shirt.

Inside, the rest of the Deadlies lined the conference table.

"Can I have everyone's attention?" Sam's silky tone was a warning to anyone who knew him. "I wanted to remind you all that we negotiate with Heaven under a flag of truce."

Greed harrumphed. "You got us out of bed to tell us that?"

"This isn't our first trade negotiation, you know." Gluttony gathered two grease-stained paper bags closer to his chest. His red-gold hair was confined in a man-bun that would have looked silly on anyone less dazzling.

What was it about Sam that made him stand out, even in a crowd of beautiful men?

"I do know that," Sam said. "I'm less certain you understand the terms of the truce, so I thought I'd check in on how each of you spent your evening."

Greed wore a plush hotel bathrobe she suspected he had every intention of stealing. "I took a cab to Wall Street," he said. "I rubbed the bull's horns for good luck."

Mostly he liked being close to where so much money changed hands every day.

"Then I bought a salad from the bodega down the street and ate it in my room," he added.

Was spending money physically painful for him? Or was the discomfort strictly psychological?

Camouflage pajamas stretched across Ornias's broad chest. He'd only been Demon of Sloth for a few years but he grew lazier all the time. Already his abs were less washboard than washtub. He looked like he might nod off at any moment. "I grabbed a sandwich from the deli next door, then came back here and watched a movie."

"I got dinner from street vendors." Gluttony spoke around a huge bite of a lobster roll.

"Did you talk to anyone while you were out?" Sam asked.

Gluttony's gaze slid away from Sam's. "No."

"Make food recommendations to some tourists, perhaps?"

"Of course not." Casually, he licked mayo off the corner of his mouth, but sweat sprang up on his forehead.

"None?"

Gluttony lifted the first bag to his nose and sniffed it, looking like he might float away on the delicious smell. "These are the best dirty water dogs in Manhattan." He pulled a spring roll out of the other bag. "And this lumpia was made from a Filipino family recipe." He offered Sam a melting smile. "I mean, I had to tell people about that, right?"

Sam picked up a metal trash can and walked over to him.

Gluttony's face turned ashen. He hugged the bags to his chest. "Come on, Sam. It took me all night to find this stuff."

Sam held out the trash can. Gluttony squeezed the bags tighter. They began to smoke.

"Please." His brown eyes were as piteous as a basset hound's. "Please?"

"You broke the truce." Sam's tone was implacable. The bags burst into flame.

With a shriek, Gluttony dropped them into the trash can. There they blazed, throwing off oily smoke.

Lilith checked the ceiling for sprinkler heads. Yes, there they were. Sam must have had the same thought because he picked up a water pitcher from the conference table and dumped it into the trash can, dousing the flames. An actual tear rolled down Gluttony's face.

Sam turned to Lust. "What did you do this evening?"

"Stayed in and watched the Orgy Channel."

That originated in Hell, so it was within the terms of the truce. With a grunt, Sam turned to the head of the Envy division. "How about you?"

Envy clutched his phone. "Just the things I do every day on social media."

Sam held out his hand and flexed his fingers. Envy looked over at Gluttony, who was staring sadly at the steaming trash can. Envy handed Sam the phone. Sam dropped it on the floor and ground it beneath the heel of his shoe. Then he turned to Wrath.

"I ate two devil dogs and walked around Central Park," Wrath said. "I didn't talk to a soul."

Sam raised one eyebrow. "Really?"

Wrath nodded, smirking.

"What about last night?" Sam asked.

Wrath stilled. Then his smirk returned, but it was a little less self-assured."I went out to dinner with Gluttony and Envy and Lust."

"And didn't talk to anyone?"

"Of course not. We're under a flag of truce."

"Not even the waiter?"

"Sure, I mean, yeah, I talked to the waiter to order food."

"What else did you talk about?"

Wrath's face flushed. "He was having problems with another waiter. I mostly listened."

"And when you weren't listening, what did you say?"

Wrath's nostrils flared. "Nothing in particular."

"You didn't say he shouldn't put up with having another waiter use his tray jack?"

Wrath threw Envy a furious glare. Envy held up his hands. "He didn't hear it from me."

"Well?" Sam said.

Wrath bared his teeth. "Who are you to be asking me all these questions?"

Sam stared at him coldly. "I am mission lead and the Devil's Advocate. In case that doesn't make it clear, let me explain. I decide whether you stay on this mission or return to Hell in disgrace. I decide whether you get punished for willfully breaking the truce. I decide whether you continue to be Demon of Wrath, in command of forty legions, or spend the next hundred years with fly larvae crawling up your ass."

Wrath balled his fists. "Only Satan makes those decisions."

"In thirteen thousand years, Satan has never once failed to deliver on a punishment I've recommended." Sam's self-control was in stark contrast to Wrath's panting. Wrath jumped to his feet.

"But if you'd like to take your chances against those odds," Sam said softly, "by all means, be my guest."

The two men were of equal height. An objective observer might view them as being of equal beauty. But there the equality ended. As much as Lilith might deride Sam's mentions of his past as a seraph, he was clearly superior to any other demon here.

Wrath puffed his chest out. Swaggering a little, he stepped toward Sam, coming to a halt only when they were nose to perfect nose.

"You want to take it outside?" Wrath asked.

"Are you suggesting fisticuffs?"

Wrath drew himself up in what was clearly an attempt to intimidate Sam. "I'm suggesting we go out into the alley and I kick your ass."

"Manhattan doesn't have alleys."

Wrath blinked. "Well, out in the street, then."

"And risk getting picked up by the police? That hardly seems like a low profile way to conduct a trade summit."

"You're afraid," Wrath sneered.

Sam stared down his aquiline nose. "Hardly."

Wrath made noises like a chicken cackling. "You're afraid to fight me." He turned to the other demons sitting around the table. "How can you follow this chicken shit?"

At that, Sam's hand shot out. His fingers closed around Wrath's throat and he slammed the other demon against the wall.

"Would you like to say that again?" he asked softly. The muscles in his arm and shoulder bulged beneath his shirt as he held Wrath off the floor. Anger strengthened his lime and leather scent. Even though Lilith stood at the back of the room, it enveloped her. She could detect no trace of the cinnamon and chili peppers that were Wrath's signature scent.

Wrath's face turned blue. His fingers scrabbled at Sam's clenched hand, to no avail. He tried to speak, but no words came out.

Sam cocked his head. "What was that?"

Lilith's pulse raced. His strength called to her like a shofar calling an army to battle.

Wrath's face darkened to purple.

With his free hand, Sam picked up a ballpoint pen from the podium. "If you're prepared to accept my leadership on this mission without further challenge, raise your right hand."

Reluctantly, Wrath lifted his right hand. His face was nearly black. Sam jammed the pen through the center of his hand and into the drywall. Wrath's eyes bulged.

"That's for the man you put into the hospital last night with your advice," Sam said.

Stepping back, he released his hold on the other demon's throat. Wrath sagged, but his impaled hand wouldn't allow him to slide to the floor. Moaning, he pulled the pen from his hand. Almost instantly, the hole in his palm healed over.

The same could not be said of the drywall.

Lilith's pulse thundered in her ears. Sam's strength, his authority over the other demons, his insistence on *justice,* were electric. She deplored the violence, but Wrath had earned his punishment by breaking the truce.

"Can you take care of this, Lil?" Sam asked.

She started. If the room hadn't been filled with demons, she would have shoved him down on the conference room table and had her way with him right then and there. From the smile that crept into his eyes, he knew it, too.

"Will do," she said, and escaped from the room.

CHAPTER 12

*L*ilith flipped on the light in the bedroom and surveyed the neatly turned-down duvet cover. Did she really want to do this? All she had to do was say "no" and Sam would sleep on the couch again. Sam wasn't the problem.

His dominance over Wrath, over all the Deadlies, had taken her breath away, but that didn't justify making what was clearly a bad decision. Just because the muscles in his arms had bulged and his dark eyes had burned like black fire and his scent had permeated the room until she couldn't detect even a whiff of the six other powerful demons there, that didn't mean she should let her desires rule her.

But she couldn't stifle her yearning to be with Sam. She'd dealt with her craving for the past ten thousand years by staying angry, but now she felt only want. Her anger had deserted her right when she needed it most.

She blew out a breath between clenched teeth. If she was going to do something stupid, she could at least minimize the potential for damage. From her lingerie drawer, she extracted a box of condoms she'd purchased after Sam started sleeping on her couch and it became clear how this would inevitably end. Sam might be immune to disease, but her welcome-to-Hell gift from Satan had included only immortality, not immunity.

After she became an operative, she'd caught nearly everything that made the rounds on Earth, including a particularly nasty case of the plague in the 14th century. It had taken her months to get over it, working the whole time because sick leave in Hell was non-existent. She'd love to do something about that, not just for herself, but for the Hades, who were also subject to disease.

Good. She was thinking like a career woman again, and not like a lovesick teenager with out-of-control hormones.

Setting the condoms on the nightstand, she stripped off the black linen sheath she'd worn to dinner and hung it in the closet. In the lingerie drawer, she located a crimson negligee. Sam had always loved her in red.

She drew it on. Scarlet lace highlighted her breasts and the matching lace around the hem barely covered the waxed area that had fascinated Sam the other night. She'd just gotten into bed when she heard the hotel room door open.

A few moments passed before Sam appeared in the doorway. His eyes sparkled at the sight of her. "You didn't need to change on my account, but I commend your excellent taste."

He'd removed his jacket and tie and his shoes. The sight of his bare feet made the room suddenly feel very small. He leaned against the doorjamb, watching her. Was there something in his hand, out of sight beyond the door?

His gaze fell on the box on the nightstand and he went still. "What's that?"

She braced herself for a contentious argument. It was hard enough to get human men to use the blessed things, and they stood to benefit as much as she did. She lifted her chin. "They're condoms. If you want me, you'll need to wear one."

His unnatural stillness disappeared. "All right."

"I realize you can't get…" She blinked. "What did you say?"

"I want you very much, so I accept your condition." His shoulder that was propped against the doorjamb twitched and a tiny thud sounded in the living room.

She cocked her head. "What was that?"

He didn't bother to look. "My phone fell off the end table."

He was lying, but she couldn't afford to let herself get distracted. "You don't have an issue with wearing a condom?"

"I was expecting it. I read an article that said modern women prefer their partner to use a condom."

He'd done research in preparation for being together again. He might be proud, but while they were together he'd also been protective of her. That he put her safety before his own pleasure was bittersweet in its familiarity.

His eyes darkened as he read her surrender, growing black as obsidian, reminding her that this was Sam, the once-in-a-lifetime love she'd suffered and longed for. She'd put that look in his eyes.

She expected him to remove his shirt and pants at demon speed, disposing of them too quickly for her eyes to follow, but he didn't. He carefully unbuttoned each cuff of his shirt and then the placket and slid it off his shoulders, hanging it on the wooden arms of the valet stand. Then he unbuckled his belt, pulled it through the loops and hung it on the hook provided for that purpose. Finally, he reached for his zipper, his eyes gleaming, daring her to look away. Her mouth went dry.

"If this is your idea of a strip tease," she managed to say, "you forgot to cue the music."

Then he was with her, naked, his knee between her thighs. His mouth was fire and honey, so hot and sweet it felt as though her bones would dissolve. The scent of lime and leather filled the room and his weight pressed down on her and it was hard to think but she shoved at his shoulder. "I don't do the bottom. You know that."

He lifted his head and his black eyes sparkled with laughter. "Obstinate woman." But he slid off her before slanting his mouth across hers fiercely, cradling her head and holding it immobile.

He held the kiss for a long time, taking her mouth so completely there was no pulling away, no drawing back, just closer and harder and hotter and no possible escape and none wanted. It was lips against lips, tongue against tongue, skimming, sliding, with every stroke sending currents throughout her body, making it clamor for more.

She ran her fingertips over his shoulders, feeling the rounded swell of his muscles before drifting to his chest, her palms gliding over his satin skin. His chest muscles felt like slabs of stone, exactly as they had that first day in Hell when he'd caught her up in his arms and tucked her against him.

He slipped her negligee over her head and tossed it aside. His lips brushed her forehead and then her eyelids and finally her cheekbones. "So beautiful."

He breathed warm breath into her ear and she shuddered. Then he kissed her again, dragging her down to a place where everything was fire and nectar and velvety black shadows, pulling her under, so that the heat and the darkness and the wanting closed over her and there was nothing in the world but the two of them, and there never would be, world without end.

When she'd lost all connection to anything but Sam's hands and Sam's lips and Sam's tongue, he pulled back, till his mouth barely brushed hers. Her heart clutched at losing him, even that much of him, even for an instant, and she was in trouble, in real danger here. His kisses turned her body into a torch, a torch that would burn until there was nothing left but ashes.

She had to put some distance between them, between her heart and him, or he'd destroy her when he walked away again. It wasn't selfish to think about the future and to know she couldn't survive losing him a second time. Within the circle of his arms, she edged backward a fraction of an inch.

Cool air filled the space between them and she was chilled at not having his body pressed against her, at not having Sam's heat setting her ablaze. He must have felt it, too, because he tightened his arms and his mouth descended on hers and he dragged her into the darkness again and she caught fire, burning so hot there would be no recovering from this when he returned to Gomory's arms and she was left alone.

The image of Gomory's flawless body writhing in Sam's arms was like a knife to the gut. The searing pain let her step back and gave her the distance she needed to survive. Now she could admire Sam's excellent technique, appreciate how well he knew his way around a woman's body without losing her mind as he shepherded her unhurriedly toward orgasm.

As though he sensed her retreat, he redoubled his efforts, kissing, licking, caressing and reality retreated until she pulled up memories of the day he left so she wouldn't get dragged under again. In the here and now he touched all the right places and stroked all the right spots, but her memory replayed a sound loop of him saying, "I've been offered a promotion in exchange for divorcing you and I've chosen to accept."

Then he licked into her and made her arch and shudder, and the pain of his leaving seemed very long ago while what was happening in this bed was here and now and very enjoyable. He located her g-spot as effortlessly as if only a day had passed since they were last together. The combination of his mouth and his hands and his scent pushed her over the edge and it was good but survivable.

It was the kind of orgasm any unattached woman would happily revisit if an old flame came to town, but wouldn't think about too much when he left again.

When the ripples of her orgasm receded, she reached for the box of condoms. "And now it's your turn."

For a climax, that was pretty anti-climactic.

Even while Lilith's body had clenched around his fingers, Sam sensed her withdrawal, as though she was enjoying herself but was trying to remember if she'd left the water running in another room.

He took the box from her hand and set it back on the nightstand. "Not yet."

She glanced at his groin. "Why not?"

His cock was hard enough to punch a tunnel through anthracite, but he wanted more. He'd had that kind of mechanical sex with every she-demon in Hell but none of them had the fire and heart of Lilith. Beneath the anger and resentment and mistrust, she still felt something for him. He knew she did. He refused to settle for dull, ordinary sex when they were capable of brilliance that put the stars to shame.

"Let's start over." This time he would draw an honest response from her, a celebration of what they'd been to each other.

"Start over?" She tensed. "I'm more of a 'press forward to the goal' kind of gal."

"Are you?" He cocked his head reflectively. "I'm more about getting it right than getting it done, I think."

"It was fine," she said quickly.

"Fine? When did you become a woman who's willing to settle for 'fine'?"

When you chose a promotion over me. The words hung in the air, but all she said was, "Learning to settle is part of life."

No, it wasn't. Nor from Lilith, not from this creature of mud and flame he had adored for ten thousand years. He traced his finger over the tip of her breast until it tightened into a rosette. "Your body likes the idea of starting over."

"My body doesn't always know what's good for it." But she sounded a little breathless.

"Or maybe it does, but it gets overruled by your head." He leaned forward to suck the taut tip into his mouth and she gasped. He repeated the experiment with her other breast and was rewarded with a convulsive wriggle of her hips.

Much better. He stroked his hand down her belly and palmed the smooth mound at the juncture of her thighs, letting the heat from his hand soak into the bare skin there.

"Very sexy." He let a fingertip steal between her smooth lips and she gasped. "For you, too, apparently."

She watched him warily, panting, but he had her attention, and that was better than the empty shell she'd presented to him a few minutes ago.

He trailed kisses along her hipbone and when she opened herself to him he moved lower, and her pants became moans. After a very short time, her head rolled back, thank Satan, because, former seraph or not, he couldn't have waited much longer.

He reached for the condom box, but she was there before him, tearing a foil packet from the roll and ripping it open. Then she smoothed it over him and the touch of her hand almost undid him.

He gritted his teeth and made himself think about his final centuries as a seraph. Just when he had himself back under control, she stroked him, her hand knowing, remembering what he liked, and he hissed, hanging on through sheer effort of will.

"Having a problem, there, Pride?" Deliberately, she repeated the action.

Enough was enough. He dragged her atop him, poising her to take him in, but she said, "No," and rolled, folding her legs around his ass and grasping his shoulders to reverse their positions.

And that was a surprise, but he couldn't stop to think about what it meant because he was spreading her legs with his knee and she was opening to him and he thrust into her. She rose up to meet him and even through a condom it was the best thing he'd felt in ten thousand years.

Her eyes were on his, shining like the stars in the night sky above their skylight and it was sublime, as it only ever was with her, as it could only ever be with her. He slid his hands under her shoulders, cupping them, and rocked into her, hot and hard, and her heat gripped him. How the heaven had he survived without her for so long?

She arched beneath him, her breasts pressed against his chest and her hands kneading his ass. Then she caught his rhythm and they moved together and it was like no time had passed. He looked into her eyes and all the old love was there and he was home.

Masses of rebellious dark curls filled his nose with the scent of sesame and anise as he pressed his lips against the side of her throat. He bit down at the juncture where her neck met her shoulder and rocked into her and as he did she rolled her hips to meet him.

He made a strangled noise. "I won't last much longer if you do that."

She surged upwards, crying out as a second climax overtook her. He gritted his teeth, trying to hang on, but being inside her after so long apart was too much. "Lilith, love—" With a shudder, he followed her they went to the center of the universe and stars whirled around them.

For a long moment, he stayed where he was, reveling in her body, warm and boneless and relaxed beneath him. She smiled up at him with no trace of the anger that seemed ever-present these days. He smoothed her hair away from her face and kissed her swollen lips and she kissed back and it was like the old days, except in the old days he'd never been on top. He'd have to ask her why that was, what had made her relax her one, immutable rule. Finally, reluctantly, he pulled out, halting in shock as fluid spattered the sheets.

He rolled to the side, staring at the mess in alarm. "I thought the condom was supposed to sequester my seed."

"It is." She struggled up onto her elbow and looked at his crotch before issuing a sound that was half-laugh, half-snort. "Well, that's one dead soldier."

The condom hung in tatters on his cock.

"What happened?"

"I think the hot demon sex was too much for it."

This wasn't a joke. What if she became pregnant? "What will you do now?"

Her amusement faded. "Do you have a reason to believe you just gave me some mutant demon version of the clap?"

He lifted his chin. "Of course not."

"Well, it's not like I'm likely to catch a baby. I mean, we tried that for two thousand years without any luck."

She was right, of course. The probability that she would conceive from this interlude was tiny.

He drew a finger down her ribcage. "Perhaps we should use two next time."

CHAPTER 13

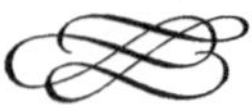

The next morning when Lilith stumbled into the kitchen, Sam was drinking a cup of coffee. Muscles she'd forgotten owning stung as she crossed the room.

"Good morning." He smiled at her over the rim of his cup.

She eyed him warily. "Good morning."

"Did you sleep well?"

They had engaged in highly acrobatic sex until around four a.m. Sam was clearly no worse for wear, but she was tired and decidedly sore.

"Well enough," she said.

He poured her a cup of coffee and she sat down at the counter, frowning at the thought of the day ahead. Gibeon would renew his attempt to pressure Sam into kicking her off the mission. How far would the angel go to get her?

"Are you still worried about Gibeon?" Sam had many faults, but a lack of perceptiveness wasn't one of them.

"A bit." She shuddered as bitter brew landed on her tongue. Coffee hadn't been invented yet when they were together. Sam apparently liked it strong.

"Avoid him," Sam said.

"I don't know if that's feasible. He seems determined to get rid of me."

"Keep track of his movements." Sam walked over to the sink and rinsed out his cup. "Wherever he is, don't be there."

She opened her lips to argue but he pulled her to him and kissed her like she was the only woman in the world and she went all squishy inside.

"I've missed doing that." He spoke so softly she almost didn't hear him.

And soon he would miss it again, though not nearly as much as she would. The thought of being parted from him again felt like half of her being torn away.

"You are a redoubtable woman." His voice was deep, and the timbre sent a thrill through her. "I have complete faith in your ability to handle Gibeon." He gave her another smooch. "See you in a little while."

She watched the door close behind him. Blessit, why did she let him do this to her? Coming out on top in the negotiations meant big things for Sam but it was less clear that it meant anything at all for her. Judging from past experience, Satan's promise, even in front of a crowd, was not anything she could depend on.

As she headed for the bathroom, deep in thought, a brightly colored box peeking out from behind the sofa caught her eye. On closer inspection, it proved to be a box of condoms. This must be what Sam chucked aside last night. He'd not only researched being together; he had prepared. Why had he hidden the box instead of showing her they were on the same wavelength? She tucked the question away to ask him this evening.

She showered to remove the lingering scent of leather and lime from her skin, then dressed quickly, donning a pair of seven-inch stilettos. They were high, even for her, but Sam had paid a lot of attention to her legs the day before, and the heels showcased her calves.

She hurried the two blocks to the U.N. complex. With the rah-rah kickoff over, they would relocate to the Secretariat building today.

She'd arranged for a breakfast buffet to be set up in the Delegates' Lounge.

Long and narrow, the Delegates' Lounge was decorated with a Scandinavian vibe. Grid curtains made of knotted yarn and porcelain beads covered the east-facing windows. Chairs and low sofas, upholstered in gray, lime green, pale purple and blue, were scattered throughout the space, along with the occasional table.

There she found both angels and demons chowing down amiably enough, though separately. At a demon table, Sam sat beside Wrath, who appeared to harbor no ill-will from their confrontation the night before. She would never understand males.

The chair on the other side of Sam was empty. She gave into a moment of weakness and sat beside him. He paused to smile at her before returning to his conversation.

Gibeon, she noticed, sat apart from the other angels. Occasionally, another angel would call him over to refill a coffee cup or replace a dropped utensil. The sight cheered her. No demon would dare to treat her like that.

After breakfast, the delegates separated into the surrounding conference rooms. Pride's negotiations were in Conference Room Four, which had an attached viewing room. Taking Sam's advice, she spent the morning there, watching him through the viewing slit. He handled the talks with the same skill and confidence he'd displayed the night before in dealing with his errant colleagues.

Her mind drifted back to their lovemaking the night before. Had she made a mistake in sleeping with him? Her body felt sated in a way it hadn't in thousands of years, but would she feel the same way eighteen days from now? Or would she feel like an addict, jonesing for a drug she could no longer obtain?

Just before the mid-morning break, she left the safety of the viewing room to check on snacks and coffee. Everything looked fine.

It felt so good to be out of the windowless room she headed downstairs to check out the garden that lay outside the building. Only a few roses were still in bloom so late in the year, but it was still lovely.

The sweetness of the rose perfume matched her mood. If she could stop herself from thinking ahead, there was no reason why she and Sam couldn't enjoy the next two and a half weeks together. It couldn't go on forever, but the scent of a rose was no less pleasing because it couldn't bloom eternally. If anything, the knowledge of their impermanence made their scent all the sweeter.

She went back inside, resolved to take this bouquet life had handed her and enjoy it while it lasted. A ginger-headed figure stepped off the escalator and strode toward her, his shoes clattering on the marble floor. Her heart clenched. For a being that floated among the clouds, Gibeon had a heavy gait. What was he doing?

She couldn't reach the escalators without passing him but there was an elevator nearby. She hastened over to it and pressed the up button, but luck was not on her side. The car was on the sixth floor. As she waited, the slap of Gibeon's hard-soled shoes drew closer. Her heart thumped. Floor five, floor four, floor three. At any moment he would round the corner and she'd have no escape.

The elevator arrived and the doors swished open. She scurried inside and mashed the button to close the doors but before they could seal, Gibeon thrust his arm between them. They bounced open again. He stepped into the car, filling it with the scent of burnt sugar. His curls glowed like copper in the confines of the elevator car.

The memory of him in the cave, screaming that her behavior would doom her baby to death, overwhelmed her. Her hands shook.

She swallowed. Last night she had forced one of the most powerful demons in Hell to respect her autonomy. If she could handle a devil like Sam, Gibeon should be a piece of angel food cake. At any rate, the elevator only had to travel a single floor. How much damage could he do in the time it took to travel one floor?

He stabbed the emergency stop button with his thumb and the elevator lurched to a halt. Despite her internal pep talk, Lilith's mouth went dry. She resisted the urge to squeeze into the back corner of the elevator.

"You can't hurt me," she said, hating the way her voice trembled. "I'm immortal now."

"A gift from Morningstar for being his whore," Gibeon sneered.

She'd never had sex with Satan, thank badness. His pride would never have allowed him to mate with a species he viewed as inferior, but she doubted Gib would believe that.

His gaze dropped to her waistline, his eyes like slits. "But is the demon spawn you carry in your belly also immortal?"

She stared at him blankly.

He lifted his eyes back to her face. The corner of his mouth curled with loathing. "You didn't even know you were with child." He made it sound like she'd given birth so often that one more pregnancy wasn't even worth noticing.

Was he suggesting Sam had gotten her pregnant last night? Fierce joy flooded her at the thought.

Gibeon spread his wings. They all but filled the elevator. His eyes went gray and colorless, like he was seeing beyond her into another world. "Your spawn is damned by having you for its mother. It is twice-damned by having a demon for a father. It is thrice-damned by being conceived in lust. The Most Holy will not suffer such an abomination to see the light of day."

Oh, right. Gibeon was a nutcase and nothing he said could be believed. Her joy evaporated.

"You are crazy," she said. "Now let me out of here." She punched the emergency stop button and the elevator moved upward again. When it reached the second floor, the doors opened and she stepped out.

"Heed my warning," he called after her. "Your thrice-damned child will not be allowed to defile the world."

"No child does, buddy," she muttered and strode away, hoping Sam would be in the lounge to offer her protection or at least some cover.

But when she rounded the corner from the elevator bank, the Delegates' Lounge was deserted. The break must have come and gone while she was smelling the roses. She hurried back to the viewing room.

For the rest of the day, she stayed there. What if Gibeon was right? What if, after all these thousands of years, she was pregnant? She pictured a little boy that looked exactly like Sam, or a little girl who also looked like Sam, except for a few feminine characteristics. The images made her smile with wonder until reality crashed back in on her. She couldn't be pregnant.

Succubi dropped children like litters of puppies but she had only ever borne one baby, little Ayelet, whom she'd conceived in Eden with Adam. Adam, who had been dust for twelve thousand years. But if she wasn't pregnant, why did Gibeon think she was? She pressed her hand against her flat belly. It was probably wishful thinking, but something felt different.

On her phone, she searched for "how can I tell if I got pregnant last night?" The consensus seemed to be that she wouldn't be able to tell for certain for at least a couple of weeks. If science couldn't tell yet, how could Gibeon?

Still, she couldn't leave the thought alone. What if she was pregnant? How would Sam react? In the early days of their time together they'd discussed having a child, but Sam hadn't seemed too disappointed when it didn't happen.

Would he be pleased? Or would a half-breed child be a barrier to the high position he hoped to achieve in Hell? Would he ignore their child as thoroughly as he'd ignored her for all these centuries? If it turned out she was pregnant, was it even worth telling him?

At five p.m. the conference rooms emptied out.

"We're having dinner with the Deadlies tonight," Sam said as Hell's delegations emerged from their various conference rooms. She knew what he was doing—keeping them under his watchful eye so they couldn't do anything else to screw up the trade talks. The Deadlies didn't look excited but his tone didn't leave any room for refusal.

"Since you're the only female, we'll let you choose the restaurant," Sam said. "Where would you like to eat?"

Lust eyed her breasts. "You can sit next to me."

She could think of few things that would make her less likely to enjoy a dinner, unless it was watching Gluttony gorge himself, or Greed try to weasel out of paying his share of the tab. "No, thanks. I'm going to go back to the hotel to order up room service and watch TV."

She turned to leave but Sam pulled her aside. "I was counting on you to help me ride herd."

"Not in my job description."

"A little extra effort tonight will help to ensure—"

She pulled her arm out of his grasp. "Not happening. I'm going to go take off these shoes and kick back."

He looked so disappointed her heart warmed. He wanted her out of bed as well as in.

He turned to the demon delegation. "Looks like it's just us."

Lilith stopped by a drug store on the way back to the hotel and bought a heating pad to ease the crampy sensation she'd had all afternoon. It was wishful thinking, but she also picked up a pregnancy test.

It was far too soon but Gibeon had seemed so certain.

Back at the hotel, she read the package directions. The test didn't promise accuracy until she had missed her period, but that wouldn't be for two weeks. If an angel could sense her pregnancy, perhaps there was something special about a demon-fathered child.

According to the box, it would be best to take the test first thing in the morning, when the hormones in her urine would be most concentrated. If she was pregnant, two lines would appear in the little window. If not, a single line. She hid the box in the bottom of her empty suitcase.

Then she ordered lobster, steak and two slices of cheesecake from room service and curled up on the couch.

Sam walked into the hotel room to find Lilith asleep on that zany couch. He slipped one arm beneath her shoulders and the other beneath her knees and carried her into the bedroom. After disrobing, he crawled in beside her and pressed a gentle kiss on her lips. She didn't wake. She must be worn out. He needed to keep in mind that she was only human.

As he backed away, her eyes opened and she smiled drowsily. "How was dinner?"

"Long. I wanted to be here with you."

Her smile broadened and the drowsiness left her eyes. "Really?"

"Really." He kissed her again. "Now go back to sleep. I know you're tired."

She pulled her pajama top over her head. "I'm not that tired."

He bent his head and she winced as he sucked on one plump breast. He frowned. "Are you still sore from last night?"

Her face got an odd look he couldn't interpret. "Must be."

He cupped them. "They feel heavier than they did last night."

She slid down his body and took him in hand. "So does this."

The next morning Lilith stayed in bed until Sam came in to say goodbye.

He arched one eyebrow. "Sleeping in?"

"Just for a few more minutes." She had to pee so bad her bladder felt like an overstretched balloon but she didn't want to take the test till he'd gone.

"You've done such a great job of setting things up," he said. "Why don't you take the morning off?"

She blinked at the unaccustomed praise. "If you run into problems, let me know."

"Will do." He bent to give her a lingering kiss.

As soon as the suite door closed behind him, she leaped out of bed, dug the box containing the test out of her suitcase and hurried into the bathroom. After fumbling for a moment, trying to wet the stick without peeing on her fingers, she set the test aside to develop while she took her shower.

As she shampooed and conditioned her hair, she told herself she was being silly. She wasn't pregnant. She couldn't get pregnant. Little

Ayelet's face was no more than a hazy memory, but the spike of pain she felt whenever she thought about her lost infant was still sharp and immediate.

Don't fall for it, she warned herself. This was probably a new way for Gibeon to torture her.

She toweled off and moisturized her skin, telling herself there was no need to be in a hurry for what would be a non-event. Despite the internal lecture, her stomach roiled with butterflies when she picked up the stick.

There were two lines.

She stared at it blankly, unable to absorb what she was seeing. Maybe she'd gotten the number of lines for a positive result confused. Maybe one line meant positive. She re-read the instructions.

No, two lines definitely indicated pregnancy. And they weren't faint, either, which might have left her in limbo. They were clear and bold. The test said she was expecting. Was it her imagination, or was her tummy slightly rounded? Her breasts were sore, and she didn't think it was from Sam's handling.

A smile spread across her face. For the first time in twelve thousand years, she carried a child. Sam's baby was growing in her belly. It would have his hair, black and shining as obsidian, and his incisive mind.

One of the reasons she'd put off sleeping with Sam when they first got together was that she'd worried they would conceive a child only to lose it, per the prophecy. When she'd finally shared her concern with him, he'd told her not to fret, that there were many ways around the prophecy. Over the years, he'd grown even smarter. He would know how to keep their baby safe.

She dressed in a trance. When it came time to slip on her shoes, she set aside her stilettos for a pair of kitten heels she'd brought in case she had to do a lot of walking. It was too early for her belly to make her off balance, but she remembered the falling-forward sensation that would come later.

What did it mean that her pregnancy was detectable so early? Was that a bad sign? She did a quick search on her phone on the way to the conference center. All the pregnancy sites assured her that an early rise in hormones was an indication of a healthy pregnancy, though none addressed a rise as early as this.

She walked into the Secretariat building like she was walking on a cloud. What would Sam's reaction be? Would he be thrilled? Would he believe it was his? Surely he'd believe her. Worst case, she supposed DemSec had a DNA test that could verify the identity of the baby's father.

Her brow clouded at that thought. If she took that test, DemSec would relay the results to Satan. Her pulse jumped. She didn't want him to know about the baby. God and Gibeon were responsible for the death of her first child, but Satan had played a role there, too. In the guise of a snake, he had lured her into the desert.

She got onto the escalator. When the Delegates' Lounge came into view, she saw Sam chatting with Jehudiel. A dozen other angels and demons clustered them. She'd have to wait to talk to him until they reached the privacy of their hotel suite tonight.

She had no more than stepped foot in the lounge when the smell of the angels' breakfast kippers made her sprint for the ladies' room. She returned a little while later to find Sam still debating Jehudiel. Gibeon eyed her, stony-faced as a gargoyle.

For a moment, fear of what he might do paralyzed her. Then she lifted her head and her jaw firmed. Lilith-the-mother-to-be might cower from the angel who had killed her first child, but Lilith-the-she-demon wouldn't give in to the same fears. She stared back at him, her gaze defiant. If she had to, she would wrestle with the angel and this time it would be the angel who broke.

CHAPTER 14

Despite her brave thoughts, Lilith spent the day holed up in the VIP room next to conference room four. By the time the afternoon break came along, she felt distinctly claustrophobic. She headed for the down escalator, figuring Gibeon wouldn't dare attack her in front of witnesses.

On the matching upward-bound escalator, Sam and Jehudiel ascended toward her, absorbed in yet another high-level discussion. She paused, allowing herself to drink in Sam's beauty, to bask in the respect Heaven's top archangel accorded him. No wonder he was doing so well in Hell. Heaven had lost a brilliant mind when they'd allowed him to get away.

If Gibeon and the pregnancy test she'd taken were right, that beauty and those brains would pass on to their child. She smiled dreamily. A child. Sam's child.

Something struck her, hard, between her shoulder blades, throwing her off balance. She lurched into space, flailing. Adrenaline flooded her system and time slowed to a crawl as she tried frantically to right herself, with no luck. She screamed.

At the sound of her shout, Jehudiel looked up. As she lost the battle to stay upright, he vaulted over the rails of the escalator, his wings spreading wide. He soared beneath her and lifted her back onto her feet before she could do a face-plant onto the gridded metal treads.

"Are you all right?" His perfect features were alight with concern.

Instinctively, she touched her belly. "I think so."

Sam met her on the first floor. He must have raced down the up escalator to get there so quickly. He took her shoulders in a comforting grasp. "What happened?"

Diplomatically, Jehudiel backed away.

"I don't know." She twisted to look upwards. Gibeon stood at the top of the escalator, his back to them. His wings were at full extension. Without turning around, he retracted them and tucked them inside his jacket.

Fury which was partly a reaction to her terror flooded her. She pulled loose from Sam's grasp. "Did you see that?"

But his gaze was on her. "See what?"

Wildly, she pointed up the escalator. but the angel had moved out of sight. "Gibeon knocked me down the escalator." She was still shaking with reaction.

Sam rubbed his hands over her shoulders, as though checking for damage. She started to relax but then he spoke. "Where were you going when you lost your balance?"

Her heart seemed to freeze inside her chest. "I didn't lose my balance. Gibeon pushed me."

"I meant, where were you headed initially?"

She'd seen him use this tactic too often not to recognize it. He hadn't ceded the point; he'd just deflected it.

"I was going outside for a breath of air." She willed her hands to stop shaking. "Tell me you're not going to let him get away with this."

"Let's discuss our best approach." Sam herded Lilith toward the street. She tried to resist, but before she could recover enough to truly dig in her heels, he swept her through the revolving door.

After the door spit them out onto the sidewalk, though, she halted.

At her sides, her hands were still balled into trembling fists. "I told you he had it in for me. What are you going to do about him?"

"We have a number of options," He steered her down the street. She'd feel calmer with a little distance between her and the scene of the accident. It also gave him time to think.

If he complained to Jehudiel, he could probably get Gibeon dispatched back to Heaven. The problem with that approach was that when Satan learned his prize was out of reach, there would be Heaven to pay, and Lilith would be the one paying. He paused beside a tiny garden of sunflowers surrounded by a wrought iron fence.

"What kind of options?" she asked.

Should he tell her of Satan's plans for Gibeon? Not when he didn't have a plan in place. He needed more time to strategize. It would only distress her further if she learned Gibeon might be joining them in Hell. There was also more than a slight chance she'd tell Gibeon's boss about his interest in changing sides.

Sam took a deep breath, knowing his words would be unwelcome. "I think we should start by asking him to explain what happened."

Her face went flat. "He'll say it was an accident."

"Probably, but we can't very well demand that they send him back to Heaven without allowing him to tell his side of the story."

"What side? That he got a cramp in his wing and had to stretch it out right behind me at the top of the escalator?"

"It's possible he didn't see you there. Try to be rational about this. When the situation was reversed yesterday, and you were the one accused of breaking the truce, I didn't send you back to Hell willy-nilly."

She wrapped her fingers around the top rail of the little fence, as though to steady herself. When she spoke, her voice held no anger, only mild curiosity. "There is nothing more important to you than success, is there?"

He drew back. "Don't you think you might be overreacting a little?"

"He tried to kill me."

"He didn't, though. He knows you're immortal. Even if you had fallen, you would have healed, good as new, by now."

Anger burned in her eyes but her tone remained conversational. "You really don't care anything about me, do you?"

"I know you don't like Gibeon, but is it truly worth throwing away all that we're accomplishing by turning this into an inter-cosmic incident?" He reached for her hand but she raked her fingernails across the back of his hand hard enough to draw blood.

"Blessit, Lilith!" He tried to reason with her but she refused to speak to him as she stalked back to the conference center. There she got on the escalator and took the moving stairs two at a time. He hurried after her.

Jehudiel met her at the top. "Are you all right?"

"Yes, I am, no thanks to him," She scowled at Gibeon.

Gibeon bowed from the waist. "My apologies. I got a kink in my wing. I didn't realize anyone was behind me."

Lilith's face reddened. "You lying little—"

Sam gripped her elbow. "Apology accepted. Isn't it, Lilith?"

Gibeon's eyes burned with a blend of triumph and hatred. Sam forced himself to pretend not to see. Instead, he focused on Lilith. The betrayal on her face said he had a difficult cleanup job ahead of him.

After the break, the delegations resumed their talks. In the privacy of the viewing room, Lilith faced reality. Sam would not do anything to protect her—not if it meant jeopardizing this mission. That might change if he knew there was a child on the way, but it might not. He had been a demon for a long time and his position in Hell was all-important to him. She had waited too long for this baby to bet its life on a demon changing his ways.

She had once again come in second to his ambitions. She was on her own. It had been thousands of years since the last time that happened, but the familiarity of the feeling was gut-wrenching.

Steely-jawed, she called the Putnam and reserved a room. Then she hurried back to the suite she shared with Sam at the Ferguson and packed up her things. Ten minutes later, a cab delivered her to her new home away from Hell.

After she checked in, she paced the floor. What should she do next? Gibeon said she was pregnant and the test said she was pregnant, but before she started planning her life as a mommy she wanted that news confirmed by a professional.

But how? She couldn't go to a human doctor. There was no telling what Sam's DNA and her immortality would do to their baby's genome. She couldn't risk drawing attention.

Then she thought of Zelda. The little Hade midwife was an expert on pregnancy in all its demonic forms. She knew more than anyone else in Hell about cambions, the hybrids that were a mix of human and fallen angel. And Hades had no problems keeping secrets from Satan.

She changed out her shoes for a pair of platform heels that would insulate her feet from the burning floors of Hell. Then she put her phone on the end table so Sam couldn't track her journey, and caught the portal from the basement of the hotel.

A short while later she was hurrying down a steep trail that made a 90-degree turn and then another before coming to an arched gateway carved into a wall of coal. A pair of yellow lanterns lit the sign above the entrance—Hadeville.

Beyond the entrance lay an expansive hallway lined with small wooden doors ornamented by brass hardware. She knocked on the fourth door on the left. Cool air poured out as it opened.

In the doorway stood a tiny Hade woman with turquoise horns and a blue-and-green striped tail. Zelda's mouth fell open. "Lilith Firstwoman! As I live and breathe. What are you doing here?"

Before Lilith could even answer, Zelda motioned her inside. "Come in, come in, you're letting the air conditioning out."

Lilith ducked through the doorway and Zelda slammed the door behind her. She inspected Lilith curiously. "I heard you were Above on a mission with Samael."

Was there a single soul in Hell who wasn't gossiping about her?

"I was," she said. "That is, I am, but I need to talk to you."

Zelda tilted her head. "To me?" She looked like a sparrow, except for her turquoise horns. She waved at Lilith to take a seat.

Lilith sat. Minus her nosebleed heels, she wasn't much taller than Zelda, so she fit easily onto the contours of the small sofa.

Zelda sat at the other end. "What did you want to see me about? I don't know anything about Aboveworld mission work."

Lilith tried to think of a subtle way of breaking her news but she couldn't come up with anything, so she blurted it out. "I think I may be pregnant."

Zelda's face lit up brighter than the lanterns back at the entrance to Hadeville. In that moment Lilith knew why she'd really come. Zelda was the one person who would rejoice unquestioningly at her news. The little woman focused on Lilith's midsection, dimming slightly at its flat condition.

"I was hoping you could confirm it for me," Lilith said.

Zelda put her hands on Lilith's belly and moved them around. She frowned. "When did you conceive?"

Lilith's cheeks grew warm. "The night before last."

"That explains why there's no heartbeat. What makes you think you're pregnant?"

"An angel told me I was."

"Is that so?" Zelda leaned in, stopping a scant inch short of burying her nose in Lilith's bosom, and sniffed, drawing in breath until her chest expanded visibly. She sat up, clapping her hands and beaming. "Yes! You're pregnant."

For reasons Lilith couldn't explain, the shock of hearing the Hade midwife say that was almost as great as when Gibeon had announced her pregnancy in the elevator. Maybe it was because sharing the reality with another female made it seem more real. Joy made the room go misty.

Zelda looked at her anxiously. "Not happy news?"

She smiled through her tears. "Very happy news."

Zelda's beaming smile returned. "Let me mix you up a protein shake. They're full of good things for the baby. What did Sam say when you told him?"

"What makes you think the baby is Sam's?"

Zelda patted her knee. "I know someone who lives in Judecca. So what did Sam say?"

"I haven't told him."

Zelda smiled comfortably. "You wanted to be sure first."

Lilith nodded, but she didn't meet Zelda's eyes. The woman's plump fingers tightened on her knee. "You do plan to tell him, don't you?"

"I don't know." Why had she admitted it was Sam's? She was a world-class liar. She could easily have told the midwife the baby was the spawn of one of her human targets. Why hadn't she lied?

"Why don't you want him to know?" Zelda asked gently.

Lilith ticked the reasons off on her fingers. "It's not like he's going to be there for me. Satan wouldn't allow that. And he wasn't exactly torn up when the boss ordered us to split up. He was seeing another she-demon within a month."

"That was a long time ago." Zelda's centuries of practice at soothing nervous mothers-to-be were evident. "He must still have feelings for you. From what my friend said, he was very focused on you that afternoon in the hallway."

Another blush warmed Lilith's cheeks. "Wanting to get laid and wanting a relationship are two different things." She got to her feet. With the inches added by her shoes, the top of her head almost brushed the ceiling. She paced up and down in front of the sofa. "I don't trust him."

Zelda's tail shot straight up. "Whyever not?"

Lilith recounted Gibeon's attempt to push her down the escalator and the way Sam had smoothed it over instead of confronting the angel. "He won't risk his promotion to protect me."

"He's going to notice you're pregnant eventually."

"I'll tell him it's a human baby, from my last mission."

Zelda shook her head. "Human babies take about forty weeks to gestate. Demon children come much quicker."

She hadn't known that. "How quick are we talking?"

"If the mother is a succubus and the father is human, three months."

"Three months?" Shocked, Lilith put her hands on her still-flat stomach. Could she really grow an infant in three short months? That didn't give her much time to prepare. "Are you saying this baby could be here by year's end?"

"I can't say for sure. I've never helped birth a child with a human mother and a demon father. Those births happen Aboveworld."

That made sense.

"There's your immortality to factor in, too," Zelda added.

Lilith stilled, hope dawning. "Since Sam and I are both immortal, the baby will be, too. Right?" Maybe she had nothing to fear from Gibeon after all.

Zelda looked doubtful. "You weren't born immortal. Satan granted that to you later. I don't know if you can pass that on or not."

Lilith's heart sank. "What about cambions? They're half demon and half human. Are they immortal?"

"I don't know," Zelda said. "I only see them when they're born."

But Lilith knew who might know. "Where can I find the succubi these days?"

"If they're not on a mission, you can usually find them in the daycare center."

"That's right. There's a daycare center in Hell. The baby can go there when I have to work." It would give her? him? a chance to play with other kids.

Zelda's lips pinched in disapproval.

"What's wrong with daycare?" Two days pregnant and already she felt defensive about her parenting choices.

Zelda's expression didn't lighten. "Go see for yourself."

After drinking a disgusting protein shake that Zelda assured her was loaded with calcium and folic acid needed by the baby, Lilith followed the midwife's directions to Hell's daycare. It was located in Ring Two, the ring devoted to punishing those who allowed passion to overrule their judgment. She was still sixty yards away when the sounds of crying infants and screaming toddlers reached her ears.

A moment later, she opened the door to a scene of total chaos. There were children everywhere. To the right, tots with scissors ran in circles till they collapsed from dizziness. To the left, toddlers sat cross-legged on the floor, striking matches and throwing them at each other. Deeper in the room, a preschooler attempted to scale a bookcase while three others watched her, open-mouthed.

At Lilith's feet, a baby crawled across a rug strewn with tiny objects. As she watched, he picked up a tiny doll's shoe and put it in his mouth. He chewed for a minute, grimacing at the taste, before trying to swallow. After stretching his neck as though he was trying to force it down, he coughed a couple of times. Then his face turned purple and his eyes rolled back in his head.

She sprinted across the crowded room and picked him up. Pressing against his diaphragm with one hand, she struck him sharply between the shoulder blades with the other. After a couple of blows, he hacked up the tiny shoe and began to scream.

She tried to cuddle him. "It's all right. You're okay."

He pushed at her arms with his fat little hands. "Down."

She set him back on the floor. "Don't put anything else in your mouth."

He made a beeline for the cluster of tiny objects.

She started after him but a gravelly voice spoke behind her. "Well, would you look what the hellcat dragged in?"

Lilith turned. In the far corner of the room, three women in slinky negligees sat in a trio of rocking chairs, smoking cigarillos. Naamah, Eisheth and Agrat were Hell's original succubi, charged with increasing the population in Hell by seducing human men into impregnating them. Though thousands of years had passed, they still looked exactly the same—satiny skin, voluptuous bodies and pouting red lips.

After her breakup with Sam, Satan assigned her to the succubi department. If her time with Sam was the best of her life, the century she worked as a succubus was the worst. Each seduction felt like it destroyed a part of her. Even worse, no matter how many children her targets had fathered in the past, she didn't get pregnant. The other succubi called her "Barrenness Lilith." She would have done anything, harmed anyone, to get out of there. Another hundred years passed before Envy recruited her to his division.

Squatting, she gathered up all the tiny objects and set them on a shelf out of the baby's reach. He stretched out his little fingers, screeching when he couldn't reach them. She patted his back. "You don't want those. They'll choke you."

He smiled up at her. His hair was golden and curly and his eyes were as blue as an Aboveworld lake, but his teeth were surprisingly pointed. He plopped down on his butt and grabbed her ankle with both hands. She smiled fondly. Then he fastened his slobbery little mouth around her Achilles' tendon and bit down with all his might.

She shrieked. Those pointy little teeth were wickedly sharp. It took all of her self-control not to haul her foot back and launch him across the room. From their rocking chairs, the succubi howled with laughter.

"Watch out for that one," Naamah called. "He's a biter."

"No kidding." Lilith tried to pry him loose from her ankle, but he had the jaw strength of a barracuda. She peeled his fat little hands from her calf with one hand while she dragged his mouth away from her ankle with the other. Then she skipped out of range before he could latch on again.

The succubi were still snickering when a crash sounded behind her. She whipped her head around. The preschooler she'd seen climbing had made it to the third shelf before the bookcase toppled over, pinning her and several other children under the heavy wooden shelves. Screams issued from beneath the bookcase, though less loudly than Lilith would have expected.

"Oh, for the hate of Satan," Eisheth set her cigarillo on an end table and stomped across the room. Grunting, she hauled the bookcase off the floor and pushed it back against the wall. Three of the children that had been pinned underneath stumbled toward her, wailing and clutching at her nighty. The one that had been climbing lay still on the ground, her forehead caved in.

Eisheth yanked her negligee from the fingers of the clinging toddlers and poked at the unresponsive child with the pointed toe of her shoe. "Wake up."

When she didn't move, Eisheth prodded her more sharply. Lilith watched, dry-mouthed. Was she…dead?

After a second, the child gasped. Her eyes sprang open. She wailed as the hole in her forehead closed and her skull knit itself back together, leaving a huge dent. Lilith had endured that kind of pain too many times herself not to recognize demon healing when she saw it. The thought of a small child enduring that agony filled her with horror.

With a grunt of satisfaction, Eisheth returned to her rocking chair and picked up her cigarillo.

Lilith lifted the little girl and tried to soothe her. At first, the child clung like a limpet but once her forehead popped back out to its original shape, she wriggled in Lilith's arms. When Lilith didn't immediately set her down, she snarled. Lilith plopped her on the ground and hastened away.

By the time she reached the rocking chairs, the child was already scaling the bookcase again. "Do you let them do whatever they want?"

Naamah picked up a glass tumbler filled with amber liquid. It smelled like bourbon. "They have to learn somehow." She took a long drink and smacked her lips.

"And they're not going to learn any younger," Agrat pointed out.

The three women threw back their heads and laughed. Their throats gleamed smooth and unlined in the torchlight. The disconnect between their youthful bodies and their cackling, crone-like laughter was beyond creepy. If she had stayed working beside them, would she have become this cynical?

"Are all of these kids yours?" she asked.

Namaah shook her head. "Some are our grandkids, some are great-grandkids, some are great-great grandkids—and so forth."

"How does this place work? Is this a co-op?"

The succubi yipped like hyenas.

"Good one," Naamah, slapped her thigh, wheezing. "Like anything in Hell is ever a cooperative effort."

She had a point. Lilith rephrased her question. "Do the mothers take turns providing care?"

Naamah shrugged. "Someone is in here most days."

Lilith frowned, not understanding. "Most days?"

"Yeah, usually. Sometimes Lust has us all on assignment. Then it's kind of fast-and-loose in here."

This was a well-supervised day? Despite the heat, a shudder wracked her body.

"There should be adults in here at all times." She couldn't stop herself from speaking up. *And they should pay more attention to keeping the children safe.*

The succubi's faces turned sullen.

"We're doing the best we can," Naamah said.

"Have you ever thought about doing things to child-proof this area?" she asked.

Agrat frowned. "Like what?"

"Like securing those bookcases to the walls. And keeping the choking hazards away from the babies. Those are all accidents waiting to happen."

"And that's a problem because—?" Agrat seemed genuinely perplexed.

"Because you don't want a room full of dead babies."

"That won't happen. Most of them are immortal."

"But not all of them?"

"The first generation of human spawn were all mortal," Eisheth said. "They died like flies. We tried cross-breeding the few that survived. In the second generation, about a quarter of them were immortal. They lived."

"That seems like a pretty inefficient way to breed demons."

Agrat nodded. "They still die a lot. We tried two demon parents, but none ever conceived."

Because, unlike the Enemy, Satan had no life-spark, although it was a sure trip to the Lake of Fire to ever say that within his hearing.

"So you're back to inter-breeding with humans?" she asked.

Agrat nodded. "We accept the high mortality rate. I mean, they're half-breeds anyway."

Lilith's insides curdled at that cold judgment. How could any mother bring her child here—especially any half-human child that was surely mortal? One thing she knew for sure—her child would never come here. She would figure out how to make a life for it outside of Hell.

CHAPTER 15

The suite was dark when Sam arrived back at the hotel that night. He flipped the wall switch inside the door and the room lit up. It felt oddly empty. Lil must have gone to bed early. In fairness, she'd had a stressful day.

He removed his shoes and loosened his tie. He hated that she was so distressed. The angel wasn't truly a threat. Once Satan spent time with him, he'd realize Gibeon was a complete loser. He'd quickly lose any leverage from being a trophy and wind up like a lot of fallen angels, drinking, gambling and fornicating to pass the time.

By the time Sam reached the darkened bedroom, he was down to his boxers. He crawled onto the bed and felt out to both edges of the mattress, groping for Lilith. Nothing. Where was she?

He turned on the light on the nightstand. The bed was neatly made up, as though she had never gone to bed. A glance around the room revealed that her belongings were gone.

Where the Heaven was she? He pulled out his phone and called her number.

It was after midnight before Lilith got back to the Putnam. When she switched on her phone she was relieved to see her only voicemail was from Sam, demanding to know where she was. She didn't call him back. Where she went in her off hours was none of his business.

She ordered koshari from a nearby Mediterranean grill. After meeting the delivery guy in the lobby, she returned to her room and climbed onto the bed, sitting cross-legged, her back against the headboard. The blend of chickpeas and pasta atop a bed of rice and lentils was exactly the kind of comfort food she needed right now. Eating directly from the container, she contemplated what to do next. As incredible as it seemed after all these centuries, she was pregnant. If only she could tell Sam.

She wasted a few minutes daydreaming that she and Sam left Hell behind and became a human couple with a family and a house in the suburbs. The yearning she felt for this totally implausible scenario shocked her. She was a she-demon, even if only by adoption, and she had been around for thousands of years. She was far too savvy to fall for the fantasy of happy family life on Earth. Divorce, death and disease made a mockery of that dream. Human nature made a mockery of that dream.

Even if it weren't a foolish fantasy, it wasn't an option open to them. To her knowledge, Satan had only ever released one fallen angel from Hell, and even that had required divine intervention. The Enemy had given Sam the highest position in Heaven and Sam had turned his back on it. She had walked away from the mate the Enemy had created for her. He wasn't going to stick his oar in for either of them.

If she couldn't leave Hell with her child, and she couldn't raise it in Hell, what other options did she have? The only one she could think of was to hide her pregnancy and hand the baby over to a human couple to adopt. It was by no means a sure thing that she could keep her pregnancy a secret, but if she was successful, she'd need to find a family to raise the child.

The thought of giving up the baby she'd waited so many millennia to conceive felt like taking a hot knife and carving the child from her womb, but that didn't matter. She had to think about what was best for the baby. They would need to be a good couple, people who liked and respected each other, and who were committed to staying together.

On top of that, they needed to be parents who had the stamina to deal with a half-demon child. Any offspring of hers and Sam's was bound to be a hellion. A smile tugged at the corners of her mouth and her heart melted with yearning. If only they could deal with their little hellion together.

Get real, she told herself. Daydreams were pleasant, but they weren't useful as plans for the future.

Speaking of plans, she still didn't know what kind of timeframe she was looking at. Based on what Zelda had told her, it would fall somewhere between the three-month pregnancies that succubi experienced and the forty-week marathons that humans endured. There had to be someone who could predict which end of the scale she fell at. If only there were a human doctor who knew something about demons.

Her hand froze on the container of koshari. Belial. Of course! The former demon was now human and working in north Florida as Dr. Ben Lyle. He could at least estimate when she could expect to give birth.

Another thought struck her. A human who was once a demon would make a good father for a cambion. Not only that, he was married to Dara Strong, a nurse and one of the Enemy's favorite people. She and Dara had butted heads, to put it mildly, but Dara would make a fantastic mother.

She grabbed her phone off the nightstand and did a directory search for Dr. Ben Lyle. All she could find was a business listing. When she called the number, Dara's voice on the answering machine told her to call 911 if it was an emergency and otherwise to try again during office hours.

You had better believe she would.

Sam was waiting in the lobby when Lilith arrived at the conference center the next morning. She wore a red suit with a knee-length skirt that didn't display nearly enough of her legs. He tried to read her face, but all he could see was fatigue. Her eyelids drooped wearily, which was unlike her. Lil had more energy than anyone he'd ever met.

He drew her into a small room off the lobby where they could have privacy to discuss the situation with Gibeon rationally. "Why did you change hotels?"

She didn't meet his eyes. "I thought we both needed space to make better decisions."

"We have so little time to be together," he said. "Can't you set the future aside and enjoy the moment?"

She straightened, looking him dead in the eye, all hint of drowsiness gone. "Are you going to ask Jehudiel to replace Gibeon?"

Any hope of compromise evaporated. "We don't know that he pushed you on purpose."

"Don't we?" she asked.

"Not with certainty."

"So your position is that accidents and gracelessness are part of an angel's normal repertoire."

Put that way, it was clear Gibeon's act had been intentional, but if he acknowledged that he would have no excuse for keeping the angel at the conference. And if Gibeon left the conference, Sam would have no chance of recruiting him, which, at minimum, meant a stint in the tar pits for Lilith. Satan might even be angry enough to take more drastic measures. Sam repressed a shudder. "Who's to judge what's normal for an angel?"

"Since you were once a seraph and you're now the Devil's Advocate, I'm going to say you have the exact knowledge required to make that judgment."

He abandoned that argument. "We have a lot riding on the success of this summit. Let's not throw that away over one unbalanced angel."

She tilted her head, looking at him like she was seeing him for the first time. "If you had ever loved me as much as you love your career, we'd still be together." She didn't sound bitter, just matter-of-fact.

This conversation wasn't going the way he'd planned. He pulled her into his arms and pressed his lips against hers, but her mouth remained stiff, her jaw closed tight. He ran his tongue along the seam of her lips, but they didn't soften.

Beneath his fingertips, her shoulder blades felt as fragile as eggshells, but the sensation was misleading. Lilith was the definition of toughness. "We only have two more weeks to be together. Let's not waste precious time fighting over the bad behavior of a low-ranking angel who's trying to impress his boss."

"He killed my baby."

"He played a role," Sam temporized.

She tore loose from his arms to glare at him. "A role?"

"It was Satan who got you lost in the desert."

She drew back as though he'd slapped her. "Are you saying I've spent the last ten thousand years working for the guy who killed my child?"

"All I'm saying is that it wasn't all Gibeon. He couldn't know Satan would drag you around the desert until you became too dehydrated to nurse."

Her face was nearly as red as her suit jacket. Her voice shook. "You know what? Just leave me alone. Don't talk to me, don't flirt with me, stay away from me." She stalked out the door and marched across the lobby to the elevator.

He followed her with a frown. Lilith had always been emotional, but she'd never been one to abandon an argument. What was going on with her?

Lilith monitored the breakfast buffet, shooing the angels away from anything that fell outside their dietary guidelines while on the inside her mind churned. So much time had passed it was hard to remember details. The trip back to Eden had taken far longer than the journey to the cave where Ayelet was born. Could Sam be right? Had she been working for her baby's murderer for all these millennia, trying to overthrow an Enemy who wasn't really her enemy?

No. It couldn't be. It was the Enemy who had paired her with Adam. And when living with him had become too much to bear, it was the Enemy who had sent three angels to order her to return. That was why she'd wound up out in the desert.

Once the talks were in session for the day, she pulled out her cell phone and tried Belial's office again.

"Lyle Family Practice, Gabby speaking, How may I help you?" The voice sounded familiar. After flipping through her mental file, she recognized it as belonging to the receptionist at the free clinic Dara used to run. That free clinic had shut down due to Lilith's machinations.

"I'd like to speak to Dr. Lyle, please."

"Dr. Lyle is with a patient. May I give him a message?"

Their last interaction had earned her the top spot on Belial's shit list. If he knew it was her, he wouldn't return her call.

"My name is Lily Furst." She picked a name out of the air. "I'm pregnant and I was given Dr. Lyle's name by a friend."

"He's not accepting new patients, except by referral."

She should have prepared a better cover story. "But I need a doctor."

"You can find a list of doctors here." Gabby recited the URL for a physicians' directory website.

"But I want to see Dr. Lyle."

"I'm sorry," Gabby said. "We can't help you."

Over the weekend, Lilith returned to Hell and hid in her apartment, leaving only to go pick up more protein smoothies from Zelda.

All the next week, while Hell's delegation negotiated for mandatory selfies, mealtime robocalls and deep-fried high fructose corn syrup, she waffled. Maybe she didn't need a doctor. She had Zelda, after all. She'd given birth to her first child without one.

And see how that had turned out?

Meanwhile, Sam did his best to lure her back to his hotel or out to dinner or even just for a walk, but to Heaven with him. His resulting frustration would have been amusing if it hadn't been one more thing to deal with.

On Thursday morning her skirt wouldn't button. She hurried to the mirror, where the glass agreed with her waistband's claim. Her waist was getting thicker and she still had no clear idea when she was due. She needed to figure that out.

After the delegations went to their conference rooms, she returned to the Putnam and took the portal to Hell. From her apartment, she collected a set of identity and credit cards for a secret persona Satan knew nothing about.

Then she went by Zelda's and asked for help locating Belial's home address in Florida. Zelda made a call and then whipped up another smoothie. While Lilith choked it down, a soft knock came at the door. Zelda hurried to open it.

Outside stood a young Hade with turquoise horns like Zelda's. His hair and eyebrows were the color of a pink baby blanket.

"This is my grandson, Phoenix," Zelda said. "He should be able to help you."

Gratefully, Lilith set down the smoothie. "I'm trying to find the demon formerly known as Belial."

The boy's face turned wary. "I don't know where he lives."

"But you can find out." From his expression, she was 100% certain of that.

"Why do you want him?"

"She's pregnant." Zelda answered before Lilith could speak. "She needs to see a demon doctor."

He apparently knew there was no point in trying to resist his grandmother when a baby was involved. He pulled out his phone and dialed. "Uncle Bad? I have someone here who needs to see Belial."

Lilith flinched. On a mission a few years ago, she had treated Bad's wife, Keeffe, abominably. There was no way he would help her.

"It's Lilith Firstwoman," Phoenix said. The silence went on much longer this time. "But—"

Zelda grabbed the phone out of his hand. "Where is Belial?"

Bad must have attempted to explain why he couldn't tell her. She cut him off ruthlessly. "This woman has a cambion on the way. She needs that address."

After writing something on a square of paper, she hung up the phone and handed the paper to Lilith. "Did you go by the daycare center?"

Lilith stretched her neck. "I did."

"And will you enroll the baby there?"

Lilith shuddered. "Of course not."

"Then what are you going to do?"

"That's what I'm trying to figure out."

As soon as Lilith got back Above, she made flight reservations to Jacksonville for Saturday morning. She couldn't use the Portal—it kept a record of everyone who used it, and where they went.

Belial would not be glad to see her and his wife, Dara, would be even less glad. That was all right. They could pray her into the tar pits, as long as they agreed to adopt her baby.

On Friday morning Sam saw the date on his phone with a feeling of frustration. Two-thirds of his and Lilith's time Above had elapsed but still she refused to return to him. He couldn't believe she was allowing that incident with Gibeon to make her throw away a once-in-ten-thousand-year opportunity.

He intercepted her on her way into the Secretariat building. She had dark circles under her eyes.

"You look tired." Could Satan have reneged on her immortality?

After an instant of icy fear, Sam relaxed. Satan wouldn't do that while Sam was still working to recruit Gibeon.

"I haven't been sleeping well," she said.

"The bed at the Ferguson is very comfortable." He lavished his best smile on her.

She opened her mouth to reply but, unexpectedly, she belched. Her cheeks turned red, as though she'd been caught doing something shameful. Maybe she had. Whatever she'd eaten smelled disgusting.

"Let me take you to dinner and the theater tonight," he said. "I bought tickets for *Hadestown* and made dinner reservations at Tavern on the Green. You can order something that's easy on the stomach."

Amusement lit her eyes for a second. "You've studied up on the modern world."

"For you." He took her hand. "Please say you'll come."

She bit her lip, considering. Inside, he rejoiced. He'd spent hours the previous evening putting together a date that would appeal to her.

Her gaze shifted away and he thought he'd lost her, but then her scarlet lips widened into a flirtatious smile. "All right, I'll meet you at the Ferguson at six."

With that, she headed up the escalator toward the Delegates' Lounge. He watched her go with the first feeling of peace he'd had in over a week. After the play and a good meal, he'd lure her back to their suite. They wouldn't waste another minute.

As soon as Sam went into his negotiating session, Lilith headed back to the basement of the Putnam. She'd had to accept his invitation. If she'd refused, he would have put all his resources into following her this weekend. That couldn't happen. She had to make sure he was out of her hair.

She was still burping when she got to Sam's office. Was there anything this baby liked? Gomory's door was open. Perfect. She positioned herself where Gomory would be sure to overhear.

"Sam asked me to pick up some cufflinks from his office," she told Estelle. "He wants to wear them to the theater tonight."

Estelle crossed her arms over her chest. "I can't let thee into Lord Samael's office."

"No, of course not. He wanted you to get them. He said they were in his desk."

To say the look Estelle gave her was skeptical was an understatement but she went into his office to look for the cufflinks nonetheless. While she was gone, Gomory appeared in her office doorway. Her chin was up, her nostrils flaring. She clearly wasn't happy that her lover was taking his ex-wife to the theater. What would she say if she knew Lilith was carrying Sam's child? The thought made Lilith smile. Gomory did not smile back.

"There be no cufflinks in here," Estelle called from Sam's office.

"Do you check his lap drawer?" Lilith called back, trying to suppress another burp. Gomory watched her unblinkingly.

Estelle returned to the outer office. "They are not to be found."

"Thanks for looking." She headed for the door.

Before she could make her exit, Gomory asked, as though she couldn't stop herself, "Did you say that Sam is taking you to the theater tonight?"

"He's not taking me," Lilith said too quickly. "We're just going together. You know, as co-workers on an Aboveworld mission."

"Is anyone else going?" Gomory's eyes were as blue and cold as gun barrels.

Lilith let her gaze dart away. "Everyone else had other plans."

Gomory's fists clenched. "We'll see about that."

Another belch escaped Lilith's lips, this one long and loud. Gomory looked repulsed. Estelle, who was standing only the width of her desktop away from Lilith, wrinkled her nose.

Lilith chuckled weakly. "I really need to stay away from those lentils." Before Estelle could ask any questions, she scurried out of the office.

"You're a little troublemaker, aren't you?" She rubbed her abdomen as she waited for the elevator to Manhattan. It had grown more convex over the past week. She'd need to start wearing looser styles soon.

Back above, her first stop was a mobile phone store, where she bought a burner phone. Back at her hotel, she used the phone and her new identity to make a seven a.m. plane reservation from Newark to Jacksonville for the next morning. She'd just finished when someone knocked at her door. She'd been expecting this.

"How did you know where to find me?" she asked as she let Sam in.

"I had DemSec track your credit card."

Blessit. She should have retrieved her other ID before she reserved this room.

"Why did you leave the conference early?" His tone held more curiosity than suspicion.

She shrugged. "There's not much for me to do now that things are rolling."

He fixed her with a penetrating glance that said he was determined to get to the bottom of this. "The projector lamp burned out in Conference Room F. I had a heaven of a time locating someone to fix it."

"But you figured it out." She adopted the encouraging tone of a third-grade teacher talking to one of her slower students. When his expression didn't alter, she added, grudgingly, "I had a couple of errands to run."

He raised his eyebrows. "Did your errands happen to include going by my office and flaunting the fact that we're going to the theater tonight in front of Gomory?"

Lilith spread her hands. "What can I say? It's the girl code."

"She's insisting on coming Above for the evening and staying over."

"Have a lovely evening."

Blessing under his breath, Sam turned and left.

Sam made it as far as Forty-Third Street and Second Avenue before it occurred to him that Lilith had been far too accommodating about his standing her up to take Gomory to the theater. It was like her to tell Gomory about their planned date—stirring shit was one of Lil's favorite pastimes. It wasn't like her to let him off the hook afterward, though.

Why hadn't she given him a hard time about ditching her? If putting him between a rock and a hard place hadn't been the point of her plan, what was? Was she punishing him for failing to act on her paranoia where Gibeon was concerned? Or did she have something more nefarious in mind?

Given that it was Lilith, he voted for nefarious. This bore investigating. He changed direction and headed for the Putnam Hotel's basement portal.

Back in Hell, Sam's first stop was his office. Gomory was gone for the day, getting ready for their date, no doubt, but Estelle was still at her desk. That was normal. It was all Sam could do to get her to go home at night.

"What did Lilith say when she was here earlier?" he asked.

"She said you wanted your cufflinks from your desk drawer to wear to the theater tonight."

"And Gomory overheard?"

Estelle's lips twisted. "That one hears everything. She likes to spy."

A true statement, but that didn't tell him anything he didn't already know. "Did Lilith say anything else while she was here?"

Estelle shook her head.

"Did she seem upset that Gomory overheard?"

Estelle's lips curled in a smile that reminded Sam why she'd wound up in Hell in the first place. She'd poisoned her boss, with whom she was sexually involved, for cheating on her with his wife. "No, she meant for her to overhear."

That matched his take. He rubbed his jaw. "And nothing else happened?"

She looked at him for a moment like she was weighing whether to say anything. "She belched."

He stared at her blankly. "She what?"

"Just before Lilith left, she belched."

He would have discarded that information as useless, but Estelle wasn't given to providing useless information. "And?"

"It smelled like those protein shakes Zelda the Hade makes."

That was clearly supposed to mean something to him, but it didn't. "What shakes are those?"

Irritatingly, Estelle chose that moment to get close-mouthed. "You should talk to Zelda."

Sam checked his watch. It was after six. He was supposed to meet Gomory at the hotel at seven-thirty. It would take him at least a half hour to get to Zelda's and as long to get back.

"You should talk to Zelda," Estelle repeated.

"I don't really have time."

Estelle picked up her phone. "I'll have her come here. She can use the Hade tunnels. It will be faster."

Why couldn't she simply tell him what was going on? "Fine. I'll be in my office."

Ten minutes later, Zelda tapped on his doorframe.

"That was quick." And a little spooky. The Hades' system of tunnels had been in place eons before the angels arrived. Efforts to create maps didn't go well. No sooner was a tunnel documented than it disappeared and another popped up. To this day, only a handful were mapped. The fact that Zelda had been able to make a half-hour trip in ten minutes suggested there was one from Hadeville that led directly here. He set that aside to think about later.

Zelda eyed him from the doorway. Being summoned by the Devil's Advocate had to be alarming for her. He gave her a reassuring smile and invited her to come in. To his surprise, she crawled into the chair across from him and fixed him with a piercing stare. Her feet dangled six inches from the floor but she did not look intimidated.

"Thank you for coming." As a fallen angel, he was unable to apologize but that was no excuse for not saying please and thank you. "I appreciate it."

"Estelle said you were asking about Lilith," she said.

He drew back, startled by her directness. How well did she and Estelle know each other? "She mentioned that Lilith might have visited you recently."

Zelda smoothed her skirt and nodded. "She came by yesterday."

Again he felt thrown off by her straightforward manner. Having his questions answered with candor wasn't something he'd had much experience with. "Did she say anything about her plans for this evening?"

Zelda cocked her head and thought about that. "This evening?" she said finally. "No, she didn't say a word about this evening."

That was clearly an evasion. Finally, his prosecutor's instincts found something to seize on. "But she did say anything about her plans?"

Zelda nodded. "She's going to Florida to see Belial this weekend."

Jealousy roared through him like a grass fire through dry brush. Before Belial had abandoned the underworld, he had been at the top of the Hellish hierarchy, on the cusp of being appointed Chief Executive Demon. He'd spurned Satan and everything Hell had to offer in pursuit of a human woman, an affair that had cost him his immortality. He was also a consummate politician. Was Lilith turning to him for help in routing her enemy—or was she just turning to him?

"Belial the Traitor?" he asked.

For the first time since she'd walked into his office, Zelda looked wary. "She doesn't think of him that way."

No, she thought of him as an old flame. Lilith had enjoyed a fling with him while on a mission to corrupt King Solomon three thousand years ago. Their affair had lasted only a short time but to the best of Sam's knowledge, Belial was the only demon she'd ever been with other than himself.

"She may not think of him as a traitor," he said grimly, "but I can assure you Lord Satan does."

In a world peopled by the angelically beautiful, Belial was exceptionally handsome, and his charm was legendary. Human women found him irresistible. Lilith was angry at Sam for refusing to wreck their mission by insisting Gibeon be remanded to Heaven. Was she visiting her old flame to make him jealous? Or did her trip have a darker purpose?

"Do you have any notion of why she's visiting him?" he asked.

"Perhaps you should go find out." She held out a scrap of paper. "Here's his address."

Once again, her forthrightness shocked him. Thanking her, he took the paper and walked her to the door. As she left, she exchanged a look with Estelle. He couldn't interpret what it meant, but it didn't matter what a pair of old biddies were up to.

He handed Estelle the scrap of paper. "Figure out when she's getting to Florida and get me there before her."

He wasn't jealous. Jealousy was an emotion for lesser demons. He was concerned. If word of her consorting with a traitor who had abandoned Hell got back to Satan, there would be Heaven to pay. And if she was asking Belial for help getting rid of Gibeon, well, that needed stopping, too, for her own sake.

Estelle didn't jump to do his bidding, which was a rarity. "She'll be traveling under an alias."

He frowned. That was probably true.

"Shall I call DemSec and get their minions working on it?" she asked.

If they called in DemSec, the request would be logged and reported to Satan. At that point, the disposition of Lilith's case would pass out of Sam's hands.

"No." He rubbed his jaw, weighing his options. "Ask Zelda to have that grandson of hers look into it."

"All right." Estelle looked relieved, though he couldn't imagine why. She barely knew Lilith. He went back into his office and called Gomory. "I won't be able to make the play tonight."

"Why not?" Gomory's voice was like the mewing of a hellcat.

When Lilith was pissed, her voice turned into gravel on slate. Just the thought of it affected him like an aphrodisiac.

"Something's come up."

"Something that can't wait till morning?"

By morning Lilith would be on her way to Belial's side to plot who knew what kind of mayhem. "No. I'll leave the tickets at the theater. Invite a friend to go with you."

"I don't know anyone who would be available on such short notice," she said. "I mean, it's not like you gave me much time to—"

"Ask Andromalius." He'd seen her flirt with the Assistant Devil's Advocate on more than one occasion. "I'm sure he'll be willing to drop everything and take you."

He hung up before she could deny any interest in Andromalius. He had more important things to pursue.

CHAPTER 16

$\mathcal{L}$ ilith would have been waiting when the boarding call came for her plane, but the baby had its own ideas. As she was heading for the gate, morning sickness overwhelmed her. By the time she'd rinsed her mouth and sponged the resulting stain off her shirt, she needed to pee. She barely made it on board before the door closed.

The gate clerk glared at her as she processed her boarding pass, "You're supposed to arrive at the airport a couple of hours before your flight time." She handed Lilith a cardboard tag with a stretchy string attached. "You'll need to leave your bag at the door to the plane. The overhead bins are full."

She considered dropping her boarding card behind the counter so the plump clerk would have to bend over to pick it up, but the life inside her made her so happy she wanted others to be happy, too. She threw the woman an apologetic grin. "I didn't mean to hold everyone up. I'm pregnant and I had to make a pit stop."

Instantly, the woman's glare relaxed into a sympathetic smile. "How wonderful. Your first child?"

Lilith shook her head. "No, I lost an infant, years ago. I'm on my way to Florida to see a specialist to make sure that doesn't happen again."

"I'm sure everything will be fine." The woman's voice was warm and comforting. "I'll keep you in my prayers. Have a wonderful flight."

"Thank you." Lilith headed down the jetway, dragging her wheeled bag behind her.

I'll keep you in my prayers. It was just an expression, but it was an expression of goodwill, which was considerably better than she usually received from humans she interacted with. How would the Almighty receive such a request? Favorably, she hoped.

"Please let my baby live," she murmured and realized, with a sense of shock, that she'd just prayed her first prayer in over twelve thousand years. Would God listen? She could only hope.

She left her suitcase at the end of the jetway and made her way down the narrow aisle toward the back of the plane. The flight was full and she tried to ignore the scowls thrown her way. If she told them why she was late, would they give her a pass, as the counter attendant had done?

When reached her row a middle-aged woman sat in the middle seat. She gave Lilith a drowsy smile. It wasn't even seven a.m. yet. Was she one of those terrified people who had to take anti-anxiety meds before she flew?

Then Lilith's eyes fell on the passenger by the window. His head was turned away, watching the ground crew scurrying around outside the plane, but his profile, with its Mediterranean complexion and aquiline nose, was almost as familiar to Lilith as her own. Shock ricocheted through her. What was Sam doing here?

Why was Sam here? And, for that matter, how had he known she'd be on this flight? She'd covered her tracks. How had he uncovered them?

"Sam?" Lilith leaned across the woman to address him directly. "What are you doing here?"

He turned his head. He smiled at her, but his eyes burned like glowing coals and his pupils were rectangular. Uh-oh.

"Visiting an old friend." His voice was as smooth as cream, but his pupils didn't round. "Or perhaps I should say an old rival."

What in the world was he talking about?

A flight attendant approached her. "Could you please take your seat, miss?"

The woman next to Sam removed her arm from the armrest and the drugged expression in her eyes dissipated like clouds in a brisk wind. "Would you like to sit next to each other?"

"No, no, we're fine." Lilith needed to sit on the aisle, with ready access to the bathroom. Slipping into her seat, she shoved her purse beneath the seat in front of her and clipped the safety belt across her lap.

"So, what's in Florida for you?" Sam leaned forward to ask the question across the poor woman in the middle seat. His tone was affable, but his pupils were still rectangular. He was livid. Well, let him throw his little temper tantrum. He couldn't intimidate her.

"Toes in the sand," she said airily. "It's been an intense couple of weeks. I decided I could use a little R and R."

"And Belial?" Sam's voice was like ice cubes in a blender. "Is he also looking forward to some beach time?"

Her head whirled. He knew where she was going. There was only one person who could have told him—Zelda. The next time she was in Hell she would have to have a chat about patient confidentiality with one small, horned midwife.

"Are you hoping your old flame can help you send Gibeon back where he came from?" Sam asked.

The poor woman in the middle pressed herself against her seatback like she hoped it would swallow her but Lilith blew out a breath of relief. He might know where she was going, but he had no idea why.

"I'm going to sit there." Pointing to an empty seat across the aisle, the woman scrambled across Lilith.

"Very nice," Lilith hissed. "You chased that poor woman out of her seat."

Sam snorted. "Like you've ever worried about making a human uncomfortable."

That was true, but now that her child might grow up around humans, she was more concerned.

The pilot came over the intercom. "Flight attendants, prepare for takeoff."

A flight attendant stopped next to their row. "Sir, could you please fasten your seatbelt?"

Sam clicked the belt closed like he thought it was a total waste of his time, which, of course, it was. If the plane went down, he'd walk away unharmed. The flight attendant moved on.

"I know you had a fling with him." Sam's eyes shot sparks across the empty seat.

She knew she was poking the bear, but she couldn't resist. "Jealous?"

He lifted his chin. "Don't be ridiculous."

"That was three thousand years ago," Lilith said. "How many different she-demons had you dated by then?"

He gazed at her like he was trying to look through the flesh and bone of her forehead and read what lay behind it. "Are you consulting him on how to get rid of Gibeon?"

"The thought hadn't even crossed my mind." And it hadn't.

"Then why are you going to see him?"

"Are you familiar with the term 'booty call'? There was no way Belial would be interested in hooking up with her, but Sam didn't know that.

Apparently, he was familiar with the term because his face turned crimson. His lips moved, but no words came out.

"You're the one who's ridiculous." She removed a magazine from the seat pocket in front of her and pretended to read it. Once they got to the airport in Jacksonville, she'd have to lose her unwanted tail.

For the duration of the two-and-a- half-hour flight, Sam smoldered. Was she rekindling an old flame? Or merely soliciting advice on how to get rid of a pesky angel, in defiance of the agreement she'd made not to undercut the mission? He couldn't let that happen. Satan would be livid.

When they landed in Jacksonville, she grabbed her purse and practically ran up the aisle while he was delayed, waiting for his luggage. When he'd gotten on the plane, he'd set it on the empty seat beside him. A few minutes later, the attendant had stowed it for him.

He assumed someone would retrieve it for him, but no one did. Finally, the young man standing behind him grabbed it from the bin and shoved it into his midsection. While he appreciated the service, the young man's manner was unacceptably rough. Sam's powers on Earth were limited, but they were enough for this situation. As he trundled his bag down the aisle, the young man's suitcase burst open, flinging his belongings far and wide.

By the time Sam got to the boarding area, Lilith was nowhere in sight. He gazed around him with something like panic. He'd done a little research the night before. Jacksonville was not like New York. There was no mass transportation, nor were there logically numbered, grid-like streets. Estelle had made his flight arrangements and hired a car to get him to the airport. She'd offered to arrange another car once he arrived in Florida but the idea of dogging Lilith's high-heeled footsteps and forcing her to lead him to her former lover's house had been more appealing.

Dragging his wheeled bag to a halt, he was fumbling for his phone to call Estelle when, ahead in the distance, Lilith appeared outside the door to a women's restroom.

Relief flooded him. It wasn't that he couldn't figure out how to go on in this brave new world that had sprung up over the past thousand years. He would simply prefer to focus his efforts on more useful things, like the illicit activities of his ex-wife. Hurrying to catch up, he attached himself to her like a barnacle.

She eyed him with displeasure. "Why don't you get a life?"

"I have a fine life," he said. "I want to see what you're doing with yours."

"You're an idiot." She strode away.

He followed her down a hallway to a counter with a blue and yellow sign. A dozen people waited for service. Lilith joined the back of the line.

"What are you waiting for?" he asked.

"My turn."

"You've spent far too much time up here. Demons don't wait on humans." He strode past the waiting crowd. At the front of the line stood a pair of young women in startlingly short dresses. Their legs were bare. On their feet, they wore sandals held in place only by a pair of v-shaped straps. They were both deeply absorbed in their phones. So much the better. He motioned Lilith to join him. She didn't move.

One of the young women looked up from her phone. "What the fuck?" Her voice had an annoying nasal quality and the volume of a taxi horn. She spoke to the other girl. "This jerk just cut line in front of us."

The second girl looked up from her phone and surveyed him disapprovingly. "You may be a hottie, but that's a dick move, dude."

Behind her, the crowd grew restive.

His scent was apparently not strong enough to penetrate the first girl's clogged nasal passages and the second must be out of range. He reached out his hand to touch the first girl's wrist but she yanked her arm out of reach. "Hands off, hot stuff. Haven't you ever heard of consent?"

A hulking man in a hooded sweatshirt loomed behind them. He was so tall he blocked the overhead light. "How about you go back to the end of the line and wait your turn, buddy?"

What was wrong with this place? He was the Devil's Advocate. He had once opened up the Earth and caused it to swallow up an entire regiment of Israelites. It was within his power to call up legions of demons and level this entire building. Unfortunately, he couldn't do that without breaking the truce. He strode back to where Lilith stood. Her lips twitched but she didn't say anything.

Twenty minutes passed before they reached the head of the line. After ten more minutes of negotiations, not one word of which he understood, she walked briskly out a set of automated doors. He could only follow her.

Outside, the first thing that struck him was the heat. The overhead sun was unrelenting. Combined with the lush vegetation, it made him feel like he was being stewed for a cannibal's dinner. Expelling a breath, he dragged the neck of his shirt away from his throat. "It's hotter than Satan's ball sack here."

Lilith crooked her index finger and brushed her nose with the knuckle. "If anyone would know that, it would be you."

He supposed he had opened himself up for that one.

A few moments later, a blue and green bus arrived. Lilith boarded it. He was right behind her. As the bus pulled out of the airport, he gazed around in frank fascination. The abundant foliage reminded him of the plant life they'd seen when she took him to the site that was once Eden.

"This is very different from Manhattan," he said.

She turned to him, eyebrows raised. "You've never worked a mission here?"

"By the time Ponce de Leon discovered the place, I was already running Legal Affairs."

The bus came to a halt. He got to his feet but Lilith remained where she was so he sat back down. A couple of passengers got off and the bus rolled forward a few yards. This time, Lilith got up.

"Where do you have a hotel reservation?" she asked.

The look he gave her was completely blank.

"Hotels. They're these big buildings where humans stay when they're away from home."

His brows drew together. "I know what hotels are."

"Did Estelle make you a reservation anywhere?"

He'd been so focused on getting to Florida before Lilith got away from him that he hadn't thought any further ahead. "No."

"Why not?" She shot him a look out of the corner of her eye.

"Because you didn't want the boss to know." She answered her own question.

That sounded like a good excuse. "What he doesn't know won't—"

"—hurt you," she finished for him. "Did you bring your phone?"

"No, I left it in my hotel room, on the charger, with calls forwarded to a burner I picked up in New York."

She turned her head to stare at him in amazement. "Look at you, getting all techie."

Estelle had suggested doing that. "I'm not an idiot."

"I never thought you were. Well, if you don't have a hotel reservation, where would you like me to drop you?"

He crossed his arms. "I'm going to Belial's with you."

Lilith typed Belial's address into the GPS on her phone and laid it on the console. Her visit would be an unwelcome surprise to both Belial and his wife. Sam's presence would only make things more difficult. Why was she letting him tag along?

Because she wasn't sure what else to do with him. Although he tried to hide it, he clearly viewed Florida as an alien jungle that might swallow him whole.

He wasn't completely wrong.

Before this mission to New York, he hadn't left Hell for over a thousand years. Even for someone like her, who frequently came Above on missions, it was challenging to keep up with the changing landscape up here. He wouldn't have a chance on his own.

Also, she wanted to see his face when he realized how far off the mark his suspicions were about her and Belial.

Who are you trying to kid? a voice sneered at the back of her consciousness. *You're still hoping that he'll step up and you'll be able to tell him he's about to become a daddy.*

To the best of her knowledge, Sam had never fathered a child before. This would be as miraculous for him as it was for her. If he demonstrated that it was safe to share her news with him, she would be delighted.

Forty-five minutes later, the sign announcing the town of Alexandria, Florida, appeared on the side of the road. Dense foliage gave way to pastel concrete block houses on postage-stamp lots.

"You have arrived at your destination," her GPS announced a few blocks later. They pulled up in front of a pale blue house. In the center of the tiny front yard sat a green plastic baby pool in the shape of a frog. An array of plastic buckets and shovels lay scattered near the pool.

"This is where Belial lives?" Sam sounded amazed, but no more than she was. Belial had once been the most ambitious demon in all of Hell. She'd assumed he and Dara had married, but she'd known nothing about them having children. She tried to picture Belial as a middle-class American dad but failed.

"You wait here," she told Sam.

"So you can plot to undermine the trade talks? I think not." He reached for the door handle but she pressed the master lock button, momentarily stalling him.

"You won the wager," she reminded him. "I agreed to support you. Do I look like I want to have my limbs rearranged?"

Before he could answer, the front door opened. A man appeared inside the glass storm door. Sam peered out the passenger window. His jaw dropped. "Is that Belial? What the heaven happened to him?"

There was no question that it was Belial. His flawlessly molded features were both beautiful and unique but the male gigolo look he'd worn in Hell was gone. There were a few lines on his face and his dark hair had grayed at the temples, giving him a distinguished look. A baby crawled up behind him and used the leg of his khakis to pull itself up, leaving a trail of drool on the fabric. He bent and lifted the child into his arms, smiling into its smooth little face. He nuzzled the child's neck until muffled squeals of glee filtered through the closed car windows.

A father who loved his child this much would surely be willing to help her. The problem was, she couldn't ask for that help with Sam eavesdropping.

"You have two choices," she said. "You can wait here in the car until I signal you."

Sam's jaw hardened. "Absolutely not."

"Or I can drive you to the nearest police station and tell them you attempted to carjack me. You know Hell has a policy against intervening in Aboveworld justice, right?"

He had made that policy. He glared at her. "How can you be sure I won't simply drive away while you're inside the house?"

"Because you don't know how to drive."

His gaze narrowed into two pinpoints. "What are you trying to hide?"

A female figure, holding a baby that appeared to be a duplicate of the one in Belial's arms, appeared in the doorway behind him. Like Belial, Dara had aged since Lilith had last seen her. She had also cut her hair. Five years ago, she had worn it in a waist-length braid. Now it was cut in a chin-length bob that was clearly chosen for ease of maintenance.

"Who is that?" Sam asked.

"Belial's wife, Dara."

It was clear on his face that his theory about why she was there had collapsed like a beach hut in a hurricane. He looked at Dara again, frowning as though bemused that she had lured one of Hell's most ambitious demons away.

"There's more to her than meets the eye," Lilith said. That was true. And she could leverage Dara's background to convince Sam to give her a moment alone with the human couple.

"She's a demon-fighter, and she doesn't like our kind. She keeps a bottle of holy water and a bag of demonweed at the ready. If you descend on her unannounced, she will view you as a threat to her children. I don't think you'll enjoy how that turns out."

Sam leaned forward to study the woman in the doorway more closely.

"Now, assuming you don't think I'm planning a threesome, could you please give me a moment alone to prepare them for our visit?"

"Five minutes," he said. "Then I'm coming in, holy water or no holy water."

She would have to talk fast.

Taking a deep breath, Lilith crossed the lawn to the front door. It was eleven-thirty a.m. on a mid-October morning. Even though it was autumn in the northern hemisphere, Florida hadn't gotten the memo. The sun beat down mercilessly from a cloudless sky. She hoped Belial's little cement oven had air conditioning. She'd been sweating like a horse these last few days. As she approached the house, he opened the storm door. The baby still rested comfortably on his hip.

"It was you who called the office," he said. "Gabby thought she recognized your voice."

He had a tiny cut on his chin, as though he had nicked himself shaving. He was human and clearly mortal.

"I'm expecting," she said baldly. If she'd felt surprised at the changes in him since the last time they met, it was nothing compared to the total and absolute shock that stilled his face at her words.

"You're pregnant?"

She nodded. "And I don't want my child raised in Hell. I came to ask you to adopt it."

He started to speak but Dara interrupted him. Without a trace of warmth in her voice, she said, "Let her in."

CHAPTER 17

$\mathcal{L}$ilith had once been burned as a witch; that experience had been more comfortable than sitting in Belial and Dara's living room. Each of them held onto one of the children, as though they were afraid to risk letting them crawl too close to her. Dara had been unable to bear children. They must be adopted.

"Cute kids," she said.

Dara looked at her coldly. "Stay away from them."

"Right. I mean, I will." A line of sweat broke out beneath Lilith's breasts.

"How far along are you?" Belial asked.

"Not very." She started to count on her fingers.

He shook his head. "How long has it been since your last period?"

That was easier. "Three and a half weeks."

He and Dara exchanged a look she couldn't interpret.

"That's early," he said. "How do you even know you're pregnant?"

She explained about Gibeon's announcement in the elevator. Dara's gaze sharpened and she set down the baby she was holding. He crawled toward a pile of toys in the center of the floor. His twin fussed and wriggled in Belial's lap. Belial grunted as he leaned forward to set the child on the floor. It was getting harder every minute to remember that this decidedly human dad had once been one of the sexiest demons in Hell.

"Was there any wiggle room in his wording?" he asked. "Angels can't lie—not and stay in Heaven—but they can skirt out to the edge of truth."

She shook her head. "He was pretty clear, but just in case I took a pregnancy test and it was positive."

He exchanged a look with Dara. "Those are usually pretty accurate."

"Also, I went to see Zelda and she agreed."

That did it. "She's probably the most knowledgeable person in Hell about human-demon pregnancies. Did she say when you're due?"

"She said there were too many factors at play to be sure. That was one of the reasons she thought I should see you."

Dara was still watching her without a hint of sympathy in her hazel eyes.

Lilith took a deep breath. "I don't want my baby raised in Hell. I've made my bed, and I'm willing to lie in it, but that's not the future I want for my child. When I tried to think of a human couple who had the skills and the knowledge and the right mindset to deal with a half-demon child, you two came to mind."

She'd hoped her frank admission would soften the other woman, but Dara's face didn't relax in the slightest degree.

Belial glanced at the door. "Sam's the father?"

"I'd rather not say." Could they just hurry up and give her an answer? At any moment Sam would get tired of waiting in the car and barge in.

Belial frowned. "If he's the father, he has a right to know."

"Especially if you're thinking about giving the child up," Dara said.

Lilith's clasped fingers tightened. "As far as I'm concerned, he's just a sperm donor."

"I know you two have a history—" Belial began.

She waved that away. "It's not about that." She told them of Gibeon's message when Ayelet was born, then about the threat in the elevator, and his attempt to push her down the escalator. She shuddered. "He wants to kill my baby."

Speaking the words aloud brought home to her how easily Gibeon could have succeeded. Her eyes welled with tears. Stupid pregnancy hormones. She blinked them away before they could fall.

"What does that have to do with trusting Sam?" Belial asked.

"He refused to do anything about it. He doesn't want to risk disrupting the trade talks." Tears threatened again but she forced them back. "If I can't trust him to set aside his ambition to protect me, how can I trust him to protect our child?"

For the first time, she detected a hint of sympathy from Dara. One of the babies crawled over to her and hauled himself up to teethe on her kneecap. She leaned forward to brush a kiss across the top of his head. Lilith watched enviously. She would never get to do that with her child.

"Time for a snack?" Dara cradled his little chin even though it was dripping with drool.

He beamed at her. "Bana."

She smiled. "We can do that." She got to her feet. "Can you get the other one?"

Belial made no move to pick up the child. Lilith was shocked to realize Dara was speaking to her. She checked to see if the holy water was visible.

"It's all right," Dara said. "I give you my permission."

Awkwardly, Lilith scooped up the other twin. His plump little body was a joyous weight in her arms. The top of his head smelled like baby shampoo. She couldn't stop herself from sniffing it. These happy, well-cared-for children bore no resemblance to the feral infants she'd seen in Hell's daycare. Dara and Belial had to adopt her baby. They just had to.

She followed Dara into the kitchen, where they settled the boys into matching high chairs. Dara retrieved a banana from a stand on top of the refrigerator.

"Bana," one boy yelled, reaching for the fruit.

"Bana," yelled the other, even louder.

Dara stripped off the peel, broke off a chunk of banana and set it on the first child's tray. He gobbled it up and grabbed for a second chunk. When Dara gave it to him, the second child shrieked like he'd been betrayed. His face turned red. As he slammed his little fists on the tray, something changed in his eyes. Lilith looked more closely. His pupils had gone rectangular.

"Are they—?" Right at that moment, the rich aroma of ripe banana reached Lilith's nose. Her stomach did a back flip. She pressed her fingers against her lips.

"Bathroom?" she gasped.

"Down the hall, second door on the right," Dara said.

She barely made it in time. After she flushed the toilet and rinsed out her mouth, she opened the door a tiny wedge. Dara and Belial's voices floated down the hall.

"Is adopting her child something you'd consider?" Belial asked.

Lilith held her breath.

"I don't know," Dara sounded troubled. "I know we've talked about adding another child to our family but what if it turns out I can't forgive? What if I can't love the child because of its mother's actions?"

Lilith cradled her mid-section against the gut punch of Dara's accusation. She had feared this would happen. It was bad enough to screw up your own life but so much worse to realize your sins were about to be visited on the next generation.

Across the hall, a door opened, followed by creaking noises and then the tinkling sound of a lullaby being played on a music box. They must be putting the babies down for their naps.

Reluctantly, she left the shelter of the bathroom. At any moment, Sam would join the conversation. She was surprised her threat had held him this long. As though on cue, a car door slammed out front.

Belial met her at the end of the hallway. He spoke in a low voice. "Dara and I talked. I need to do an exam and an ultrasound to determine your due date."

She twisted her fingers together. "What about adopting the baby?"

"Let's take this one step at a time."

A firm knock sounded on the front door.

"We'll come back to the topic of father's rights." Belial ushered her into the living room. "Let's get your exam out of the way first. That will require a trip to my office."

Sam knocked louder.

She bit her lip. "I'm not sure how I can get away from—"

Dara stepped into the hallway, closing the boys' door behind her. "Leave that to me."

Like a ship sailing into battle, she headed into the living room and opened the front door. Sam stood outside with his fist raised to pound on the glass again. Dara eyed him coolly through the storm door. His hand fell to his side.

She opened the storm door. "Samael?"

He nodded, nonplussed.

"I am Dara Strong-Lyle. If you agree to adhere to my rules, you may enter my home. Do you agree?"

As Lilith could have predicted, Sam's face grew wary. "What are your rules?"

Dara ticked them off on her fingers. "You may not attempt to win anyone over to your master's way of thinking. You may not lay your hands on or physically touch any human beings while in this house. You may not use your pheromones to alter anyone's mood or perceptions."

Belial chuckled under his breath. "I remember hearing this warning."

At the sight of Sam's shocked face, Lilith choked back a laugh, but Dara didn't so much a smile. She picked up a spray bottle from a table next to the door. "This bottle contains holy water. If you break any of my rules, I will spray you with holy water until your face liquefies. Then I will take a picture of you with your face melted and post it on the dark web for all your friends to see, destroying your credibility and wrecking your future."

Sam's eyes were the widest Lilith had ever seen them. She snorted. He was right to be cautious. Dara was the most take-no-prisoners human she had ever met.

"Do you understand the house rules as I have explained them to you?" Dara blocked the door, her spray bottle aimed directly at his face.

Sam nodded silently, as Lilith had expected he would. Direct confrontation was never his favored approach. He was more about finding the wiggle room behind the words.

"I'd like a verbal assent, please," Dara said.

"I understand your house rules as you have explained them," he said. "And I agree to abide by them on pain of being sprayed in the face with holy water until my face melts."

"Then we understand each other." She opened the door.

Belial's wife was fascinating. Her face had remained as serene as a fourteenth-century Madonna's even as she threatened to dissolve his face. Though her gaze stayed tranquil, her brow unruffled, he did not for one instant doubt that she would carry out her threat. On the surface, she appeared soft, loving and maternal, but he suspected that what lay inside more closely resembled an iron cross.

The backs of her hands were thick with scar tissue and he glimpsed additional scars at the base of her rounded throat but somehow they didn't detract from her appearance. Hers was a beauty built not on pretty features—although they were attractive enough— but on character. Fortunately for both of them, he had no desire to harm her or her family. He simply wanted to find out what Lilith was up to.

One thing was clear. There was no way Lilith was pursuing a liaison with Belial. This woman would never allow that. That meant she was here to enlist him in her crusade against Gibeon.

Trying to look as unthreatening as possible, he entered the house and took a seat on the small sofa Dara directed him to. She and Belial occupied a larger sofa directly opposite his and Lilith sat in a wing-backed chair that was perpendicular to the sofas. His position did not give him a clear view of Lilith's face, so he focused on the human— how odd to think of Belial as human—couple.

"What are you doing these days?" he asked in a jovial tone.

"I'm a doctor," Belial said.

Sam stared at him blankly, unsure he had heard correctly. "A doctor?"

"A physician. I treat humans for disease and try to help them live longer and more enjoyable lives."

Sam smiled politely. What a total waste of time. Humans had the life spans of mayflies. What difference would a few more years or a few less fevers make?

Perhaps that wasn't Belial's real motivation. American doctors were supposed to be quite wealthy. Sam glanced around the room, assessing the contents. The furniture appeared to have been mass-manufactured and the upholstery showed wear in places. Dara wore no jewels—only a plain gold wedding band. There was nothing here to indicate that Belial had achieved any material success, despite being well-positioned to do so.

"Ben's practice includes a high proportion of indigent patients who can't afford to pay for treatment." Dara seemed to read his mind.

Maybe that was what was why Lilith was here. Maybe Belial wanted to access the riches of Hell to improve his circumstances?

How the mighty were fallen. The Belial he'd known in the old days wouldn't have wasted his time on people who were in no position to pay for his services. He tried to exchange a glance with Lilith, but she had curled into a corner of the chair with her eyes closed. She appeared to have nodded off. That was unlike her. Could she be ill? His hands turned clammy. Was that why she'd come to see Belial—to seek medical care? He shook off the thought. That was ridiculous. Lilith was immortal.

"How about you?" Belial asked. "Still running the Legal Department?"

Sam drew in a breath, making his chest expand. "I'm the Devil's Advocate."

"Right," Belial said. "You got that promotion ten centuries before the Son was born, didn't you?"

Had it been that long?

"Once these trade talks are concluded," Sam said, "Wrath and Envy will report up through me."

He expected to see a spark of envy in Belial's eyes at the news of his promotion, but the look the former demon gave him seemed more like pity. He frowned. How could this grubby little human feel pity for *him*?

They chatted for a while longer, but nothing Belial said provided any insight as to what Lilith was up to. As far as Sam could tell, she'd shown up here unannounced. She continued to slumber until the sound of whimpering came from down the hall.

"The kids are awake," Belial told Dara. She nodded.

In her chair, Lilith blinked and straightened. She gazed around the room, looking slightly bewildered.

"Did you have a good nap?" Sam asked sardonically.

"Don't be ridiculous," she said. "I never sleep in the daytime."

Dara and Belial exchanged a look. Sam froze. Satan had granted Lilith immortality but this wouldn't be the first time he had given a gift only to later wrest it from the recipient's hands. Perhaps he thought if she died while on an Aboveworld mission, Sam wouldn't connect her death back to him. Was this why she'd wanted to see Belial?

"Would you like to join us for lunch?" Dara asked.

"Thank you. We would," Lilith said before he could answer.

Thousands of years had passed since the last time Sam sat down to dine with humans. In their high chairs, the babies ate noodles in tomato sauce. He chuckled as they tried to grip the tiny circles of pasta with their chubby fingers. Within moments, sauce covered their hands and faces.

"They seem like fine little fellows," he told Belial.

"Their names are Thomas and Timothy." Belial was clearly proud of his progeny.

"Lilith and I hoped to have children," Sam said. "But it wasn't to be."

The room grew quiet, as though he'd said something either profound or profoundly boorish. He tried to catch Lilith's eye across the table to get a read on which it might be but her charcoal-tinted eyelids shaded her eyes from view. Despite her nap, she had bluish circles beneath her eyes. His palms started sweating again. What was going on?

As they rose from the table, Belial said, "Would you like to see my new physician's office?"

"That sounds like an excellent plan." Sam was relieved at the opportunity to move out of the reach of Dara's spray bottle. "It's always interesting to see what my old friends are up to."

"Actually, I'd like you to stay here and help with the babies while I clean up the kitchen," Dara said.

He opened his mouth to refuse, but nothing came out.

"Please," she added, but it clearly wasn't a request. It was a ruse to allow Lilith to pop off somewhere with Belial without Sam accompanying them. But why?

He opened his mouth to decline but what came out was, "Of course." Although it wasn't clear how much help he could be since she wouldn't allow him to touch her children.

"We won't be gone long," Lilith said and followed Belial out the door like she was escaping from Hell.

Dara got to her feet and stacked his empty plate on top of her own.

"How do you know Lilith?" he asked.

She added Lilith's plate to the stack. "She and Ben came here five years ago on a mission to corrupt and destroy me."

It was shocking to hear her sound so matter-of-fact about it. Clearly, they'd failed at their task. "But you married Belial and you have a fondness for Lil?"

"I did marry Ben." She added his plate to the stack and carried them over to the kitchen sink, where she scraped off any remaining food before opening the shiny door to a small white cave with racks inside. She loaded the plates into the lower rack.

Her non-answer confirmed what he'd suspected. She didn't care for Lilith. That wasn't a surprise. Few women did, and none who'd been the object of one of Lilith's missions.

"If you don't like Lilith," he said, "why did you allow your husband to go off alone with her?"

She turned on the tap and then flipped a switch behind the sink. A deafening roar filled the kitchen. Startled, the baby nearest Sam began to wail. The other quickly joined him. Sam reached out to comfort them but pulled his hands back as he recalled Dara's threat.

She flipped the wall switch again and the noise died away.

"All done," she cried gaily.

The boys stopped crying. With red sauce crusting their hair, hands and clothes, they looked like infant mass murderers. Dara brought over a cloth and began to wipe their faces but after a moment she abandoned the effort. "They're going to need more than a washcloth."

He doubted a fire hose could do the job.

"The bathroom is down the hall on the right," she said. "Would you please run bathwater for them?"

Had he entered an alternate universe where, instead of being the Devil's Advocate, he was somehow in training to become a nursemaid?

"Of course," he heard himself say again.

The bathroom was a small room with a yellow-and-white tile floor. A white shower curtain sprinkled with yellow daisies concealed the bathtub. A basket filled with brightly colored plastic animals sat on the floor beside it. One small window filled the room with muted sunlight. He turned on the faucet and let it run for a moment, then adjusted it for temperature, allowing the water to pool a few inches in the bottom of the tub.

When he returned to the kitchen, Dara had removed the tray from Thomas's high chair. She unfastened the strap that held him in place and lifted him from the chair. Holding him away from her body, she offered him to Sam.

Sam stepped back.

"They're cambions, so the argument could be made that they're not fully human." Dara's tone was casual but her gaze was like a cutting torch.

This was a test, but what kind of test? It wasn't as though he were actually planning to become her nanny. Still, he allowed her to place the child in his arms. Thomas immediately tried to rub his sauce-spattered face against Sam's white golf shirt. Sam recognized his intentions in time and held the baby away from his body, as Dara had done.

It was, to Sam's knowledge, the first time he'd ever held an infant. The child was surprisingly solid. His little round face, with its snub nose and smooth-gummed mouth, looked up into Sam's face fearlessly, squealing with delight at his new playmate. With a messy hand, he grabbed Sam's nose. It was clear that he had known only love in his life. His eyes were dark brown and his hair as black as Sam's own. If he and Lilith had been able to have a child, it might have looked much like this one.

Nearby, Dara watched him closely. She lifted Timothy from the other chair and led the way to the bathroom. Balancing the baby on one hip, she checked the temperature of the water. "Perfect."

Ridiculously, Sam felt a flush of pleasure at her praise.

"Strip him and put him in the tub," she directed.

Despite Thomas's flailing arms and constant escape attempts, Sam managed to remove his clothes and place him in the tub next to his brother. Dara gestured at Sam to have a seat on the toilet while she settled in on the floor next to the tub where the babies splashed and squealed.

"I can see the resemblance to Belial," he said.

Dara smiled serenely. "We adopted the boys from a patient of Ben's."

Sam tried to process that. "Is Belial—Ben—the father?"

"No. We have a monogamous relationship."

Many people falsely believed that about their relationships, but, in this case, he thought it was probably true. She seemed remarkably clear-eyed for a human.

"How did he happen to have a patient who was pregnant with cambions?" The likelihood of that happening by chance seemed slim.

"Ben's practice is made up of women who have been impregnated by demons."

Relief flowed from his shoulders outward. Lilith wasn't ill. Belial's unusual medical practice must be the reason she had come to Florida. But why, exactly? What was her interest in expectant mothers of demon hybrids? Was she hoping, like Dara, to adopt a child?

More information about Belial's practice might yield clues. "Are there enough of those women locally to constitute an entire practice?"

Dara rubbed a soft cloth across Timothy's face. He shook his head violently, trying to avoid the cloth, but she simply held it still and allowed him to flail until he rubbed his face clean. Then she looked at Sam thoughtfully, as though she were weighing how much to reveal.

"We run ads nationwide," she said finally. "We invite women who find themselves in pregnancies with odd timelines to contact us."

Sam cocked his head. "Odd timelines?"

She repeated the wiping process with Thomas. "Cambion babies gestate much quicker than humans. It makes it difficult for the mothers to find good prenatal care. They can't get their doctors to believe them about their conception dates and the progress of their pregnancies."

More from courtesy than curiosity, he asked, "But Belial—Ben—does believe them?"

She nodded. "Depending on which genes dominate, cambions can be born in as little as ten weeks. That's one quarter the time that it takes human babies to gestate."

Sam considered that. "The doctors are going on what they learned in medical school, no doubt."

"It's more complicated than that. The majority of the women are prostitutes. Because of the nature of their sex lives, doctors discount everything they have to say about their conception dates. They rarely see the same doctor throughout their pregnancy, so they have a similar problem convincing them that their pregnancy is progressing with abnormal speed."

His attention honed in on the first part of her statement. "Did you say that most of the women that come to you pregnant with cambions are prostitutes?"

Dara nodded a touch bitterly. "They're easy targets. The demons don't have to put forth any effort to seduce them. They pay them a few dollars and leave them with a demon baby in their belly."

Sam was outraged. "This is pure slacking. The Lust division's budget is built on the assumption that it may take an incubus several weeks to seduce his target. If they're shortcutting the process by simply picking up prostitutes, where is all that extra money going?" He would have a few choice words to say to Lust the next time he saw him.

Dara fished the bottle of holy water from her smock.

He held up his hands. "Sorry. I tend to be a little work-obsessed."

She didn't smile or lower the bottle. "I can see that."

"I wasn't like this when I was with Lilith." Now, where had that come from?

He was relieved to see her finger relax on the trigger. "What were you like?"

"It was a long time ago. Longer than a human could conceive."

"But you still remember."

He cast his mind back over the thousands of years that had passed since their split. "Half of me—the playful half, the laughing half—left with her." Although, if he were honest, that change had started long before they split.

"Satan separated you?" she asked.

He nodded. "We were what is called a 'power couple' up here. Together, we represented a threat to his domination of Hell." Her expression seemed to question that, so he added, "Before joining Lucifer, I was a seraph."

She didn't look impressed.

"Seraphs are the top tier of the angelic hierarchy," he said.

"Yes. I know." Her expression still didn't change.

"There was no way around his decree, but Lilith is not a woman to give in easily."

Her lips flattened. "I've experienced that with her."

"Then why did you send her off with your husband?"

"I trust my husband."

He nodded. "As long as we were together, I never looked at another woman. After we split, I knew she would never accept the situation as long as she thought we might reconcile. I took up with another she-demon so she'd know we were over and let go."

"Are you still with that she-demon?"

"Not her, nor any of the hundreds of she-demons since."

"Why not?"

"They weren't Lilith,"

He was surprised to see a wealth of compassion in Dara's eyes. "Sometimes you have to go through Hell to find your Heaven."

Sam laughed bitterly. "There is no heaven for Lilith and me. For us, there's only Hell."

CHAPTER 18

ilith watched as Belial retrieved a tube of transparent green gel from a drawer in a little table with a screen mounted on top. He uncapped the tube and squirted the gel on her belly. She gasped as the cold gel touched her skin.

"Sorry about that," he said. "This helps me get a clearer picture."

She wasn't sure which was more difficult to accept—a former demon apologizing so effortlessly, or one working as a doctor.

From a holster built into the tabletop, he took a wand connected to the screen by a thick cord. "This is the transducer probe. It bounces sound waves off the baby to let us see detail."

She watched his calm, sure movements, fascinated by his transformation from one of the least empathetic demons in Hell to a caring physician.

He angled the screen so she could easily see it and dragged the broad head of the probe across her belly, spreading the gel as it went. On-screen, in the center of a wide cone of gray swirls, a shape that looked a bit like a tadpole with a giant head appeared, surrounded by a pool of black.

"The first thing we'll do is a heart tracing." Graph lines appeared on the screen. With his free hand, he made a note. "The heart is beating at 149 beats per minute."

Lilith watched the agitated lines, frowning. "Is that because it's half demon?"

"No, that's perfectly normal. Human fetuses have fast hearts. Now I'm going to take measurements to determine how far along you are."

"I know exactly when I conceived—eleven days ago."

He moved the ultrasound probe around, making notes as he went along. "Eleven days? You're sure?"

"One hundred percent."

He pursed his lips. "Based on its current development, this baby is eighteen weeks along."

"Is this proceeding faster than a normal human pregnancy?"

"Yes, but it's not a human pregnancy. It's a hybrid pregnancy." He explained his practice.

"What a wonderful thing to do." She truly meant it.

"We think so."

"Is there a way to tell if the baby will be immortal?"

He looked regretful. "None that I know of, other than waiting to see whether he or she stops aging."

Well, that wasn't helpful. She looked back at the screen. "Can you tell if it's a boy or a girl?"

"I'm not sure—" he began, but as he spoke the tadpole on the screen did a backflip and pressed its genitals—its decidedly feminine genitals—against the spot where the probe pressed against Lilith's belly. Belial burst out laughing.

"She's a girl," he said. "And as shameless as her mother."

Lilith watched the screen in wonder. A girl child, just like little Ayelet. She could almost feel the sensation of the nursing baby's mouth tugging on her nipple. She drew a deep breath. That couldn't happen. To keep this baby was to doom her.

"A girl would make a nice addition to your family," she said casually.

Belial's left eyebrow arched. "Tell me more about why you're reluctant to tell Sam he's going to be a father. From what he said at lunch, he'd be happy to take on that role."

"He can't be trusted."

"I understand why you feel that way," he said. "But try to look at the situation objectively. The only reason you connected Gibeon pushing you to the baby is because of his threat in the elevator. Sam doesn't even know there is a baby, much less a threat to it. I don't live by Hell's rules anymore, but it hasn't been so long that I've forgotten. Satan would have Sam's ass if he wrecked these trade talks merely because a she-demon was being harassed. True?"

"True," she said grudgingly. "But if there was a threat to Dara, even if it didn't involve the children and even if it didn't put her life at risk, would you let her take her chances?"

"No." His response was instantaneous.

"That's what I thought." She stared at the screen, watching her little tadpole float happily in its cone of gray soup. "She looks healthy."

"Are you going to tell Sam about her?"

"No, but I think he deserves to know he's going to be a father."

She checked the clock on the wall. Sam had spent over an hour alone with Dara. "Is Dara telling him now?"

Belial shook his head. "This is for you two to work out."

When Lilith and Belial arrived back at the house, they found Sam lying on his back on the living room floor. The babies crawled over him and pulled his hair, giggling when he yelped. From a nearby chair, Dara placidly watched her children torment the proudest demon in all of Hell. Even Belial seemed a little taken aback.

"You're quite the demon-whisperer, aren't you?" Lilith said to Dara. She couldn't prevent the slightly acid note in her voice.

"I just bring out what's already there," Dara said. "Would you like to stay for dinner?"

"Thanks, but we need to catch our flight back to New York." She had no flight reservations. She hadn't been sure how long it would take to work things out with Dara and Belial so she'd left it open, but it was clearly time to get Sam out of here.

"Ben, why don't you show Sam the backyard?" Dara said.

Belial stared at her blankly. "The backyard?"

"I'm sure he'd like to see where we're thinking about installing the patio," she said.

He blinked. "The patio. Right." He led Sam out the back door.

Sam, Lilith noticed, made no effort to avoid this clear attempt to sideline him, following Belial out the door without argument. He must have reached a conclusion about why she was here. "Did you tell him?"

Dara shook her head. "That's between you and Sam."

"Then what did you want to talk to me about?"

"My grandmother."

Shame washed over Lilith in a hot wave. "I'm... I'm..." The word wouldn't come. She'd lost the ability to apologize the day she'd joined Hell.

"I'm not interested in an apology, even if you could give one. I simply want to know what happened that day."

"I didn't kill her," Lilith said.

Dara's face was implacable. "Tell me what happened."

"She had a stroke."

"Was she afraid?"

"Esther Perdue?" Lilith said. "Are you kidding? She was praying me down—quite successfully—when her body went slack. She died a Viking's death, sword in hand." She heard the admiration in her own voice and knew it to be justified.

Dara processed that and finally nodded. "Thank you." She took a deep breath. "Ben and I are willing to adopt your child under one condition."

Lilith felt a rush of relief. The idea of giving up her child was painful but this was the best outcome she could hope for. "What condition?"

"Sam has to agree."

Well, that was no good. She shook her head. "If Sam knows about her, Satan knows about her."

"You're underestimating him."

"I think I know him a little better than you do."

"You know the demon he is far better than I ever will," Dara said. "But I have a better grasp of the man he could be."

Lilith crossed her arms. "Sam isn't Belial. Belial hated Hell. He knew right away he'd made a mistake following Lucifer. He was thrilled to get an opportunity to do something better. Sam's not that guy. Sam is all in for Satan. Always has been."

"Sam needs to be all in for something," Dara said. "Right now it's Satan because that's his only option. Give him another option."

Lilith shook her head. Dara didn't know Sam.

"Your child's welfare is at stake here." Dara's tone was implacable.

"I know exactly what's at stake." Lilith thought about Hell's daycare and shuddered. "If I tell Sam about her, there's a chance it will get back to Satan. I won't put her at risk by exposing her existence to Satan."

"Fathers have as much right to their children as mothers do."

"Men have spent thousands of years knocking up women and then hitting the road. That tells me it's not a right they care to exercise."

"That's a small minority of men."

"You see the best in people." She envied Dara her strength, her ability to cut to the heart of a matter without backing down or second-guessing herself. She was a worthy successor to her grandmother.

"He deserves the benefit of the doubt." Dara was unyielding. "We have a policy."

Lilith shook her head. The risk was too high. "So, those adorable little tykes of yours—did Mommy notify Daddy about them?"

Dara went still. She'd hit a nerve. After a moment, Dara cleared her throat. "The policy only applies when the father can be identified."

"DemSec has the DNA of every demon in Hell in their database. If you'd wanted to know who the father was, you could have found out."

"Neither Ben nor I have any contact with that world."

"Maybe not," Lilith said, "but I'd bet my Ferragamos Belial has stayed in touch with Bad."

Dara's soft mouth tightened, telling her she was right. Belial might not have any direct contact with Satan's minions, but the former head of DemSec kept tabs on what went on Below.

"If you change your mind," Dara said, in a tone that said she was ending the discussion, "we're here."

If she couldn't convince them without getting Sam involved, she'd have to find another set of prospective parents.

CHAPTER 19

From the passenger seat of the rental car, Sam watched as Lilith pulled into the flow of traffic on the interstate highway. He still didn't know whether she'd gotten the information she'd come for or why she had come to see Belial in the first place, for that matter.

"Let's get a hotel room and stay over." Extracting information from Lilith required deliberation and subtlety. It wasn't a conversation to hold in the chaos at an airport gate. Chatting over dinner and a bottle of wine would be much more productive.

She shook her head. "I need to get back to New York. I have things to set up for next week."

"We could fly back tomorrow morning. If you need an extra pair of hands, I could help."

She caught her lower lip between her teeth. She was tempted. He doubled down. "We could find a Greek restaurant and enjoy a candlelight dinner." He made his tone a caress. "Are Kalamata olives still your favorite?"

"These days they give me heartburn." Her lips twisted into a tiny smile.

She always claimed he got heartburn when he was keeping secrets.

Apparently, so did she. Maybe if he came at this obliquely he could pry a clue from her. "What was Belial's office like?"

She blinked at the sudden change of subject but answered readily enough. "Like any doctor's office. Exam rooms and old magazines."

"You came all the way to Florida, traveling under an assumed name and getting rid of your phone so Satan couldn't easily track you. That's a lot of effort simply to look at old magazines."

"What can I say? I'm a sucker for 'Who Wore it Best?'"

He looked at her blankly.

She shook her head. "You need to get out more."

Exactly what he'd been thinking earlier, but he wasn't about to let her derail him. The fact that she'd sidestepped his question said he was on the right track. "You had an opportunity to show me what modern medicine looks like, but you passed it up."

"I thought it would be more useful for you to get a glimpse of a typical modern family."

"Dara and Belial's family is hardly typical. The boys are cambions."

Her hands went tight on the steering wheel. Deliberately, she relaxed them. "Really? I didn't notice."

She had absolutely noticed that the boys were half-demons. The fact that she lied about it said he was narrowing in on the true purpose of her travel. There was one way to get her to talk. He pumped his scent into the closed cabin of the car. When she inhaled, her shoulders relaxed and the corners of her lips lifted in a soft smile.

Then her eyebrows snapped together. Shooting him a glare, she pressed a button on her armrest. All four windows descended, turning the cabin into a maelstrom. The wind battered his face and neck. Lilith's hair blew so wildly he wasn't sure how she could even see to drive.

"Close the windows," he shouted.

"Are you going to stop pushing pheromones at me?" she asked.

"Yes!"

She pressed another button and the windows glided closed.

"What did you discuss at Belial's office that you're not telling me about?" he growled.

"Nothing. He was showing off his clinic."

"Why didn't he want me to see it?"

"He would have been fine with you seeing it but Dara needed help with the twins."

Dara had needed his help with the twins about as much as Lilith needed his help navigating the streets of Manhattan.

"What did he recommend you do about Gibeon?"

"Gibeon?" Lilith spat his name like it left a nasty taste in her mouth. "We did not discuss Gibeon."

Lilith was a good liar, but Sam was pretty sure she was telling the truth.

If she hadn't come here to fornicate with Belial, and she hadn't come for advice on Gibeon, why had she made the trip? What purpose could she have in visiting an obstetrician who specialized in cambion births? Shock slammed through him as the picture came into focus.

"They're working to raise a cambion army, aren't they? They plan to mount an offensive to shut down Hell."

She stared at him for a long, silent moment. Then she threw back her head and laughed and laughed. When she could speak again, she said, "Can you seriously see Dara Strong sending children off to fight a war against Satan?"

"You mean the woman who threatened to melt my face?"

"You're not a child."

"Belial was within a hair of becoming the Chief Operating Demon of Hell when he abandoned the field to become mortal. I can readily imagine him using whatever means necessary to accomplish his goal."

"Dara wouldn't, though."

She was right. He scowled in frustration. He wasn't accustomed to being the only player who didn't know the game being played.

"If that's not what's going on, what is? Why are they going to so much trouble to attract a horde of women who are pregnant with cambions? And what does it have to do with you?"

"It's called a ministry. These women need help, so they help them." She flicked on her signal and made the turn into the airport.

"My final question still stands. You're hardly a woman to involve herself in charity work."

She shrugged airily. "I thought it would be fun to lead you on a wild goose chase."

He glared at her, outraged.

She chuckled. "And I have to tell you, it so was."

He didn't believe her. This wasn't the end of the matter. Not by a long shot.

The aisle seat was empty when they boarded the plane home, but instead of taking the window seat, Sam plopped himself in the center seat and commandeered the armrest. The only way Lilith could keep her arm from rubbing against his was by folding it across her body. Since she didn't want to spend two and a half hours watching a mental porno of herself and Sam, she gritted her teeth and kept her arm in her lap.

As seemed to happen every time she sat still for more than five minutes these days, she fell asleep. Before she dozed off, Sam was staring out the windows into a solid mass of clouds as the plane moved smoothly through the air.

She awoke to a plane that jumped like the hounds in Ring Seven.

Overhead, the pilot came on the intercom. "Folks, we've run into some turbulence, so I'm going to have to ask you to take your seats. Flight attendants, please secure the cabin."

Sam's gaze honed in on her. "Is the plane going to crash?"

She shook her head. "It's an air pocket. Pilots deal with them all the time."

Across the aisle, a little girl tugged on her mother's sleeve. "I don't feel good, Mommy."

"Try not to think about it, sweetie." Despite her words, the mother pulled a paper bag from the seatback pouch in front of her and held it open.

The baby in the woman's arms began to fuss. She kissed the top of his head and he quieted, watching her with solemn baby eyes. No sooner had he stopped crying than the little girl threw up. She burst into hysterical tears and so did the baby.

"Having children certainly isn't for the faint of heart." Sam was surprisingly sympathetic.

Don't fall for it, Lilith told herself. In all their years together, Sam hadn't seemed to mind her inability to conceive. His comment to Dara and Belial, suggesting he regretted not having children, was simply an attempt to connect with them.

"It's okay," the mother said soothingly. It wasn't clear which child she was talking to. She rooted through the baby's diaper bag with one hand, holding the baby against her chest with the other. After a moment of digging, she produced a container of wipes.

"Let me clean you off." Mom was still smiling. The little girl pulled away, screaming. Mom's smile wilted a little around the edges.

"Can I help?" Lilith asked.

Mom thrust the baby across the open aisle between them. "Can you hold onto him for a minute while I clean her up?"

"Of course." Lilith took the baby, reveling in the weight of his little body in her arms. He stopped fussing to stare up at her. He wasn't more than a couple of months old.

Unfortunately, the hiatus lasted less than thirty seconds. Then he opened his mouth and screamed again.

To Lilith's utter amazement, Sam reached over and plucked the baby from her lap.

"That's enough of that, little man." His voice was soft but firm. The baby's almost non-existent eyebrows drew together in puzzlement, but he stopped crying.

After she finished cleaning up big sister, Mom reached for the baby. "He responds well to men's voices."

Sam handed him across the aisle, shrugging off the woman's thanks. He turned his gaze to the plane window. Outside, masses of water vapor whizzed past. He leaned forward, all but pressing his nose against the double-paned porthole. His eyes narrowed.

"That little shit." He pulled his phone out of his pocket and typed a text.

"What's going on?" Lilith tried to look past him, but all she could see was a section of the plane wing and lots of clouds.

"Nothing." He kept typing.

It didn't sound like nothing. "What did you see?"

When he still didn't answer, she leaned across him. Something appeared to be perched on the back edge of the wing but she couldn't see what it was. She released her seat belt to crawl across him to the window seat for a better look but the airplane chose that exact moment to buck again. Her body rose up in the air nearly a foot. Sam caught her and pressed her back into her seat. With shaking hands, she refastened her belt.

Something moved outside the window, something human-shaped, but white and semi-transparent. Was that—? She leaned across Sam to get a better look. The armrest bit into her ribs but she ignored the discomfort. The being on the wing had red curly hair. Her blood seemed to freeze in her veins. Could that be—? The figure crawled to the front edge of the wing, above the jet engine, and became solid. It was Gibeon, all right. "What is he doing?"

"I think he's trying to take out an engine." Sam sounded so calm he might have been saying, "take out the trash." He pressed send.

"Who are you texting?"

"Estelle. I sent her instructions to send the retrieval team, just in case."

He thought the plane might crash. They were both immortal, so their bodies would reanimate, but every broken bone and every crushed organ would have to regenerate, a process best accomplished out of sight of humans.

"What about all the other people on the plane? What about that baby you were just holding? What about his sister?" Her stomach felt like a fist had clenched around it. The children would die in a fiery plane crash. And not just them, but every other child on board.

Sam rubbed her hands, his face sorrowful. "There must be someone on board the Enemy wishes to punish."

The impact with the ground would shatter all of her organs, including her womb. Her lips went numb at the thought. Her half-human baby might be mortal. If so, it wouldn't survive the crash. Terror pumped adrenaline through her system. She clutched Sam's knee. "You have to stop him."

From outside the window came a horrific grinding noise. The plane bucked again. People screamed. A shock of white feathers shot out the back of the engine. Gibeon couldn't possibly have—

Sam's jaw dropped. "He just fed himself through the engine."

Around them, people wept and prayed. The pilot's voice came over the speaker system again. "Nothing to worry about folks. We just had a bird strike."

"At twenty thousand feet?" someone yelled.

"You're perfectly safe," the pilot went on. "We could complete the flight with a single engine but as a matter of policy, we'll be landing in Atlanta to have the plane checked for damage. Once we're on the ground, our customer service team will help you book a flight home."

She grabbed Sam's wrist. There was so much screaming and crying around them she didn't need to worry about being overheard but she spoke softly anyway. "You have to stop him."

He squeezed her hand. "You know I can't do that. Interfering with an act of retribution is grounds for war. That would kill a lot more people than the number on this plane."

"This is not an act of retribution," Lilith said.

"It looks like retribution."

"It's not coming from the Enemy. It's coming from Gibeon. And it's aimed at me."

"I know you think he has it in for you—"

"I don't think it. I know it."

The plane jumped again and then plummeted before leveling out again. Around them, the level of hysteria rose.

"Think about this logically," Sam said. "He knows he can't kill you. To take out that other engine he's going to have to incarnate again and then grind himself up—again. He'd have to go through twice what he puts you through—and kill all these other people—simply to deal you a little temporary pain."

She opened her mouth, but he cut her off. "The Enemy must have judged someone on this plane warranted the death of all the others."

"He doesn't do that," Lilith said. With surprise, she realized she believed what she was saying. The Enemy wasn't behind this. "God doesn't kill a plane full of people because he's pissed at one."

"Of course he does. He annihilated seventy-thousand people just because David took a census he didn't like."

"He didn't wipe out seventy-thousand people on a whim. I was there. A plague got loose in a society that lived at close quarters and didn't know the first thing about public health and stopping the spread of disease."

Across the aisle, the mother clutched her children tightly in her arms, her face pale. Beyond her, outside the porthole, a translucent shape began to form. Lilith's heart jumped into her throat. Sam had to take action or everyone on this plane, including his own child, would perish.

But he didn't know that. He might regret the early deaths of the people on board, but he believed the risks of breaking cosmic law by interfering were much worse. The only thing that would motivate him to put a stop to Gibeon's actions was learning about his own child. Back at Dara and Belial's, he'd said he regretted not having children. It wasn't much, but it was all she had.

She clutched his arm. "Sam, I'm pregnant."

His face went blank. "What?"

"I'm pregnant."

His face remained as expressionless as the back of a tombstone, but she knew him well enough to know that behind that empty mask his mind was moving a thousand miles an hour.

"That's why you went to see Belial," he said.

How like Sam to focus on slotting the last puzzle piece in place before reacting to the news he was about to become a father—if his child didn't die in a fiery plane crash first.

She nodded. "If this plane goes down, she may not survive."

"She?"

"Belial said she was a girl."

He nodded. No smile, no delight at learning he was about to become a daddy. With a sinking feeling, she wondered if the news was unwelcome.

"What do you want me to do?" He took out his phone and keyed in a search.

"I don't know. Call down lightning and knock him off the wing."

"I lost the ability to call down lightning when I left Heaven. Control of the sky lives with the other side."

Of course. She'd forgotten that. "We own the ground. Do something with the ground."

"Like what—have the plane slam into it? I think Gibeon already has that covered."

The plane bucked wildly. Around them, people screamed and prayed. She tightened her grip on his arm. "Turn the earth below us into a honeycomb."

"At the speed this plane will be traveling when it hits the ground, there is no substance soft enough to cushion the blow."

She stared at him in terror. "Text Jehudiel and tell him Gibeon is in violation of the truce." He started to argue but she grabbed his arm. "I don't care about the trade negotiations. I just care about my baby."

His search returned a schematic of a 737 airplane, like the one they were on. He studied it for a second and nodded. Then he handed her his phone. "You text him." He closed his eyes and steepled his hands.

"What are you doing?" she asked.

Without opening his eyes, he said, "Stopping Gibeon."

"How are you going to—" she began, but the body beside her slumped, unconscious, against the window. Sam was gone.

After disapparating, Sam dived under his seat into the return air vent, emerging in the hold beneath the cabin that housed the air conditioning pack. He was still stunned at Lilith's news. He was going to be a father. He and Lilith would finally have the child they'd longed for. That is, *if* he managed to save the babe from Satan's death sentence.

But that was a challenge for a future day. Today's test was to stop Gibeon. According to the schematic, the shortest route to the wing was via the bleed air isolation valve. Taking a deep breath, disapparated a second time and fed himself into the valve.

He arrived on the wing as Gibeon solidified into his angel form. The angel knelt above the jet engine, preparing to somersault into the roaring turbine. There was no time to waste. Sam shot toward him and oozed up his nose.

Inside Gibeon, it was spectacularly bright, much like Heaven itself. And he had wings again!

Gibeon was so intent on crashing the plane that he did not immediately notice Sam's presence. It was only after Sam loosened Gibeon's grip on the rim of the engine port and let the wind drag the two of them away that the angel realized he'd been invaded.

What are you doing here? Gibeon's panicked thoughts blared. *Begone, demon!*

I'm trying to stop you from making a mistake that will end your career.

If Lilith bears that child, that will end my career.

The plane had flown on without them. It was now a tiny dot on the horizon. Gibeon rocketed forward and screeched to a halt, alighting on the wing again. Hands seemed to grab Sam's shoulders. They tried to push him out through the envelope of Gibeon's physical manifestation. He hunkered down.

I was a seraph, he reminded Gibeon. *You are a mere messenger angel. You cannot dominate me.*

You are a demon, Gibeon screamed back, struggling to dislodge him. *You have no right to invade God's messenger.*

If you were a faithful messenger, I wouldn't have been able to enter you.

As the truth of that hit home, Gibeon screamed with rage. He made a dive for the engine but Sam dragged him back. Fury coursed through the angel's veins. Sam steeled himself to withstand another dislodgment attempt. Instead, the angel's body dissolved around him, melting into a pool of silvery white liquid.

Now what? He couldn't very well possess a puddle. Then he relaxed. He might not be able to possess Gibeon in liquid form, but puddle-Gibeon couldn't destroy the engine, either.

Clouds whipped past as the plane flew on. The sound of the remaining engine changed. He looked down. The ground was getting closer. He breathed a sigh of relief. All he had to do was keep Gibeon out of the engine until they landed and Lilith and her child would be safe.

Without warning, the puddle flowed up the wing to the base of the engine and reformed. Blessit! Sam rushed toward him, managing to get inside barely in time to prevent Gibeon from throwing himself into the engine.

The angel screamed in vexation. *She must not give birth. Her child will ruin everything. Surely you can see that?*

I see nothing of the sort.

Gibeon returned to puddle form and coursed across the surface of the wing to a hinged flap at the back of the wing. Sam didn't know anything about how airplanes worked—he wasn't convinced they even should work—but if Gibeon was targeting the flap, it must be necessary to land.

Spikes of frost darted out in all directions. He was using the expansion created by frozen liquid to tear off the flap. Sam pressed his essence into the opening. The cold was bone-chilling, He visualized the heat of Hell and the metal warmed around him. Gibeon tried to escape but Sam held him in place.

Now all he had to do was keep Gibeon right here till the plane reached the runway.

CHAPTER 20

When the plane finally taxied down the runway, the other passengers cheered as the pilot announced their safe arrival. Lilith released a huge breath of relief. Sam had done it! He had wrestled with the angel and brought them to the ground unharmed. She prodded the unresponsive body beside her. How in the world was she going to get him off the plane?

The seats ahead of her emptied with the usual jumble of passengers hauling their suitcases down from the overhead bins, barely missing hitting other people in the head. When the seats had cleared as far back as her row, she motioned for the people behind her to go ahead. The mother with the small children across the aisle paused as she was gathering their things. She eyed Sam's comatose body with concern. "Is he all right?"

Lilith forced a chuckle. "All that turbulence made him nervous. He took something and it must have knocked him out."

The woman smiled sympathetically. "Should I find someone to help you?"

"That's kind of you." And it was. "I think I'll wait until the plane is empty. If I can't wake him then, I'll ask an attendant for help."

With one last look back, the woman shepherded her daughter

down the aisle, the baby sleeping in a sling across her chest. The rest of the passengers streamed past Lilith but there was still no sign of Sam. She bit her lip. He knew so little about the challenges of modern life. Had the wind dispersed him too broadly for him to be able to re-apparate? She'd heard stories of that happening, where it took hundreds of years for the demon to coalesce again. Her heart clutched at the thought.

The last passenger left the plane. From the gangway, a flight attendant came down the aisle toward her. The attendant did not look happy. "What's the problem, ma'am?"

Should she request a wheelchair? Before she could speak, a tiny cloud of smoke issued from the vent above her head. Sam!

Lilith stood. "My husband is a bad flyer. He needs a few more minutes to get himself together."

"I'll get you a wheelchair," the attendant said.

***"

"That won't be necessary," Sam said firmly.

Lilith's eyes flew to his face. Her relief was impossible to miss. Following her into the aisle, he reached into the open overhead compartment and pulled down first his suitcase, then hers.

She waited until they reached the gate before she grabbed his arm and dragged him to a halt. Then she rose on her tiptoes and pressed a big, smacking kiss on his mouth. When she stepped back, her eyes sparkled with tears. She took his face between her palms. "You saved our child's life."

She kissed him again.

This was the Lilith he remembered, the one who looked at him like he was still a dazzling seraph. Then his heart seemed to shrivel in his chest. He didn't deserve her praise. When she discovered that their baby was still in danger and there was nothing he could do to save it, she would turn away from him in disgust.

To postpone that discussion, he said, "Should we go get rebooked?"

Her face fell but she led him to the end of a nearby line.

"How in Hell's name did you wind up pregnant?" he asked.

She gave him a cheeky grin. "The condom broke. Remember?"

"Of course, I remember. But why this time and not any of the thousands of times we made love without a condom?"

"Who knows? Maybe God doesn't want women getting knocked up in Hell. Maybe he knew we were finally ready for a child. Maybe… never mind."

He riveted his prosecutor's gaze on her. "What?"

She lifted one shoulder. "Maybe because of the position."

"The position?"

"Think of it like this: we made gravity our ally instead of our adversary."

For a moment he was puzzled. Then he gave a crack of laughter. "You mean because you finally agreed to be on the bottom."

Her cheeks reddened. He laughed even louder. "Did you just figure this out?"

"A few centuries ago."

"Then why haven't you had a baby before?"

"I never wanted a child with anyone but you."

He pulled her into his arms and kissed her, long and slow this time. When he finally released her, he said, "When were you planning to tell me?"

She looked at him thoughtfully, as though she was trying to decide how honest she wanted to be.

"I wasn't," she said finally. "I planned to arrange for a human couple to adopt her."

The puzzle finally came together. "That's why you went to see Dara and Belial."

"You have to admit, they'd make wonderful parents. And they're willing to adopt her if you agree."

He didn't agree. He didn't want anyone raising their child but them. But no way could that happen.

"Unless you would be willing to relocate and change careers for the baby?" Lilith stared up at him hopefully.

"What did you have in mind?"

"May I help you?" The ticket agent interrupted them. Probably better to hold this discussion in a more private place, anyway.

"We were on the flight that lost an engine," Lilith said.

The agent apologized profusely. "We're bringing in another plane to take everyone who was on that flight to New York. It will be here in a half-hour. I can book you on that if you like."

"Is there a flight tomorrow," Sam asked. "Preferably later in the afternoon?" He turned to Lilith. "We need time to figure things out. We can do that better off the grid."

A few minutes later they were booked on a flight that left Atlanta the next day.

"Satan doesn't know you're pregnant?" Sam closed the drapes in the hotel room to block out the Atlanta sunshine.

"No. The only people that know, other than us, are Dara, Belial and Zelda the midwife."

"You're sure of that?"

Lilith reclined against the headboard of the king-sized bed. She was exhausted and her ankles were puffy but she was happier than she'd been in a long, long time. "And Estelle, maybe."

"Estelle, definitely, but she's not a problem," Sam paced up and down at the end of the bed. "Since Heaven insisted Satan not appear Aboveworld while the talks are ongoing, that gives us six days to figure out how to prevent Gibeon from exposing our secret."

Lilith smiled.

He stopped pacing. "Why does that make you smile?"

"You said 'our secret.' You can't imagine how good it feels not to be on my own anymore."

He winced. "I should have been by your side from the instant you learned you were pregnant. I'm—" He coughed and tried again. "I'm—"

She eyed him in amazement. The Demon of Pride had actually tried to apologize?

"That's okay," she said. "I understand."

He returned to his pacing. "Come Friday night, the conference will be over and that restriction will go away. We need to figure out why Gibeon is so determined to prevent you from having a child." His tone grew pedantic. "Let's review the information we have and see if we can make sense of that."

He was such a nerd sometimes, but he was her nerd.

"The starting point, I believe, was the birth of your daughter?" He threw her a questioning glance.

She nodded.

"What did he say? Please be as precise as possible."

"It's been twelve thousand years."

"Do the best you can."

She squinted, trying to cast her mind back over the centuries. "He told me I had to return to Eden. He said that if I didn't, Ayelet would die and I would lose every other child I ever gave birth to."

"Those were his exact words?"

"As best as I can remember."

"And what did you do?"

"I returned to Eden, but when I got there, Adam had already replaced me with Eve. Then Satan, in the guise of a snake, invited me to join him in Hell, so I did."

"And that's all?" Sam asked.

"That's the last I saw of him until he showed up at the conference."

Sam wandered over to the window and twitched at the drapes. Then he turned to face her. "As it happens, I've met him before, too."

What? She sat up straighter. He described Gibeon's prophecy of the child who would usurp Satan's throne and her arms curved protectively around her belly. "If Satan believes that, there's no way he'll let this child live."

Sam nodded. "We must ensure he never finds out."

Understanding struck her like a bolt of lightning. "Is this why you dumped me?"

Sam looked shamefaced. "He was already pressing me to divorce you. After he heard what Gibeon had to say, he threatened to end you unless we split up."

"To *end* me?" Her voice came out in a squeak.

He nodded.

"Why didn't you tell me that at the time?"

"I was afraid you'd confront him and he'd lose his temper and kill you."

"I can be a little hot-tempered, but I'm not suicidal." She narrowed her eyes. "You didn't want anyone to know Satan got the best of you."

"It had nothing to do with—"

"Bullshit. You kept that secret to save your pride."

He actually hung his head. "I did. Please don't walk out and take our child away from me."

"Are there any other big secrets you're keeping from me?" When he hesitated, she slid her legs off the bed, feeling around with her toes for her shoes. "This is your last chance."

"Gibeon has expressed an interest in joining Hell." He spoke quickly. "Satan tasked me with recruiting him to our side."

She stopped trying to find her shoes. "Is that why you took him to dinner?"

"It is."

"Do you think he's serious about joining us?"

"No, I don't, and this is why: are you familiar with Deuteronomy 18?"

She shook her head. "Doesn't ring a bell."

"It says, 'If a prophet presumes to speak a word in my name which I have not commanded, that prophet shall die.' The Almighty has no tolerance for false seers."

Everything fell into place. "That explains why he's so keen to get rid of me. Once I'm dead, he'll no longer have to worry about being exposed as a false prophet."

"It does, but Satan doesn't plan to end you if you get pregnant." Sam combed his fingers through his hair.

"That sounds like a good thing, but you don't seem very happy?"

"Before we came Above on this mission, he told me if I knocked you up, he wouldn't have to kill you to keep the prophecy from coming true. He'd only have to kill the baby."

Anger swept through her. They weren't taking this child from her. She curled her lips back, baring her teeth. "Let him try it."

"I'd rather we didn't."

"Then we'll just have to stop him. Are you prepared to give up your position in Hell to start a new life Above?"

"Of course."

She sighed in relief. It was going to happen. They were going to move Above and raise their daughter together. "If we give up our immortality, I think Satan will allow us to leave Hell peacefully."

He stopped pacing. "Do what?"

"Give up our immortality. If you volunteer to give up yours and I allow Satan to remove mine, we won't be a threat anymore. He'll let us go."

Sam stared at Lilith, stunned. If he gave up his immortality, he would no longer be the highest-ranking former angel in all of Hell. He'd be an ordinary, pathetic, mortal human—like Belial. "I wouldn't be too sure about that. I am his left-hand demon, after all."

"As much as he likes the work you do, and the cachet of having recruited a seraph away from Heaven, he's also jealous and threatened. And his character flaws generally win out over his more positive emotions."

She was right, but what she was suggesting was crazy. "I can't do that."

The smile drained from her face. "Why not?"

It was intuitively obvious why not. "Because if I did, I'd die in a few years."

"If we go to live on Earth but remain immortal, everyone around us will die while we never age."

He nodded. Obviously. "Will our child be immortal?"

"No one seems to know. Apparently, first-generation cambions are usually mortal. It's not clear whether my immortality changes that. If not, we'll have to watch her grow old and die."

He flinched. It was an unpleasant thought, but the alternative was too ridiculous to contemplate. Immortal beings didn't simply jettison their everlastingness.

Belial had.

Sam squirmed, feeling uncomfortable in his own skin. Belial had given up his immortality because he'd loved Dara more than he'd loved being immortal. The thought made him feel small and unworthy.

"We won't age," Lilith went on. "Which means we'll have to keep moving around as human technology and bureaucracy make it increasingly difficult for us to remain undetected."

The picture she painted, of a catch-as-catch-can existence, wasn't very alluring. "Why would we need to remain undetected?"

"If we're discovered, we'll be captured and treated like lab experiments." Her tone was matter-of-fact.

"The way DemSec treats hellrats?"

"Exactly."

"That's appalling."

"True, but Earth is still a better environment for our child, and our possible grandchildren and great-grandchildren and great-great-grandchildren, than Hell."

The fate of future generations was not anything he'd ever had to consider before, but the possibility of his life ending in a few short decades was too ridiculous to contemplate. "We'll figure something out."

"I have money and jewels cached in various banks around the world." Lilith spoke persuasively. No wonder she was Hell's most prolific operative. "We will be able to establish a comfortable life up here."

"Not without leaving a trail that would lead Satan straight to us."

"True, but I know someone who could give us new identities."

She had this all figured out, and the connections to make it work.

"Why can't we move Above but retain our immortality?" Even as he asked the question, he knew the answer. Satan wouldn't allow the kind of threat they posed to simply walk out of Hell. And he'd never let Lilith leave Hell with a child that could grow up to supplant him.

"So, what are you going to do?" Lilith asked.

"I don't know. I need time to consider our options."

She looked at the clock on the nightstand. "I'll give you until this time tomorrow. If you haven't come up with a workable plan by then, I'll contact Belial and tell him we want them to adopt the baby."

"Agreed."

That gave him twenty-four hours.

CHAPTER 21

On Monday morning, Sam wrinkled his nose as Lilith filled a thermos with a smelly green liquid from a stoneware pitcher. She'd taken to wearing a flared jacket that hid her thickening waistline. He still couldn't quite believe they were to have a child.

"What in Hell's name is that?" he asked. "It smells truly foul."

"I try not to breathe while I'm pouring it. Or drinking it." She screwed the lid onto the thermos and put the stoneware pitcher back in the little refrigerator. "But Zelda says it's good for the baby."

He put his arms around her and kissed her hair. "You're going to be a marvelous mother."

She cuddled against him. "I'm going to do my best, anyway."

They left the hotel and set out for the U.N. Conference center. All around them taxis honked, and the air was ripe with the smell of foods from a dozen countries. Almost immediately, Lilith started looking a little green around the gills. He took her phone. "I'll get us an Uber."

A few minutes later, in the back seat of their ride, she perked up again. "What are you going to say to Gibeon?"

"I'm going to make it clear that any further effort to harm our unborn child will result in a diplomatic incident. Not to mention the potential for inter-cosmic violence."

When they arrived at the Delegates' Lounge, Gibeon was nowhere to be seen.

"He can't hide forever," Sam said when Gibeon still hadn't appeared when the morning sessions began. Sam escorted Lilith to the viewing room. "Are you going to be okay in here?"

"He's never followed me in here, so I think so. If you hear me screaming, though, please investigate."

His jaw tightened. "You can count on it."

Skulking in the viewing room had kept her safe from Gibeon before, so Lilith resolved to stay put. Unfortunately, she'd been in the room less than an hour when her bladder demanded relief. She opened the door cautiously, checking the Delegates' Lounge for her enemy. There was no sign of him, so she hurried to the ladies' room.

When she returned to the viewing room a few minutes later, the sight of her thermos reminded her she hadn't drunk Zelda's protein smoothie yet. She opened the lid. It smelled faintly minty. Zelda must have added flavoring to make it more palatable.

She took a drink and nearly retched. The mint flavoring was no doubt well-intended, but it actually made the taste ten times worse. She forced herself to swallow it all before screwing the cap back on and settling in front of the viewing window.

Next door, Sam and Jehudiel were debating whether exaggerated social media claims fell under Pride or Envy. Sam's argument for pride eventually won the day. He handled the stubborn angels as masterfully as he did the Deadlies.

An hour later they had moved on to discussing whether, under a doctrine of free will, Heaven had a right to intervene in individual choice when a belly cramp bent her double. She gasped as a wave of pain grabbed her with red-hot pincers for a long moment before receding. She smoothed her hand over her belly. She'd take far worse to have a healthy baby.

A half-hour passed before a second cramp hit. This time, she recognized it as a labor pain. Panic sparked along her nerve endings. It was too soon for the baby to come. She breathed through her teeth, whimpering, until the giant claw squeezing her womb released its grip.

A moment later, the viewing room door opened. "I thought I heard something." Sam eyed her closely. "Are you all right?"

"I-I'm not sure." She sucked in another breath. "I think I'm in labor."

He hurried to her side. "Isn't this early for labor?"

Nodding, she fought back tears. Maybe the Enemy wasn't through punishing her. Maybe he was deliberately tormenting her by holding out this hope of a child only to tear it from her.

"Shall I summon Belial?" Sam asked.

Even assuming Belial would respond to such a call, it would take too long for him to get here. She shook her head. "Get Zelda."

"I'll send for her." Sam's brows drew together. "Can you make it back to the hotel?"

She grabbed her thermos and her purse. "I think so." He escorted her to the elevator and then out to the street.

Back at their hotel, another pain rolled over her as the elevator reached their floor. Sam picked her up and carried her to their room.

Inside the suite, nausea overwhelmed her. "I'm going to be sick."

He carried her to the bathroom and set her in front of the toilet before disappearing. She figured his stomach wasn't strong enough to deal with her illness, but he reappeared a few minutes later and held her hair while she ejected the smoothie.

"Zelda's on her way," he said when she finally stopped vomiting. "She said it's probably Braxton-Hicks contractions—your body is ramping up to deliver that baby."

Dampness seeped between her legs. Terrified, she touched the crotch of her panties. Her fingertips came back tinged with red. Another cramp, harder than any that had come before, gripped her.

She grabbed a towel and shoved it into her mouth to stifle her scream. When the cramp finally released her, blood spotted the floor. Despair filled her.

"It's too soon." Tears ran down her cheeks. "Belial said I wouldn't deliver for another three weeks."

Sam carried her to the bed and helped her undress, placing a towel under her hips. Then he returned to the bathroom and retrieved the trash can and set it next to the bed. Tenderly, he smoothed her hair back from her forehead.

The cramps grew harder and longer. Tears leaked from the corners of her eyes in a continuous stream. She couldn't lose Sam's baby. Not after waiting so long.

After what seemed like an eternity, a knock sounded on the suite door. Sam hurried to answer it. Zelda's short figure, carrying a satchel and decked out in a sweatshirt with the hood up, came into the bedroom. She flipped back the hood. Her face creased with concern as another wave of pain ripped across Lilith's midsection. When it finally let up, she consulted her watch. "Forty-five seconds."

"Is that bad?" Sam asked.

Lilith swallowed, waiting fearfully for her answer.

"It's a little long for a Braxton-Hicks contraction." Her voice was carefully neutral. Then she ran her hands over Lilith's belly. The baby kicked at her palm and her expression lightened. "There can't be too much wrong with her if she's kicking like that."

Lilith breathed a sigh of relief, only to despair again when the little midwife caught sight of the bloody towel and frowned. "Let's see what's going on here."

She returned from the bathroom after washing her hands and dragged Lilith's panties down. Beside the bed, Sam's cheeks grew ruddy. He studied the ceiling.

"There's no privacy when you're pregnant," Zelda said cheerfully as she pulled a pair of rubber gloves from her satchel. After a few uncomfortable moments of feeling around, she said, "Snug as a bug in a rug,"

Relief washed over Lilith. Another cramp seized her a few minutes later, but it wasn't as strong as the ones that had come before. Fifteen minutes passed before there was another, and it was even weaker.

"Do you have any idea what brought on your contractions?" Zelda asked.

She shook her head. "I drank some of the smoothie you gave me." She pointed at the thermos on the end table. "And about an hour later, I started cramping. Could it have gone bad over the weekend? I kept it in the refrigerator."

Zelda removed the lid and wrinkled her nose. "Did you add mint to it?"

"No. I just poured some out from the container you sent home."

Sam retrieved the stone pitcher from the refrigerator. Zelda removed the lid and sniffed the contents. "This doesn't smell of mint."

Sam frowned. "I don't remember smelling mint when you poured it this morning, Lil. Could someone have doctored it when you weren't looking?"

"No. It was never out of my sight." She stopped, remembering. "Except when I went to the ladies' room. When I got back, I went to drink it. That's when I noticed the mint smell."

"Pennyroyal," Zelda said grimly.

"Pennyroyal?"

"It's an abortifacient. Someone added pennyroyal to it to make you miscarry."

There wasn't much question about who that would be. "Gibeon," Sam said.

Zelda's lips pinched in disapproval. "That is one nasty angel." She watched Lilith for a long moment before her face brightened to its usual cheerful expression. "Well, one good thing came out of it."

"What's that?" Sam looked anything but cheerful.

"Now you know for sure—your child is immortal."

Lilith blinked. "She is?"

"She wouldn't have survived the pennyroyal otherwise."

Sam was elated. "She's a chip off the old block. "

Zelda packed up her things and Sam left to escort her to the Portal.

Lilith worried the duvet cover, pleating and unpleating it with her fingers. Was immortality a good thing for the baby? If she were mortal, she would have represented no threat to Satan. As an immortal, she seemed to bear out Gibeon's prophecy. The road ahead was murky and threatening.

Sam had promised to have a plan to get their family out of Hell by this evening. If he hadn't come up with anything, she needed to move ahead with arranging to have Dara and Belial adopt the baby.

And there was another question: would Sam agree to that? If he didn't, would Dara be willing to adopt the baby over his objections? And if she didn't, who else might be willing to adopt a cambion baby? An immortal cambion baby who would live forever?

And that was assuming that Satan didn't learn of the baby's existence and put an end to her. Which in turn assumed that Gibeon didn't tell him about the child before she even had a chance to be born. By the time Sam walked back into the room, Lilith was in tears.

"What's wrong?" He hurried to her bedside. "Are you bleeding again? Should I get Zelda back?"

"How are you going to get us out of Hell?" she sobbed. "How are you going to keep Satan from killing our baby? How are you going to keep Gibeon from telling Satan about her?"

He sat on the edge of the bed and pulled her into his arms. "Is that what this is about? You're not bleeding again?"

She shook her head. "No, we're okay." She sniffled. "For now, anyway."

He tightened his arms around her. "All right. Stopping Gibeon from telling Satan about the baby. I plan to lodge a diplomatic complaint about him violating the diplomatic truce."

She breathed out a long sigh. She already felt better. "You mean, trying to down the plane?"

"Exactly."

"Does that mean we don't have to worry about him anymore?"

"Unfortunately, no. The Enemy already knows what he's doing and he's not stopping him, so that doesn't bode well for us. But, given the way Heaven operates, it should tie Gibeon up for a bit while his boss sorts out what happened.

"And how are you going to get us out of Hell?" When he didn't immediately answer, she added, "You said you'd have a plan by this evening."

"And I do," he said. "I'm going to do what I do best. I'm going to file a lawsuit against him."

CHAPTER 22

On Friday, the trade talks ended. After far too many long-winded wrap-up speeches, the angel brigade marched out to the plaza and formed a matrix next to the Peace Bell. Once in place, they unfolded their wings. Gibeon tried to skulk at the back, but Gabriel grabbed him by the collar and dragged him into the formation.

Lilith came to stand next to Sam. "Gabriel does not look happy."

"Apparently trying to down an airliner full of humans is frowned on in Heaven."

"Really?" she said. "In Hell, you win awards for things like that."

"Are you going to miss that?" Sam asked.

Her hands moved to her belly. "No," she said firmly. "I'm done with that life."

After putting Lilith on an airplane to Jacksonville, Sam returned to the Putnam and took the Portal back to Hell. Since there was no telling how long Gibeon would be restricted from leaving Heaven, time was of the essence. When he arrived in Ring Nine, he headed straight for the throne room.

"Heaven agreed to leave social media and the wealth gap as they are." He pulled a scroll from his jacket and offered it to Satan. "We agreed to let them intervene in climate change unhindered, but it will be an uphill battle to get humans to abandon the comforts of air conditioning and internal combustion engines, so that's a lost cause." He was considerably less happy about that than he would have predicted three weeks ago.

Satan took the scroll but didn't open it. "What about Gibeon? Is he coming down here?"

"I think he'll be in touch soon." But not too soon, Sam hoped.

"Excellent." Grinning delightedly, Satan broke the seal and unwound the scroll, scanning its contents. As he read, his smile disappeared and his face darkened to maroon. "What is this?"

"It's a summons," Sam said. "I'm suing you."

Satan was so shocked it would have been comical if he wasn't also furious. "Don't be ridiculous. You can't sue me." He glared at Sam. "What are you suing me for?"

"False representation. When you brought me here, you stated that this organization would operate as a direct competitor to Heaven. You indicated people would fight to get in our doors, but they actually do everything they can—hair shirts, deathbed confessions, last-minute conversions—to avoid coming here."

Satan's shoulders rose till they were practically around his ears. "That's not my fault."

Sam ignored him. "I left a very prestigious position in Heaven on the strength of your representations, only to learn that they were lies."

"Join the crowd."

Sam steepled his hands. "I place the value of my lost position at one dollar."

Satan's shoulders relaxed a little. "That's nothing."

"Plus one percent interest, compounded annually, for the intervening thirteen thousand years."

"One percent?" Satan's shoulders relaxed even further. "What does that come to—a couple of hundred bucks?"

He had never been a math guy.

"It's 1.6358 times ten to the forty-third power, but let's keep things simple and call it a trillion dollars, payable in gold bullion."

At the word "trillion," Satan's horns fired up like chimneys at a third-world factory. "I'm not giving you a trillion dollars," he howled.

"That's for a jury to decide." When Sam had codified the law in Hell, he'd made it a point not to exempt Satan from liability.

Satan's face grew darker and so did the smoke from his horns. Before he exploded, Sam added, "Or we can do things the easy way. I'm willing to settle out of court, with no financial award, provided you meet my demands."

Satan's eyes narrowed. "Which are?"

"I want to leave Hell and go live Above without interference." At least, no more interference than anyone else Above experienced.

Satan's skinny eyebrows rose till they almost invaded his hairline. "This is about the dust wench, isn't it?" He glanced around the throne room. "Where is she, anyway?"

"She's taking a well-earned vacation."

Satan grunted. "I hope it's a working vacation if she wants that directorship."

"She doesn't," Sam said. "She wants to live Above, with me."

Satan's face grew thunderous as realization dawned.

"Well?" Sam said. "Do you want to do this the easy way? Or take your chances in front of a jury of my peers?"

The demons who would sit on the jury were fallen angels who had been lured to Hell under the same false pretenses as Sam. They might not be his friends but nature, even Below-world nature, abhorred a vacuum. If he left Hell they would all jump at the chance to grab his power.

"You think you have this all sewn up, don't you?" Satan said.

Courtrooms were Sam's turf. It was, if not quite a sure thing, as close as you could get to a sure thing in a place like Hell. It would have been nice to leave here with the riches he'd amassed down here, but the gold and jewels Lilith had cached Above would get them by until he got his law practice up and running. The important thing was to settle this before Gibeon was released from angel jail and informed Satan of Lilith's pregnancy. Surely self-interest would tell Satan that it was wiser not to risk losing big in court.

But Satan shook his head. "If I let you get away with this, every demon down here will think he can pull the same thing. I'll see you in court."

The trial date was set for a week later. Sam spent the intervening days polishing his opening statement and cursing his failure to sweeten the pot enough to keep Satan out of court.

He didn't dare contact Lilith for fear of giving away her sanctuary. Nowhere was completely safe from Satan, but the home of Dara and Belial, two seasoned demon warriors, was the safest place he could think of. He hoped the delay wouldn't make him miss the birth of his child.

He went to the Legal Affairs office, only to find himself barred from entering. It appeared that his assistant prosecutor, Andromalius, had moved into his office. Without access to his computer, Sam would have been out-of-touch with the other side's trial preparations but Estelle smuggled messages to him via the Hade network. From her, he learned that Andromalius and Gomory had teamed up to represent Satan. He relaxed a little. They were talented attorneys, but he was better.

When the day finally arrived, he entered a side door into Courtroom 9Z dressed in a black suit, snowy white shirt and his favorite red power tie. The courtroom Satan had chosen lay at the bottom of the Ninth Ring of Hell, only a stone's throw from the Lake of Fire. The stench of brimstone was so strong it made his eyes water.

Taking his place at the plaintiff's table, he gave the boss points for a brilliant choice of venue. There was no way to ignore the implicit threat of the Lake when it burned your lungs with every breath you took. Still, he was sure the Deadlies would find for him. Not only was it in their best interests but he was the Devil's Advocate. He had never lost a case.

At the defendant's table, Andromalius made notes on a yellow legal pad. He looked much like any other fallen angel—beautiful form and flawless features—except for the boa constrictor that continuously wove its way down his torso before slithering back up to his shoulders. Occasionally he would stroke the serpent's head and murmur something. Each time he did, the snake turned in Sam's direction and hissed threateningly.

Gomory sat next to Andromalius. Vual occupied the center aisle of the gallery. The camel's snores thundered through the courtroom.

Satan wasn't with them at the defendant's table. Where was he?

At that moment, the bailiff, a massive demon with the body of a man and the head of a bull, shouted, "All rise for the ruler of Hell."

The door next to a massive onyx judicial bench opened and Satan swept into the room, dressed in a black robe. Perched atop his head he wore a white barrister's wig with his horns protruding through the front corners. At his entrance, everyone in the courtroom—everyone with legs, anyway—rose. Those who had hands burst into applause.

Sam was outraged. "You can't preside over a trial in which you're the defendant."

Satan looked at the defense attorneys. "What say you?"

"We have examined the courtroom procedure documents which were written by the plaintiff himself," Andromalius said. "Nowhere does it say that a defendant may not also serve as the judge."

Sam glared at him. "But it does say that the judge may not preside over a case in which he has a personal interest."

Satan crashed his gavel on the bench. "Overruled. Make your opening statement."

Seething, Sam got to his feet. As he approached the jury box, he tried to shake off his frustration. Out-of-control emotions weren't helpful when you were trying to persuade a jury.

He surveyed the demons in the jury box. Wrath scowled at him. He had remembered being chastised while they were Above. Beside him,

Gluttony apparently hadn't gotten over his forfeited hot dogs. Sloth was half asleep and Lust was covertly looking at porn on his phone. Satan would have already bribed Greed. His best opportunity was Envy.

"Demons of the jury, today I plan to prove that the defendant, Lucifer Morningstar, did knowingly and intentionally lie about this organization and the opportunities it presented and thereby defraud me and other demons like me of our rightful place in Heaven.

"I intend to show that his misrepresentations caused me to forsake Heaven, where I was a seraph, the top tier of the angelic hierarchy, in exchange for a vastly inferior job in Hell. As a seraph, I had the respect of every angel in Paradise. Angels stepped aside when I walked the streets of gold. Some even doffed their halos."

It was an opening molded specifically to Envy, who had always been in awe of Sam's celestial beginnings, so he was taken aback when Envy rolled his eyes and elbowed Wrath. Wrath grinned. What was going on?

Warily, he continued. "My quarters overlooked all the most attractive spots on Earth—Mount Aetna, the Great Barrier Reef, the Grand Canyon, the Ganges Delta. God was pleased with my work, and he rewarded me accordingly."

In the jury box, Envy made a jabbering motion with his hand. Wrath snickered, though he quickly sobered when Sam glared at him.

"Over the course of this trial, I will reveal how Satan lured me from that position with lies about a start-up organization that would compete with Heaven. I will show that he targeted me because of my background as a seraph, knowing I would be invaluable in recruiting other, lesser angels. I will demonstrate that his false promise to give me the top leadership position in this new organization caused me to abandon the best job in the universe."

"Which he's spent thirteen thousand years telling us was bor-ing," Envy sang the last word under his breath. The Deadlies sitting on either side of him guffawed.

Sam waited for Satan to call them to order but nothing happened. His opening statement wasn't connecting. Why not? In his mind, he could hear Lilith saying, "No one wants to hear about how much better you think you are than them." One look at the jurors confirmed she was right. He revised his approach.

"But I am not the only victim of this scheme. Every demon that left Heaven arrived here completely deceived. Instead of living among the clouds with a view of the best Earth had to offer, we found ourselves hunkering underground like moles. Instead of sunshine and clean air, we found darkness and brimstone. Instead of the freedom to mold a new world, we stepped into an organization with no opportunities for growth. Instead of a wise and loving leader, we found ourselves working for an angry, petty bureaucrat who makes the worst human dictator look like a benevolent uncle."

He scanned the jury box. The faces looking back at him reflected the sense of grievance he wanted them to feel. This case wasn't solely about his future. It was about all their futures.

"Demons of the jury, this case is your opportunity to redefine the conditions under which you work. It's your chance to rebuke Satan and to design a new version of Hell, where you're no longer slaves but masters of your own destinies.

"Over the next few hours, I will show you one demon's experience in Hell, and the damage Satan's foul lies did to his life, but I want you to keep the broader context in mind. This was a crime, not because I suffered, but because we all suffered.

"Rule in my favor and the future of the underworld is yours. Side with Satan and you'll live forevermore at the beck and call of a tinpot, would-be god who despises you."

When he finished speaking, they were with him. He would present his evidence, calling witnesses who were there when Lucifer unspooled his many lies, but that was just theater. He'd already won, and Satan knew it. His face was so red it was nearly black under his silly wig. Then his color faded and a smile twisted his lips. Sam watched him warily. What did he have up his sleeve? He gave Andromalius the nod and the defense attorney stood.

"Your honor, I move to dismiss this case on the grounds that the statute of limitations has expired. The time limit for fraud in human venues is five years. Samael is seeking damages for something that happened before humans were walking upright."

There was no time limit in the fraud statutes for Hell. Sam had written them himself and he'd left that loophole in case he ever needed it.

"What happens in human courts is not germane," Sam countered. "In Hell, fraud has no statute of limitations. We're on an eternal timeline here. It's one of the things that makes this place Hell. If you choose a limit of five years, you might as well choose a limit of five seconds."

Andromalius didn't even glance his way. "Your honor, if we allow demons endless time to get around to suing each other, our courts will become as clogged as human courts."

"Then we need to change the law," Sam said. "We can't simply alter it in the middle of a trial."

From the bench, Satan smiled his triangular smile. "Of course, we can. To quote your own words, that is one of the things that makes this place Hell." He banged his gavel. "Case dismissed."

Anger flooded Sam. "This isn't a court, it's a circus."

As though to underline his words, Vual loosed a loud, stuttering stream of flatulence. The demons in the gallery hooted with laughter. Satan joined in, clearly delighted at having bested Sam.

He eyed his former boss with contempt. "You can rule against me, but you can't stop me from leaving Hell." Aboveworld was full of places to hide. If Satan couldn't find Lilith, he couldn't remove her immortality. Sam picked up his briefcase, intent on making a quick exit, but before he could depart, the doors at the back of the courtroom flew open.

His mouth went dry as Gibeon entered. The angel's white robe was torn and filthy and his battered sandals bore testimony to his harsh journey down the Rings. His wings had molted half their feathers. Sam flung himself at Gibeon, trying to reach him before he could speak, but the bailiff blocked his path.

"Is this the trial of the she-demon, Lilith?" Gibeon's red curls shone like copper under the sconces on the courtroom walls.

"No, it was a civil case brought by the former Devil's Advocate, Samael, and it's over," Satan said. "Why? What has Lilith done?"

"She has betrayed you." Gibeon's irises spun like pinwheels. He'd lost whatever sanity he ever had. "She is shortly to deliver the child that will usurp your throne."

Satan's face turned maroon. He scowled at Sam. "You thought to keep this from me. Where is she?"

Sam folded his arms across his chest. "I will not tell you."

But Gibeon smirked triumphantly, "In Alexandria, Florida, in the home of the traitor Belial."

For a moment, Sam thought Satan's head would explode, but he grew strangely calm. "You two." He pointed at Wrath and Gluttony. "Go bring her back."

"The child is no danger to you," Sam said. "We'll raise her Aboveworld. You won't ever have to see her."

"Go," Satan ordered. "And hurry."

"And whatever you do, don't let her have that baby," Gibeon added.

Sam watched them go, his heart in his shoes. He'd just lost his last appeal.

CHAPTER 23

*L*ilith was in the backyard at Dara's house, soaking her swollen ankles in the baby pool where Thomas and Timothy splashed joyously when Wrath and Gluttony arrived. Their eyes grew big as saucers at the sight of her belly.

Dara and Belial had been on high alert since she'd arrived in Alexandria, determined to keep her safe, but that morning Belial had gotten a call saying a patient was in labor. A week had passed and they hadn't heard anything from Sam, so she'd encouraged him to go deliver the baby. He'd promised to be as quick as he could.

"The boss wants you back in Hell," Wrath said.

Dara moved between her and the demons, holding her spray bottle of holy water in one hand and clutching demonweed in the other, but it was hopeless. There was no way one human woman could defend three people, one pregnant and the other two babies, against a pair of determined demons.

"Don't try to resist," she said. "I'll go with them."

Dara fumbled for her phone but Lilith motioned her to put it away. "He couldn't get here in time and I don't want to risk the twins getting hurt."

"What about your baby?" Dara asked, looking at once furious and helpless.

If Wrath and Gluttony were here, then Sam had failed. She tried to come up with an escape option on the fly—bribing her escorts, threatening them, somehow escaping while en route—but nothing came to her. One puny human had no chance against supernatural forces.

"I have to believe the Enemy—I mean, God—has a plan here. We're going to have to trust him." She didn't quite believe that, but Dara seemed comforted and that was what she'd been going for anyway. She hoisted herself from the lawn chair and wriggled her swollen feet into her flip-flops. Of her thousands of pairs of shoes, they were the only ones that were comfortable these days.

Wrath helped her into the back of a beat-up-looking Jeep and got into the driver's seat.

"You're not planning to take me back via the Rings, are you?" she asked.

"Why not?"

"Because if you jounce me over that rough road, I'm gonna drop this kid in your backseat."

Wrath exchanged a look with Gluttony.

"Where's the closest Portal?" Gluttony asked.

"There's one in Manhattan," Lilith said, praying Dara had gone ahead and placed that call to Belial in spite of her direction. If she could delay them long enough, maybe he would arrive and, together, they could stop them.

Gluttony pulled up the PortalFinder app on his phone. "There's one in St. Augustine."

"That thing is four hundred years old," she said. "I don't remember the last time anyone used it."

"Where's the next closest one?"

"Miami," Gluttony said.

"It would take us all day to drive that far," Wrath said.

"It's only five and a half hours," she said. "Seriously, it's a better bet. The one in St. Augustine hasn't worked in centuries."

Wrath put the car in gear. "Well, you better hope it works because, otherwise, you're going to give birth right there in that seat."

Two hours after they left, Wrath and Gluttony returned with Lilith in tow. She stumbled along between them, her belly straining at the stretchy top molded around it. Sam raced to her side. "Are you all right?"

She nodded, shifting uncomfortably from one foot to the other. Her feet, toes meticulously pedicured as always, looked like little sausages in her open sandals. He swept her into his arms, just as he had the first time he saw her, and she relaxed against his chest just as she had then. He couldn't fail her. He couldn't fail their baby.

Satan's eyes had bugged out at the sight of her enormous belly but he had quickly recovered. "I hereby declare Lilith a traitor and sentence her to mortality."

"She's entitled to a trial," Sam said. She had a lot of friends down here and even the most hardened of demons would have a tough time finding her guilty of treason solely because she got pregnant.

"Not for treason, she's not," Satan said.

With a sick feeling, Sam remembered the statute that allowed Satan to declare a demon guilty of treason by decree. At the time, it had seemed like a way to avoid lengthy and polarizing trials. With a look of triumph, Satan raised his hands to rescind her immortality but Gibeon stopped him.

"The babe is immortal," he said. "Even if you mortalize Lilith, it will survive."

"In that case," Satan said, "I sentence Lilith to death by Lake of Fire."

"You can't change sentences mid-stream like that," Sam said.

But Satan was riding high on his successes. "I can do whatever I want down here. This is my empire and I alone decide what can and can't happen."

And Sam had helped make that so. For the past thirteen thousand years, he had worked with Satan to build this evil empire. He could blame Hell's ruler for being power-hungry and too thin-skinned to handle even the mildest of criticism, but a lot of the blame lay at Sam's own feet. If he hadn't been so determined to keep his position on the top rung of Hell, he could have used his influence to put guardrails around Satan's sovereignty. Ten thousand years ago, Lilith had warned him that his pride would be his destruction. Today her prediction was coming true.

"What if I give up my immortality?" he asked desperately. "If I'm a mortal and Lilith is a mortal, we aren't a threat to you."

Satan actually seemed to consider that but Gibeon said, "The child is still immortal and she's the threat here. You can't let her be born."

"She's not a threat to Satan," Sam said. "She's just a threat to you because you made a false prophecy and if she's born it will show you for the sham you are."

"He's lying to save the life of his child," Gibeon told Satan.

One look at Satan's face told Sam which way he would decide.

"I'll renounce the child's immortality, too," he said. "A mortal child can't possibly take your throne."

"He can't do that," Gibeon rocked forward on his toes. "The child can only do that for herself, after she reaches seven, the age of reason. By then it will be too late to save your throne. You need to throw Lilith into the Lake of Fire before she gives birth."

His reasoning was so obviously self-serving Sam was sure Satan would see through it, but the Lord of the Underworld gave the bailiff a curt nod. "Escort the prisoner to the Lake of Fire."

The bailiff tore Lilith from Sam's arms. He tried to pull her back, but being able to resist Thrall and being able to overpower a much larger demon were two very different things. His former seraph-hood did him no good in this situation. The monstrous bailiff tromped out the door and headed for the Lake of Fire, dragging Lilith. Her silent tears tore Sam's heart from his chest. This was his fault, him and his damnable pride. Satan strode along beside him and Gibeon fluttered beside Satan, his sandaled feet almost dragging the ground.

Lilith's lips were white and she shivered despite the Hellish heat.

Sam tugged at the bailiff's other elbow. The bailiff set her on the shore of the Lake and waited for Satan's signal to push her in.

It couldn't end like this. They couldn't end like this. Frantically, he tried to dive past the bailiff and get to Lilith. If she went into the Lake, he would go in right behind her. "The Enemy can take away the child's immortality."

Satan snorted. "The Enemy isn't interested in saving a child of yours."

Sam closed his eyes. For the first time in thirteen thousand years, he allowed himself to remember the days he'd spent adoring the Most High, of celestial music and ecstatic dance and rapturous light and total connection. It had only become boring when he started to chafe at the bond that tethered him to the Almighty.

The cavern brightened and a voice Sam hadn't heard in thirteen thousand years spoke. "You called to me, Samael?"

Sam's face burned with shame. Now, after turning his back all those centuries ago, he wanted help. What if he asked and God said "no?" It would be no more than he deserved. He'd have to take that chance. Lilith and the baby were too important to lose because he refused to ask for help.

"My child, whom Lilith carries in her belly, is immortal. I petition you to make her mortal so that Lilith and I may live Above and raise her in love and hope."

"If I do that, she will live only the lifespan of a human," the voice warned.

"I understand." The thought was anguish, but he kept his voice steady.

"And according to the treaty between Heaven and Hell, I can't guarantee she won't die of an accident or an illness before her time."

Sam swallowed. "We'll take our chances, as humans do."

He had a sense of being assessed. Desperately, he hoped he would be found worthy.

"It's done," the voice said.

"So, the child is now mortal?"

"All three of you are."

Gibeon's figure brightened until it looked like someone had focused a spotlight on him. He glanced around fearfully.

"By my mercy, Gibeon, you are also mortal," the voice said.

He wriggled his shoulders, trying to open his wings, but they were no longer there. He dropped to his knees, clasping his hands. "Please let me return to Heaven, Lord."

The cavern cooled several degrees. "No. You don't belong there anymore."

Then the cavern returned to its normal sweltering temperature. The bailiff made no move to stop Sam as he took Lilith's arm.

"This is her fault," Without warning, Gibeon hurled himself at her. "I shall not suffer a whore to live!"

On instinct, Sam swung her out of the way, so that Gibeon's palms encountered only air. His scream of rage turned to a scream of terror as, carried by his own momentum, he tumbled into the lake. The surface bubbled in a frenzy of chemical reaction but he didn't reappear.

It took the Lake of Fire three days to dissolve an immortal. This quick death must be what God meant when he spoke of his mercy.

"I warned him to stop calling me a whore," Lilith said, but her body shook with reaction.

Lifting her into his arms, Sam addressed Satan. "We're leaving."

Satan waved them off. "You'll be back."

"No," Sam said firmly, "we won't."

EPILOGUE

*I*t was a heck of a party.

Near the back fence of Sam and Lilith's yard in Jacksonville, Florida, a group of second-grade girls sang karaoke while an audience of enthusiastic parents recorded the performance on their cell phones.

At a table on the left side of the yard, Lilith scooped shaved ice onto paper cones and topped them with flavors of their guests' choosing. On the right side, Sam stood guard over a magnificent pink bouncy castle, making sure the children removed their shoes before entering and keeping an eye out for roughhousing. Nearby, a pink sheet cake decorated with princesses and seven candles wished their daughter, Zoë, a happy birthday.

He had just zipped the castle door behind Zoë and the Lyle twins when a forty-something guy with thinning hair and a slight paunch wandered up. "I'm Matt Miller." He stuck his right fist out. "Charlotte's dad."

Sam had no idea which of the three dozen children running around the yard was Charlotte, but he bumped the man's fist anyway.

"I chair a group of public-minded citizens," the man said. "Your name has come up a lot lately. You've been on quite a winning streak since you opened your practice. Your opponents say you're very creative."

Sam shrugged off the compliment. Knowing the law made it possible to manipulate the law and no one knew it better than he did.

"Have you ever considered running for public office?" the man asked.

Shrieks emanated from the bouncy house. Sam looked through the screen. Thomas and Timothy had synchronized their jumps, sending Zoë flying into the air. No one was bleeding and they were all giggling, so he supposed they were okay.

"I appreciate the compliment," he said, "but between my law practice and raising our kids, Lilith and I have our hands full." Four years ago, Lilith had given him a son. Recently they'd learned she was pregnant with their third child.

"We're looking for someone to run for county prosecutor. We think you'd make a great candidate."

"Thanks but no thanks." After a hundred lifetimes of dealing with politics in Hell, Sam had zero interest.

But Charlotte's dad wasn't ready to let it go. "We think you have the ability to go places. After a term as county prosecutor, you could run for state Attorney General and then Governor. Twenty-five of the seventy-eight people who have been president were once governors."

"Twenty-seven."

Charlotte's dad grinned. "I stand corrected." Then he sobered again. "We need a viable candidate if we're going to win next November. We're prepared to put all of our resources behind you."

For an instant, Sam visualized a future of increasing fame and recognition. Being President of the United States was the most powerful job a human could hold. He had only a few years left on this planet. Perhaps the best use of his time would be in a position where he could effect change.

"What are you boys talking about?" Lilith seemed to appear from nowhere.

He jumped at the sound of her voice. "Nothing."

Her eyes narrowed. "Looks like something."

"We were talking about what a little demon your Zoë is on the soccer field," Charlotte's dad said.

She smiled. "And off it."

Charlotte's dad looked confused, but he chuckled anyway. "Think about it," he advised Sam.

Lilith watched thoughtfully as the man walked away. "What was that about?"

Sam had hoped she'd let it go. He should have known better. "They want me to run for D.A."

She tilted her head. "Is that something you're interested in?"

"I told him we have our hands full with the kids and my practice."

"That wasn't my question."

He pictured himself taking the oath of office as President while Lilith gazed up at him in adoration,

"No," he said finally. "It feels like the first step in a rat race no one wins. Why? Would you like to be First Lady?"

"I was First Woman. Now it's enough to be your woman."

He pulled her into his arms and kissed her. "And you always will be."

Dear Reader,

Thank you for reading *The Demon's Secret Baby*, the third book in my *Touched by a Demon* series.

I know that your spare time is limited, and I'm thrilled that you chose to spend it with Sam and Lilith.

If you enjoyed the book, please consider leaving me a review on Amazon, Goodreads, Bookbub, or your blog or website. Word of mouth is also good—please tell your family, friends and fellow readers.

To be notified of upcoming releases, author interviews, appearances, blog tours, and giveaways and to receive special content that's for newsletter subscribers only, please sign up for my quarterlyish newsletter at www.jeanneestridge.com. The newsletter signup form is in the center of the page.

To follow me on Facebook: www.facebook.com/JeanneEstridgeFanPage

To follow me on Goodreads: www.goodreads.com/Jeanne_Oates_Estridge

To follow me on Bookbub: www.bookbub.com/profile/jeanne-oates-estridge

To see what I'm posting on Instagram (mostly pictures of wildflowers and birds and Reels of my puppy: www.instagram.com/jeanneestridge/

Again, thanks so much for reading!

Jeanne Oates Estridge

ACKNOWLEDGMENTS

Acknowledgments

When you spend three years writing a book, it's difficult at the end to recall everyone who helped along the way. If you are one of the many people who contributed thoughts, ideas or just a listening ear and I fail to mention you, please accept my abject apologies.

First and foremost, thanks to Jilly Wood, who has been on this journey with me from page one. If you like Sam, and how he arcs over the course of the book, thank her. He is a demon, and consequently kind of an asshat, and she has been unrelenting in her pursuit of a hero readers can root for—like the kind you'll find in her high fantasy romances.

Next, Tracy Brody, who pushed me to build characters readers can identify and empathize with (like her military suspense guys and gals), and who pointed out that a satisfying romance arc requires more than lust and banter. If the romance in this book works for you, thank her.

Also, Ginger Kenney. Our daily sprint sessions over the past couple of years have yielded far more words on the page than I've ever accomplished alone. Having someone who expect you to show up everyday is a great motivator! Check out her sci-fi romance stories.

Also, Central Ohio Fiction Writers Plotting Groups (both East and West). Their interest and unfailing encouragement helped me make it over the finish line.

Finally, Pauline Persing, who has listened to me plot every single book I've written approximately a hundred times before I've settled on a story that I like.

Despite all the assistance I got from these people, I suspect there are still many mistakes. Any errors are not on them, but a result of my failing to ask the right questions or correctly understand their answers.